NOTHING BUT THE TRUTH

"You've got to admit, we've got some serious chemistry," he remarked.

"We are clearly attracted to each other," Kate agreed. "But it doesn't change anything."

"What doesn't it change?" he questioned. "Our relationship?"

"Yes."

He smiled. "So you admit that we have one?"

"But we shouldn't," she said hastily. "We're working together."

"I quit," he said instantly, leaning toward her.

Other books by Roberta Gayle

SUNSHINE AND SHADOW
MOONRISE
WORTH WAITING FOR
SOMETHING OLD, SOMETHING NEW
MAD ABOUT YOU
"Just in Time" in SEASON'S GREETINGS
"The Gamble" in BOUQUET

Published by BET/Arabesque Books

NOTHING BUT THE TRUTH

Roberta Gayle

ARABESQUE
BET
BOOKS

BET Publications, LLC
www.bet.com
www.arabesquebooks.com

ARABESQUE BOOKS are published by

BET Publications, LLC
c/o BET BOOKS
One BET Plaza
1900 W Place NE
Washington, D.C. 20018-1211

All Kensington Titles, Imprints, and Distributed Lines are
available at special quantity discounts for bulk purchases for
sales promotions, premiums, fund-raising, and educational
or institutional use. Special book exerpts or customized
printings can also be created to fit specific needs. For details,
write or phone the office of the Kensington special sales
manager: Kensington Publishing Corp., 850 Third Avenue,
New York, NY 10022, attn: Special Sales Department,
Phone: 1-800-221-2647.

First Printing: August 2001
10 9 8 7 6 5 4 3 2 1

Printed in the United States of America

ACKNOWLEDGMENTS

For all my friends, male and female, who challenge me with their views about politics, current events, and issues (of race, sex, and the human condition). These characters are you. Their words are yours and mine. A very special thank-you to my brother and my father, who debated with me the longest—and the loudest—right to the end. I love you Rebel and Mel.

One

The Fluffy Pastry Café on Seventh Avenue and Fifty-seventh Street was a great spot for people watching. Businessmen, and women, dressed in dark suits and darker leather shoes, scurried from meetings in oak-paneled board rooms to meetings in tasteful, expensive restaurants. Wealthy matrons from both the Upper West Side and the Upper East Side strolled along, on their way, Kate figured, to the theaters, or to the chic cafés that abounded in this area—such as the Trattoria del Arte one block over on Broadway. Residents of the neighborhood walked briskly to and from the park dressed to jog, bike, sunbathe, Rollerblade, or walk the dog. Of course, tourists also littered these streets, probably on their way to or from trendy sites like Jekyll and Hyde, the Hard Rock Café, or bustling Times Square.

Kate Ramsey took in the scene as she sipped her coffee, feeling slightly guilty because she'd abandoned her laptop in the middle of a weekday. In her case, observing people wasn't just a hobby . . . it was a calling. She had spent her entire adult life finding the threads that linked things as disparate as this cavalcade of strangers and knitting them together into whole cloth.

Her old friend Jennifer Collier walked into the café as

if she owned it. "Quaint little place," she said sarcastically after she kissed Kate hello and sat down.

"Hi," Kate said. She crumpled her chocolate-stained napkin in the palm of her hand to hide it until she could discreetly dispose of it. Under the sardonic eye of her former college roommate, Kate suddenly felt responsible for every discarded coffee cup, scrap of wax paper, and cellophane wrapper that littered the tables around them. "When I'm in this neighborhood, I have to stop in here for a chocolate cream puff."

"Here?" Her friend looked around at the nondescript little eatery, with its worn vinyl floor and Formica tabletops, and clearly didn't get its appeal. Nonetheless, Kate liked this little place. It felt comfortable, unpretentious.

"Here," Kate said firmly. "They're filled with real whipped cream, not custard. The cream puffs. And it's real coffee."

Jennifer shrugged, nonchalant. She had an air of elegance that made Kate feel like some dowdy, unsophisticated drudge in comparison. But Jen had no idea of the effect she had. It was completely unconscious on her part. Whether she even noticed the other patrons in Fluffy's was doubtful, though most of them certainly noticed her.

"May I help you?" the counterman called over to them. Jennifer rose, with fluid grace, and went to the counter to survey the bakery's goods.

"May I have a cup of black coffee and a croissant?" she requested.

"I'll bring it over to you," he offered, smiling tentatively.

Kate shook her head in amazement, hiding her own smile. The man never came out from behind the counter. Never. She was sure he didn't mean to be unobliging, it was simply a matter of self-preservation. New Yorkers were very demanding patrons—whether ordering coffee at

Starbucks or buying an original Picasso at Sotheby's. Salesgirls at Macy's who started out as helpful and enthusiastic young women were rendered completely uncooperative within a year. An accommodating counterman would be deluged with requests he couldn't possibly fulfill (such as the time Kate had seen an old woman insist that a shop owner actually go behind the counter and make her an item that wasn't even on the menu). It was smarter, if one worked in a service industry in New York, to offer as little extra to customers as possible.

However, Jennifer Collier awakened some chivalrous instinct in men. She was not demanding, or even particularly hard to please, but she did accept their attention as her due. Unlike Kate Ramsey, Jennifer stood out in any setting. Her family had come from the West Indies just a generation ago, and she was an exotic island beauty with her glowing amber skin; long, lustrous black hair; large almond-shaped eyes; thin, almost Caucasian nose; and lips that were not too full, and not too thin, but that lush width that white women tried to achieve by injecting collagen into their own lips.

Kate, on the other hand, was as ordinary as could be. She was a little short of average height, and perhaps ten pounds overweight, which wasn't likely to change anytime soon. Kate scorned the very idea of StairMasters and treadmills. She guessed it was lucky that she enjoyed walking since it was the only form of exercise that she did regularly. There wasn't much point to doing more. Even if her body was perfect, she didn't think she could make any heads turn. She simply didn't have that kind of "oomph."

She had a round, chocolate-brown face, and mahogany eyes hidden behind big, thick, tortoiseshell glasses that rested on her flat, round nose. Her full lips were her best feature, according to Jennifer, but she could only see them as big and round, too. Kate wished she had her friend's panache, at least, but no amount of makeup could give her that elegant finished look. She worked out of her home and usually wore jeans and T-shirts. For convenience's sake, she usually had her shoulder-length hair styled in simple box braids, which she could tie back easily. Aside from choosing a scrunchy that matched the color of her shirt, and occasionally switching square garnet earrings for small tearshaped amethysts, or thin gold hoops, she barely bothered with her appearance.

She was just Kate, and since there wasn't a thing she could do about that, she accepted her God-given attributes, good and bad, as a relatively apt reflection of her inner self. She was a woman who enjoyed the simple things—a good cup of coffee and a clear view of the street, as now. Kate Ramsey was pragmatic about her appearance. It wasn't important like her work or her friends, or exposing the truth. She didn't want to attract undue attention after all. She liked to observe those around her as unobtrusively as possible, so it was really a blessing that she was so average-looking. She didn't even think about it much, unless Jen was around.

It had amazed her when the spectacular, and sought-after, Jennifer Collier had chosen her for a friend and confidante in their second year at college—seemingly out of the blue. It had taken only one day together for Kate's fascination with the untouchable sophomore to be transformed into sympathy for her new friend, whose outward self-confidence masked deep-seated insecurities that outweighed even her own. They had remained friends because they were strangely compatible. Different as they were, they complemented each other perfectly.

Men were attracted to Jennifer like bees to honey. She introduced those candidates whom she thought promising to her best friend, Kate, whom they found sympathetic and easy to talk to. It would not have been hard for either woman to become jealous of the other, but instead they fell into a routine that suited them both. Kate befriended the men who were drawn to Jennifer's beauty. She asked questions, observed and rated them and shared the results with Jennifer, who organized their social calendars so that neither woman ever lacked a suitable male companion for a date.

Kate introduced Jennifer to her circle of women friends, who had assumed that Jennifer's self-possession was conceit, and her cool composure was unfriendliness. Talking to her quickly changed their attitudes. Jennifer was quite sweet beneath the cool veneer she donned for self-protection. She could be a great friend to have—loyal and understanding. She was also a lot of fun. Jennifer and Kate both loved lively, intelligent conversation, dancing and, above all, school They both felt privileged to be attending college and gloried in academic debates about everything and anything. And they both hated pretentious jerks. If Jen didn't share Kate's enjoyment of chocolate cake and C-Span, Kate thought her best friend's shoe fetish ridiculous; but they could satisfy their need to share those hobbies with other friends. Their relationship was solid without being exclusive at all.

Kate thought they had remained such good friends after college *because* each woman challenged the other to see the world from a completely different perspective. Jen was completely pragmatic while Kate was an idealist. Jennifer was supremely ambitious, and Kate shared her triumphs and failures, and reminded her that there was more to life than money and power. Kate wanted only to write—preferably about the things that mattered—and it was Jennifer's idea that she apply to the journalism program at Columbia University.

After college, when Jennifer took a job in public relations, Kate should have deplored the hype that her best friend fostered and promoted. Instead Kate loved to listen to Jen talk about the glamorous parties, ostentatious displays of wealth and power, and all the other trappings of success. She cheered at every review the publicist's clients received, and commiserated at every perceived insult. Kate did everything she could ethically do to bolster her friend's reputation with the newspapers.

For her part, nothing would have pleased Jen more than to use her skills to publicize her best friend's achievements. She wanted Kate to have it all. It was incomprehensible to Jennifer that anyone would spurn fame. It wasn't that Kate balked at receiving the recognition she deserved, it was just that being a celebrity did not seem very attractive. To Jennifer, the only possible reason for Kate to avoid the spotlight was shyness, and Jen had no patience for that. She did not approve, and she voiced her opinion on the subject at every opportunity. Kate knew her criticism was meant to be constructive, and she braced herself for the usual lecture, since Jen's well-intentioned meddling was appreciated for the love and genuine friendship that lay at the heart of it. But Kate soon found that Jen had not arranged this meeting in order to deliver her usual lecture.

Once the counterman had served her, Jennifer focused on Kate. "Did you see the newspaper this morning?" Jennifer asked, handing Kate a copy of the *News*.

"You know I don't read this . . . stuff," Kate answered, glancing down at the glaring headline without interest. She occasionally read the sensationalist newspaper for professional reasons, but she avoided it whenever she could. She got her news over the wire services such as Reuters and the Associated Press.

"Page three," Jen directed her. "Julio Gonzalez is dead."

"And that's why you called me?" Kate asked, still completely in the dark.

Jennifer reached over the table and opened the newspaper to the story. "You remember him, don't you?" She pointed at a short article with the headline "Strike Organizer Killed in Auto Accident."

"I don't believe I ever met the man."

"No, you didn't meet him," Jennifer said impatiently. "You saw him, and heard him, though. At that town meeting last fall. You couldn't miss him. He was the big mouth who said a strike was inevitable." She waited expectantly as Kate processed this bombshell.

Kate skimmed the article as she considered Jennifer's unprecedented interest in these events. She'd thought it odd when Jennifer had invited her to the town meeting. When the discussion about Jennifer's biggest client, Leopold "Skipper" Arnold, turned into a heated debate, she had assumed her friend was trying to help her by turning her on to the story. Kate did vaguely remember the burly union spokesman who had spoken so heatedly at that town meeting. Julio Gonzalez whipped the members of the Professional Steelworkers and Welders Union of America to a frenzy with his inflammatory comments. She didn't appreciate his tactics.

"Do you remember him now?" Jen asked.

"Yeah, I remember."

The debate had been about the ethnicity of the union laborers on Skipper's latest construction site. Mr. Arnold, the most successful African-American building developer in the state, had won a highly contested city contract to build a municipal parking garage and, halfway through its construction, a debate began within the steelworkers union. A faction of the P.S.W.U.A. were upset at the underrepresentation of laborers of Hispanic descent in their union. Since Skipper was African-American, and presumably sympathetic to the inequality suffered by his brown-skinned brothers they—nominally headed by Gonzalez—suggested that the developer should try to rectify the situation. Skipper proceeded to do so . . . by hiring a nonunion company that employed primarily Hispanic workers. His decision came under immediate fire—by the city, the press, and of course, the union. At the town meeting, the union leadership accused him of being motivated by financial considerations, rather than by a feeling of social responsibility. Kate believed the union was correct. Mr. Gonzalez was the first person to suggest that the union might be forced to strike.

Since that time, the union had indeed gone on strike. Kate didn't cover the story and hadn't subsequently followed it. Jennifer, as head of public relations for Leopold Arnold Construction, Incorporated, would presumably have been affected by these events, but Kate didn't see why she was so excited by this particular item in the newspaper.

It was an article on the death of Julio Gonzalez. The piece reported that he was drunk when his vehicle skidded off the road and into a cliff along the side of the Saw Mill River Parkway, a winding, dangerous road that connected New York to its northern suburbs. There were a lot of accidents on the Saw Mill. This one was bad. Julio's chest had been crushed by the steering wheel. The article included that he'd left behind an ex-wife and two small children. Kate felt sorry for the kids, but it didn't change the fact that she had not liked the man.

When she'd seen him, he had aggravated an already-tense situation with his bombastic rhetoric. She believed he purposely sought to set the African-American and Hispanic contingencies against each other. It was a tactic Kate hated. It was a common enough strategy in big business and in politics—split the vote by setting the minorities against each other—but she especially abhorred the practice when it was utilized by those who were supposed to be fighting for people who didn't feel empowered, such as union representatives.

"So, what do you think?" Jennifer asked.

"It's sad." Jennifer didn't look satisfied. "What do you want me to say?" Kate asked. "It's a good thing there was no one else on the road, so he didn't kill anyone but himself."

"They don't usually report on accidents like this, do they? Not unless the victim was a celebrity or something."

"Maybe it was the strike. He had gotten a lot of publicity with his muckraking," Kate theorized. She couldn't help but pity him after reading about how he died. The *News* had probably printed the story because of the gruesome nature of his fatal injuries. "Or maybe they just thought the story would interest some of their more morbid readers," she offered diplomatically.

"That makes more sense," Jennifer said, nodding. "It's pretty graphic."

Kate grimaced. It was too nice a day for such a depressing conversation. Gonzalez might not have been her favorite union rep, but no one deserved to die that way. Especially not somebody's father. Her mind flashed to her father's funeral, and she pushed the memory away quickly. This guy was nothing like her sweet, uncomplicated, helpless old man. Gonzalez was a loudmouth, with a huge chip on his shoulder.

If Julio Gonzalez was truly trying to help his brothers, he had chosen the worst possible way to do it, in Kate's opinion. She had to admit that, in this case, she did have something of a bias. Like every African-American she knew, Kate had been asked often enough to represent her race, and her sex, and even—as in this case—minorities in general. It wasn't fair that Skipper had been targeted by the Hispanic leadership of the union just because he was the only minority developer who was important enough to actually affect union policy. The coalition of Hispanic members of the P.S.W.U.A. could have forced this issue with any of the many white developers whom they worked with, but chose to force the issue with Skipper Arnold solely because he was black. Julio Gonzalez attacked Skipper because he chose to use nonunion labor—even though he was one of the most vociferous among those who had originally complained about Hispanic underrepresentation in the union.

It was a complicated issue. The black members of the union had worked hard to break the barriers that had once kept them on the outside, and many were sympathetic to their brothers' struggle. But no one wanted to give up the security they had fought for to the nonunion Hispanic workers who were willing to work for less. Julio Gonzalez's solution—that they admit a group of Hispanic laborers into the union even though they hadn't earned it—didn't appeal to many of the union members either. They had sweated and starved for the privilege of joining the union, and they didn't want to forfeit work, or pay, to an influx of new members who hadn't even apprenticed. Gonzalez was paid out of union dues. He wouldn't sacrifice any of his annual income if his plan was accepted, Kate thought cynically, but his proposal would cut into Skipper's profits, as well as the paychecks of the existing union members.

"Do you think it could have been something other than an accident?" Jen pressed.

"Other than an accident?" Kate repeated confused. Then, as she realized what Jennifer was saying, had been hinting at since she'd shown her the article, "Do you realize what you're implying?"

"You saw him at that meeting. He was a man who inspired strong feelings. He had enemies," she answered.

"Do you have anyone specific in mind?" Kate couldn't help wondering if Jen recognized that her questions might embarrass her own client. "You'd better be careful with accusations like that. Someone could just as easily point the finger at Skipper as at anyone else." Leopold Arnold was Jennifer's biggest client.

"Why not?" Jennifer suggested, jokingly. "You know Uncle Skip doesn't give a damn about the complaints of the Hispanic community." Kate knew Jennifer's opinion of her adopted uncle. For years she'd hinted that he might be less than honest. "He was thrilled to be handed the opportunity to hire non-union labor and blame the union members themselves." Jen continued unabated.

"But Jen, I just can't picture it." Kate couldn't imagine the successful, debonair Skipper Arnold even considering murder as a method to increase his profit margin.

But Jennifer was clearly distressed. "You know more about this than I do. Is there stuff they're not including in this article? Does it seem to you like it could be a cover-up?"

"What are you suggesting?" Kate asked, shocked.

"Nothing. But he was one of the most outspoken advocates of the strike," Jen pointed out. "And that strike is costing Skipper money. A lot of money. Not to mention the bad publicity."

"You're not trying to tell me you killed the man because of some bad media coverage, are you?" Kate tried to joke.

"Even I wouldn't go that far," Jennifer said. "And if I did, I sure as hell wouldn't confess. Not even to you, Kate."

"Jen, honey, this is a serious accusation. . . ."

"It's just that this is the second union rep who's died since the strike started," Jennifer said speculatively.

The scenario the publicist painted was an ugly one, but, in spite of herself, Kate found that little fact intriguing. "Really? Who was the other one?"

"Walter Chapel, the guy who retired in January when he found out he had cancer."

Kate had read about that. "The man was riddled with cancer."

"I know," Jen said, shrugging. "It just seems a little too coincidental to me. The only two guys who might have stopped the strike just happen to die within a couple of months of each other."

"Skipper Arnold has always been a very lucky man. He couldn't have gotten where he is today if he hadn't been," Kate mentioned, her interest waning.

"There's luck, and then there's luck," Jennifer said. "Uncle Skip has got to be the luckiest black man in the world."

Kate decided to try a logical approach. "I think you've lost it, girl. Why would he risk it? He'll make a ton of money on this project no matter what happens. You know that, and I know that. Everyone knows that. Do you even know what effect the strike will actually have on his profits? I mean exactly how much difference does it make?"

"I don't know," Jennifer said uncertainly.

"This is your Uncle Skip we're talking about," Kate said, pounding the point home.

"I know."

"Do you honestly think he'd have a man killed just to make a few more bucks?"

"I love him, but . . . I also suspect he's done things he wasn't proud of. You know that. I told you about it a long time ago."

"In college. I remember. But then you went to work

for the man. How could you do that if you thought he was the kind of guy who has people killed?"

"I can't. That's why I have to know for sure," Jen replied. "You're a reporter. This should be right up your alley."

"He's your mentor. You're the one with the contacts in the business. You can find out all about him from the inside, much more easily than I can."

"I can't investigate him. I've never done anything like that. It's what you do, Kate. I need your help. Please." Kate had never seen Jennifer like this. The woman kept her cool in every situation. That, more than anything else, made Kate weaken. She couldn't conceive of Jennifer imagining all this. She never lost her composure, not even when she'd ended her engagement to her high school sweetheart, Dell Johnson.

"Even if I wanted to, I wouldn't know where to begin. This is very convoluted, Jen," Kate said feebly.

Jennifer smelled victory and pounced. "I can point you in the right direction, and I'll help all I can. I can't go around asking questions because everyone knows me. They'll want to know why. You can stick your nose in anywhere you want. You're a reporter."

"But they'll never tell me anything. I won't even know the right questions to ask." Kate argued.

"No problem. I've got just the guy for you." Jennifer smiled, pleased. She knew she had won. "Brant Fuller is young, successful, and he works in construction. Skipper contracted work out to him before."

"If he's a successful contractor who works with Skipper, don't you think he might be in on whatever is going on? *If* anything is going on," she said skeptically.

"He's perfect. He knows this biz inside and out," Jen replied, ignoring Kate's tone.

"And you think he's straight?" Kate inquired again since Jen hadn't answered the first time she asked.

"I'm sure of it. He drips integrity," Jennifer assured her.

"He's working with Skipper on the parking garage?" she asked, resigned.

"We've subcontracted a few jobs out to him. He thinks Skipper hung the moon."

"So what makes you think he'll help me?" Kate was dubious.

"If you find out anything, he'll want to help. I told you, he's dripping with integrity."

"I guess . . ." Kate couldn't bring herself to say it aloud, but Jennifer's satisfied expression made it clear that her friend understood. She had her.

Kate felt like the scruffy white-and-gray terrier tied to the parking meter in front of Fluffy's. He sat panting in the spring sunlight, his head turning to watch each person pass by, his big brown eyes searching hopefully for the one who would free him. She was bound by her promise to her friend, and didn't know how, or even if, she could extricate herself from this mess. But she was hopeful that a solution would present itself. Like the dog searching vainly for its owner, she just didn't know where to look.

Two

Rather than heading straight home to 110th Street, Kate decided to take a stroll over to the highly publicized site of Skipper Arnold's latest project. On the way there, she considered whether or not to back out of doing Jennifer's story. Her friend was clearly distraught, and it worried her.

Despite Kate's unease over her friend's uncharacteristic behavior, she couldn't help but enjoy the walk. Spring had finally arrived, and the balmy air was welcome after the razor-sharp winds of the winter months.

The slender gingko trees, which grew all over the city, were covered with tiny yellow-green buds, making the hearty survivors look deceptively fragile, and bringing a touch of nature to the austere city streets. A handful of building managers fought to enliven the few feet of sidewalk that fronted their properties by cultivating those tiny patches of soil left bare of cement, and the bulbs they had planted the previous autumn now yielded golden daffodils, which swayed on slim green stalks in the gentle breeze. Most New Yorkers were probably too busy to notice. Kate didn't see anyone else admiring the lacy yellow flowers. Their only acknowledgment of the change in season was the slight slowing of their frenetic pace from a shuffling flat-footed run to the brisk walk, which, to Kate, characterized native New Yorkers. They hurried past her on the streets and wended their way up and down the subway stairs.

When Kate reached the construction site, she found a ten-foot wooden wall, painted gray, surrounding the lot. Its stark facade was unadorned except for a series of notices that had been posted at ten-foot intervals and which were completely incomprehensible to her. They may have contained information of great importance to the construction workers and strikers, but she quickly gave up on trying to decipher them. She crossed the street and stood looking up at the eight-foot inflatable rat that symbolized the struggle going on at the site. The handful of picketers nearby had propped their signs up against parking meters and fire hydrants. They didn't march, but stood on their side of the small police barricade drinking coffee out of Styrofoam cups and chatting desultorily with one another. They occasionally glanced over at the site of midtown's soon-to-be newest parking structure, but they didn't seem at all hostile.

She'd passed the spot before, and had seen it on the news—the big gray rat and the men posted around it, huddled in thick coats during the last frosty weeks of winter and in the rain and wind of early spring. They seemed less pitiable now, and surprisingly, less hopeful than they had then. Perhaps earlier in the strike, they thought they'd been more effective, had been more driven, but as the weeks stretched into months, they protested more for form's sake than anything else. Work on the structure across the street had continued on, after all, and their sacrifices did not seem to have changed a thing. Her Spanish wasn't up to the test of translating the three simultaneous conversations going on at the moment, but she gleaned enough of the content to know that these men were discussing their families, and friends, and other personal matters unconnected to the events that had brought them there.

After listening for a couple of minutes, she turned her attention to trying to get a sense of the men working on the other side of that wooden wall. Each time a truck rolled through the gates, she caught a glimpse of the sandy expanse of the unpaved lot and, behind that, the sturdy concrete bones of the structure that was slowly going up in the midst of all the controversy. Next to that building, four stories high and covering half a city block, the men who worked there looked tiny and rather insignificant. But they were the ones who gave the story meaning. She looked around her at the very ordinary men whose replacements worked hard on the other side of that implacable gray wall across the street. They were very ordinary men. Though they fought, and froze, and were occasionally photographed by television camera crews, their lives went on as always. Hardly the stuff of legends, and yet . . . they were heroes in their way.

New York City was the best backdrop she could imagine for telling stories, and it provided a wealth of characters and material. Even when she was dodging manic cabbies or pushing through an immovable crowd, she loved this town. Manhattan hummed with activity, twenty-four hours a day, 365 days a year. The seething excitement behind every act, whether it was a mundane walk across town or the opening of a Broadway musical, provided all the inspiration she could ever need for doing what she loved best—writing. Now she just had to decide whether to take on this story, and whether it was fact or fiction.

Kate went into the office the next day for her bimonthly meeting with Charles Grover, her senior editor.

She didn't know if he'd buy the story idea, but it contained all the elements he liked best: money, power, corruption. Most importantly, it featured Leopold Arnold. The wealthy developer was always of interest to New York's readers—sometimes people called him the black Trump. The biggest problem she'd face would be Charles's exasperation at learning she'd changed focus halfway through her assignment. She was supposed to be working on a story she'd pitched to him two weeks ago, about the unethical policy, practiced by the owners of single-room occupancy hotels, or SROs as they were more commonly known, of renting rooms to the homeless at exorbitant rates.

As she stepped into the newsroom, she took in the busy scene with an appreciation born of nostalgia. Rather than the cubicles that were so often constructed in the airless inner portion of New York City office buildings, the space was divided by wide tables that served as desks and large open surfaces for collating and layout and any other task that required spreading out pages of print. Each station was also equipped with a computer, file cabinets, and bookshelves. Best of all, the folks that worked there had an unobstructed view of the windows that looked out over the city.

Here was where she'd gotten her first full-time job as a reporter, and she still thought of these offices as home. Her writing was, after all, the only thing of real importance in her life. She hadn't kept in touch with her extended family after her father died, so she was on her own. Many of her girlfriends were busy settling down and starting families. The men she had chosen to date had not wanted to compete with her career. Though one or two of them had been pretty good prospects, she lacked the proper motivation to spend the time or energy necessary to pursue a long-term relationship. Her work was satisfying, if demanding. Relationships were just as demanding, but not nearly as rewarding. Men, in her considered opinion, were a nuisance.

She spotted Jeremy Hallston as she stepped into the reception area, and grimaced. For a short time, she had thought he was one of those good prospects. In fact, he had been anything but. She'd suffered through a short-lived relationship with her colleague early on in her tenure at the paper and it didn't look as if she was ever going to get the chance to forget it. She tried to avoid making eye contact, but he made a beeline straight toward her. He was very good-looking, with his sleek curly hair, deep-set eyes, aquiline nose, and square jaw, but he was a pig. Jeremy would tell a person right out that he wore nonprescription glasses because it was more important to look intelligent than to actually know anything. Kate still couldn't believe it had taken her four whole dates to realize what a jerk he was.

"Hey, babe," he greeted her.

"Hey, yourself," she responded, and without breaking stride, she walked around him and down the hall that led back to Charles's corner office. Sadly, Jeremy didn't give up and leave her alone. He pivoted and fell into step beside her.

"I'm working on a story that's distantly related to your piece on the SROs," he said offhandedly.

"Distantly related, my ass," Kate muttered under her breath. Aloud she said, "Don't even think about honing in on my story, you toad." He'd stolen a story idea on the school board back when they were dating, and she'd never forgiven him. It not only broke up their fledgling relationship, but she'd seriously wished she could take out a contract on his life.

"Do you have anyone I can talk to at the Coalition

for the Homeless?" He steamrolled on, ignoring her warning. "I need to do some fact-checking."

"If you think I'd ever give you the name of any of my contacts, especially on a story I'm currently working on, then you are an even bigger idiot than I thought," Kate spat.

"Okay, no problema." Jeremy backed off. "See ya."

He left her at Charles's office, and Kate counted to ten to calm herself before she knocked on the door.

Still, she couldn't help but vent a little to her editor. "Charles, if you let that loser, Jeremy, anywhere near my homeless hotel piece, you'll never see another word from me again," she ranted.

"Nice to see you, too, Kate," he replied, coming from behind his desk to give her a kiss on the cheek. His thin red hair was turning gray, and his widening paunch made him look increasingly pregnant, but she had never gotten over her first impression of the man. When she first started working for him, she thought he was the most knowledgeable, most frightening, most impressive man she'd ever met. Now that they'd known each other for six years, their relationship had moved from that of editor and neophyte journalist to friends.

"You wouldn't seriously consider letting that fool touch my story, would you?" she demanded. "He'll screw it up. He can't write. He doesn't even understand the ramifications of half the news he reports on. And he's a moron. I didn't know how he manages to dress himself in the morning."

"He delivers," Charles said firmly. "On time." As she was about to argue further, he raised a hand to forestall her. "It's your story, Kate," he said patiently. "Where are you with it?"

Kate's ire faded. In her rage at Jeremy's presumption, she forgot that if she wanted to pursue the Skipper Arnold item, she'd have to put the article on single room occupancy hotels on the back burner.

She backpedaled, embarrassed. "That reminds me . . . I'm actually waiting for some more information on that one. And I've got a really great item to replace it with," she said.

Kate didn't wait for his response. She plunged right into her pitch on the Skipper Arnold piece. "My source is pretty sure there's something fishy going on with the L.A.C. Parking Garage strike. Two people are dead, and Skipper Arnold may have something to do with it. Walter Chapel was supposed to have died of liver failure due to cancer. Julio Gonzalez totaled his car on the way home from a hard night's drinking, but could they have been helped along?"

Charles, as always, sat stoically, listening until she was done. "Changing horses midstream again, Ramsey?" he commented blandly.

"I think it's going to be a really hot story," she persisted.

"It sounds good, but can you get it fast enough to replace the SRO piece?"

"I've already set up a meeting with Mr. Arnold for next week," she lied, praying that Jen wouldn't let her down. "And I did a quick background check."

"Is he going to be indicted?" Charles asked.

"Julio's death has been ruled an accident, so the police aren't investigating." The editor's mouth turned down at the corners. "Yet," she added quickly. "That's what will make this so big. It will definitely be exclusive, and it should get action."

"If you can prove any of it," he retorted. "Who's your source?"

"A friend. But I won't write it if I can't confirm it. You know that," she assured him.

"I know. And if you don't, I won't have anything to print," Charles said dourly.

"I'll get something. Even if there aren't any charges, there's something hinky going on with Arnold and the union, and I'm going to get it," she vowed. All of her reservations were forgotten in the face of his reluctance. Her passions were always aroused at any sign of opposition. It was her nature.

This was a big story, real news, which was just what Kate loved best. "Okay?" she asked.

"Okay," he agreed, reluctantly. "If you get the story, I'll read it. But I don't care how unethical or immoral the guy is. If you can't back up these allegations, you don't have an article—you have an editorial. I don't want or need an opinion piece from you. I've got editors who write those for me." Inwardly, she flinched. To him, she presented a confident smile. "And, Kate . . ."

"I know, Charles." She tried to forestall the warning that she knew was coming. This was not the first time she'd gone out on a limb chasing a big story. Usually it paid off, but not always. Her editor had a long memory. "I need a story," he insisted. "I don't care about ramifications. I want an article. Three weeks. Or, freelance or not, so help me, I'll—"

"Fire my ass," she finished for him. "I know, I know. You always say that." She rose from her seat and leaned over the desk to shake his hand. "You'll have the story," she promised.

She walked to the door, opened it, then turned back to him. "But you won't ever fire me, you know. You love me."

"Get out of my office," he commanded, but there was a smile playing around his lips.

Kate stopped in to visit a friend on her way out of the building. She had graduated from Columbia University's journalism program with the editor of the style section, Miranda Collins. The fashion guru was on a deadline, as usual, but the women chatted for a few minutes while Miranda vetted some advertising layouts.

"What are you doing here?" Miranda inquired, barely looking up from the glossy photos spread across her desk.

"Meeting with Charles. I've got a new idea for a story."

"Yeah? What?" she asked casually, with an editor's disregard. A reporter would have gotten excited at the mere idea of a new story. An editor needed more detail before he or she summoned up enthusiasm.

"Skipper Arnold," Kate announced.

"Wow!" Now Miranda looked impressed. Unfortunately, it was not for the right reasons. "Will you introduce me?"

"He's sixty years old, Miranda," Kate said chidingly.

"So? He's rich. He's powerful. That's sex appeal, baby," she said cynically. "Anyway, he's cuter than a lot of younger brothers."

"He's no Taye Diggs, or Denzel Washington."

"If we're going to talk movie stars, look at Jack Nicholson or Sean Connery. They're in the right age range," Miranda shot back at her. "They get their pick of women my age."

"In the movies, girlfriend. Not in real life."

"You want to bet? They just snap their fingers, and they can have any woman they want. Do I have to mention Catherine Zeta-Jones's marriage to Michael Douglas?"

"Not every woman goes for that senior citizen action. I wouldn't date a man who was more than twice my age," Kate insisted.

"Different strokes for different folks," Miranda replied. "You have your turn-ons and I have mine."

"And what would yours be?" Kate teased.

Miranda shrugged. "I don't know. As my dear old mummy used to say, 'How do you know whether you'll like something if you don't try it?' I sure wouldn't mind *trying* Skipper Arnold."

"I don't believe you. You wouldn't," Kate proclaimed.

"Yes, I would. You always think you know better than everybody else," Miranda accused without rancor.

"No, I don't," Kate objected. "But I do know there's something weird going on with his latest construction project, and he's right in the middle of it," Kate informed her.

"How do you know?"

"I've got an excellent source."

"I hope it is excellent because he's got a lot of influence in this town," Miranda admonished.

"I know that."

"Just be careful, okay?" Miranda warned.

"Of course. I don't want any trouble," Kate asserted.

"Ha!" her friend snorted. "You love trouble. You're addicted to it."

"I am not!" Kate protested. "I just want to write."

Kate could have taken the same route her friend had and been an editor. When she worked at the *New Amsterdam Press* as a staff writer, she had had editorial duties like everyone else. It was standard procedure for a reporter who was good at his or her job to be offered an editorial position eventually. Kate chose writing full time over editing—so she'd gone the freelance route. And she was happy with her choice. She didn't have an office like Charles or Miranda, but her computer was connected to the office network so she had access to the news services and wires and other amenities the paper offered. For example, she could download her articles directly into the newspaper's computer server. Her home was her office, which suited her perfectly.

She never wanted to sit in some cubicle pounding away at other people's reportage. Kate enjoyed digging up facts and bringing them to light. And this exposé on Skipper Arnold was her kind of story, like the one on the city suspending school funds, or her investigative report on subsidized housing for families. This time, though, she was going to make a real difference—not just get a few lower echelon slobs fired while the fat cats walked away unscathed. She was going to make this one count. If Skipper really had had a man killed, her story could put him in jail. There would be no simple slap on the wrist, and there definitely wouldn't be a cover-up. She, personally, would see to it that Skipper, not some scapegoat, would pay.

Kate's preliminary research turned up a number of articles about Skipper and his construction projects, as well as a couple of interviews with the more prestigious journalists of the last twenty years. But it was one small reference to a much younger Leopold Arnold that convinced her that his reputation for honesty might not be completely deserved. Uncle Skip was an ex-con. His name first appeared in print not long after he'd first arrived in New York from the islands, but it wasn't in connection with his meteoric rise as a contractor. In a small item a crime was reported—a robbery committed by a small group of young black builders who had been cheated by an exploitive subcontractor. Leopold was arrested and convicted of breaking and entering, though the burglary charge was dropped. He pled guilty and did eight months at Riker's.

Kate would go to the party Jennifer had invited her to attend to meet him and see what her gut told her about the man. And she'd try to find out how he'd gotten a

contract from the city with a criminal conviction on record, which was definitely not standard procedure.

It was a fascinating angle for a story on a self-made
man of color who'd started out with no money, no con-
nections, and no apparent means for acquiring either. Kate
didn't know what she wanted to write, or even whether
she actually would write a story about Jen's uncle Skip,
but her interest was piqued. She wondered if he'd comment on the jail term if she did get an interview with
the man. If so, it would be a first, and that was definitely
worth looking into.

Three

For the party the next night, Kate dressed in her most elegant little black dress. The velvet bodice molded itself to her breasts and torso, the taffeta skirt flared out slightly from her waist and over her hips, its hem landing midthigh. She finished off the ensemble with a pair of sheer black stockings and strappy expensive heels she'd bought with Miranda's assurance that they'd never go out of style. Her only jewelry was a necklace of pearls and rhinestones in a setting as ornate and old-fashioned as the dress was sleek and modern. Kate appraised her transformation from duck to swan and was quite pleased. Even her hairstyle was classy; the hairdresser she had visited that morning had gathered the thick mass into a shining French twist, leaving the back of her neck bare except for a few tendrils over her nape and ears.

Not too bad, she thought, glancing in the hall mirror one last time before she left. "Get down with your bad self," she said aloud to her mirror image. She grabbed her purse on her way out of the apartment.

The party was in full swing when she arrived. If her reception was any indication, the attendees had already partaken quite liberally of the refreshments offered at the bar. A gentleman she had interviewed briefly the previous year met her just inside of the door and insisted on kissing her hand.

"If you had looked like this when you cornered me in that elevator, I couldn't have refused to answer any question you wanted to ask," he said flirtatiously. Kate could have told him he answered her questions anyway, but she didn't want to start an argument with him.

She racked her brain for his name and finally remembered it. "Nice to see you again, Mr. Draper," she said politely, forcing a perfunctory smile as she tried to sidle around him.

"Paul, please," he urged. With his name, her memory of her past association with the self-important little weasel came back to her. He'd been a minor source on a story, and he kept trying to get Kate to promise that what he told her was "off the record." She tried to explain to him that she didn't protect sources whom she had to hound, confront, and finally force to divulge information, but he hadn't seemed to comprehend her. "We can be friends now. Unless you're here to do another story on me." He'd been barely a footnote in the last story, but Kate was too eager to get away from him to waste time correcting the drunken wannabe Lothario.

"I'm supposed to meet some friends here . . . Paul," she explained, once again trying to slither past him.

He blocked her way. "Don't run away, my Nubian princess. Stay with me," he pleaded. "This could be the beginning of a beautiful friendship."

"I'm sorry," Kate told him without remorse. "I've got to go find my friends."

"I just told you," he insisted, listing slightly to one side. "I could be your friend."

"Thanks, but no thanks," Kate responded, as politely as she could. She feinted to the left and, as he lurched over to stop her, she stepped nimbly to the right and maneuvered around him and away. Liquor loosened most people's tongues, and she was not above taking advantage of the fact to do a little research on Skipper that evening, but Paul Draper was not likely to know the developer. Luckily there were plenty of people in the crowd who did.

These businessmen and politicians were not her usual sources, but she did recognize a number of them. Her stories were usually about grittier subjects than the philanthropy of New York's elite. In fact, the majority of these glittering beautiful people had little firsthand knowledge of the misery and suffering their charity would be used to relieve. Most of the people at the five-thousand-dollar-a-plate dinner were white, upper- and upper-middle-class socialites who were born to their money and position.

A few darker-skinned guests stood out from the crowd, and Kate tried to guess which of the younger black men might be Jennifer's friend Brant. She was amazed to see that there were a half-dozen handsome, smooth-looking brothers in the ballroom.

"Ninety percent of the time, a black man looks better in a tux," she commented when her friend suddenly appeared at her side. Jen looked fantastic in a long satin backless gown. Its shimmering cream color complemented her golden brown skin.

"Everyone looks better when they dress."

"I thought I looked good until I saw you." Kate was accustomed to being outshone by her old friend, but she wished that, just once, she could have been the glamorous one.

"You look beautiful," Jen complimented her.

"You look stunning," Kate replied. Despite a twinge of jealousy, she was proud to know such a dazzling woman.

Jennifer hardly seemed to hear her. "Okay, no small talk," she said wryly.

"Huh?" Jen asked, distracted.

"Nothing. Who are you looking for?" Kate asked, wondering if Jen's odd mood was connected to the evening's covert activities. She, herself, felt on edge.

"Brant. He's around here somewhere. I saw him a little while ago." Jen's eyes darted about the room, but she barely seemed aware of their surroundings as her gaze swept the crowd, settling on Skipper Arnold. "Come on and say hello to Uncle Skip," she commanded, and strode away without giving Kate a chance to answer. Kate hurried to follow her.

"Skipper, you remember my old friend Kate Ramsey," Jennifer said as she joined the dignified old man whose photographs Kate had so recently downloaded from the Internet.

Leopold "Skipper" Arnold looked exactly like what he was: a wealthy, powerful, forceful man who built buildings that touched the sky. He included Kate in the warm smile he bestowed upon his adopted niece. "Are you having a good time?" he asked genially.

"It's a lovely affair," Kate murmured, shaking the hand he proffered.

"Jennifer's done a lovely job organizing this thing, as always. I don't know what we'd do without her."

His question emphasized his position as one of the hosts for the evening. Kate had read in the material she'd dug up on Skipper that, among his many other good works, he served as the chairman of the board for Haven House, the charity for which this party was being thrown.

Kate tried to ignore the pang of guilt she felt as she remembered she'd donated nothing to the orphanage in whose honor all these guests had ostensibly gathered. Who was she to judge the man whose magnanimity made this evening possible? At least *he* wasn't here tonight under false pretenses.

As if she sensed that she was wavering in her determination to request an interview with her quarry, Jen jumped in. "Kate was thinking about doing an article about you for the *New Amsterdam Press*. Do you think you might be able to give her an interview?"

"Sure," Skipper answered without hesitation. "You two girls set it up."

"Okay," Jennifer agreed.

"Thank you," Kate said quickly, then let Jen lead her away. "Well, that was easy," she commented as soon as they were out of earshot. "I noticed when I did my research that he doesn't do a lot of interviews, and those he has given have been with the heaviest hitters in the media."

"A coup for you, then," Jennifer said. "Just don't forget who arranged it."

"Of course not," Kate spoke soothingly, unsure why her friend sounded so severe. "I wouldn't do that."

"And just don't forget why," Jen hissed sharply. "This isn't going to be some whitewashed puff piece, right?" Her eyes glittered like diamonds in the low light.

"I'll print the truth, but I've got to tell you, Uncle Skipper sure doesn't look like a man with anything to hide. In fact, I'd say he doesn't seem to have a care in the world."

"Maybe he does and maybe he doesn't," her old college roommate said mysteriously. "And maybe that's because of what he's been doing on that new job."

"Has something happened?" Kate asked, keeping her voice low. "Have you found out something you're not telling me?"

"No," Jen replied harshly. "I haven't learned anything new."

"Why are you so—?" Kate started, but Jennifer silenced her abruptly by nudging her sharply in her side.

"Brant! I'm so glad to see you. This is Kate Ramsey, whom I was telling you about earlier."

"Hey, Jenny." The tall, well-built man didn't seem to find anything odd in Jen's demeanor. He took the hand she offered him and tucked it possessively into the crook of his arm as he surveyed Kate.

Kate had to control the urge to gape openly at the man. She couldn't believe Jen hadn't bothered to mention that the man was incredibly handsome. Brant Fuller was movie-star material.

"You're the reporter?" It didn't sound like a question exactly, more like an accusation. His dark eyes examined her. She felt her back stiffen under his curious regard. His high forehead and arched brows gave him a questioning, intelligent air that she instinctively perceived as a challenge.

"You say that like we're some kind of strange exotic breed," Kate answered, not sure if it was hostility she sensed in his voice or something else. "It's just a job." His mouth quirked in an ironic little smile, drawing her attention to his full lips and strong jaw. She stared, feeling bemused. No man should be this beautiful. It made Kate feel off balance.

"Don't be so modest, Katie," Jen interjected. She turned to Brant. "She's won awards for her reporting."

"You must be good at what you do, then," he commented. She hadn't been mistaken; there was definitely a sarcastic tone to his voice. It was just her luck that they were meeting under these circumstances rather than on a moonlit beach. It had to be at a business function where, for professional reasons if nothing else, she was forced to keep her distance. Not that she was likely to attract his interest.

It's just as well, she thought. *He doesn't like reporters.* She shot a venomous look at the woman who had arranged this meeting. How could Jen have failed to tell her that the man was sexy as hell?

"And you want me to help you with what, exactly?" Brant asked.

This kind of "help" she didn't want. "If it's an inconvenience, I don't need—"

Again Jennifer cut her off. "I thought you could fill her in on the state of the business, the lingo, introduce her to people she might want to talk to."

"Of course," said Brant. "Anything I can do to help." Although the words were polite, his tone made it clear that he was less than enthusiastic about working with her.

Annoyed with his hypocrisy, Kate replied just as insincerely, "Your business is fascinating."

"The media does seem to have an interest in a couple of aspects of construction," he said wryly. "The more . . . shall we say . . . colorful aspects, anyway."

"That's what we do," Kate said lightly, trying to hide her irritation at his obvious prejudice. "Report on those colorful aspects of life in the big city."

Jennifer looked from one to the other of them curiously, then smiled. "Ahhh, this should be fun. I had a feeling about you two." She knew how to press all the right buttons. Her obvious enjoyment at their animosity was not, perhaps, her most endearing quality—but it was the first time that night that she had seemed somewhat happy, so Kate resigned herself to being the entertainment. For the moment.

"I've noticed that the media tends to focus primarily on the negative aspects," he continued. He was gorgeous, but he was also a jerk. That should have been enough to turn her off. Unfortunately, Kate couldn't get over how incredible he looked.

Mentally, she shook herself. "I don't know about that. We try to be objective," Kate replied.

"Do you?" he asked sardonically. "So it's your readers who were more interested in Mayor Dinkins's grandkids' college funds than in his campaign to reeducate racist police officers."

Just what she needed. Another angry black man who thought the media existed to malign his heroes. There was no way she could win with this guy.

"I knew you guys would hit it off," Jennifer said, smiling.

Kate wasn't in the mood to perform for her anymore. In fact, Jen's smug, patronizing tone set her teeth on edge. She saw right through Ms. Collier's stratagem, but it didn't seem to matter. It still worked. Her old friend knew how to get her riled.

Kate looked back up at Brent, absolutely determined not to argue with him anymore. No matter what he said, she would keep her cool. "Our readers determine what we write about, for the most part."

"I've heard that." His tone made it clear he didn't believe it. "I've also heard it's the advertisers who decide what the readers want to read."

"The advertisers don't edit the newspaper," she averred.

"But it's their money that pays the editors' salaries, right? And yours?"

She wanted to slap him. He was insufferable.

Kate decided to ignore the insult. Patiently, she explained, "Our circulation has to stay up, or advertisers don't buy space in our paper—it's true. But it is news that sells newspapers, and we cater to our audience in choosing what to report—to keep them buying."

"You don't think the readers' interests are shaped by how you choose to report the news?"

"I doubt it," Kate answered. "Have you ever heard of

journalistic objectivity? We're supposed to be unbiased. I'm not saying that we're perfect. Who is? But usually what that means is we include a quote from the opponent as well as the facts as presented by the principals in the story." Perhaps she could change the focus of this conversation. "You seem just as interested in my business as I am in yours. I have done a little research of my own," Kate mentioned. "I'd love to hear what you think about the situation at the L.A.C. Parking Garage construction site."

He didn't back off; she had to give him that. "The strike's gotten quite a bit of coverage on television," he said. "The union's certainly done its job there."

"So you think it's the union that's at fault?" she pressed.

Jennifer finally stopped the debate. "Kate, I don't think this is the right time or place for an interview, do you? Let's get some more drinks, all around, and the two of you can discuss this during business hours. I want everyone to enjoy themselves tonight. In fact, I went to a lot of trouble to make sure this party would swing." Just then, the band struck up the opening notes of its first song. If Kate knew her friend, she'd planned it that way. Jen was back to herself again.

She gave Kate a smug, self-congratulatory smile, and asked Brant to dance. Kate watched them head out onto the dance floor. They were a striking couple. Brant's large dark hand splayed over the supple bronze skin left bare by Jennifer's open-backed gown. They moved gracefully over the gleaming marble floor, gliding effortlessly to the strains of big band music. Kate wondered briefly if their relationship had ever been more than friendly, but she quickly discarded the thought. It was not her concern. All that mattered to her was how she was going to get out of this. She couldn't work with that man. He was impossible.

Kate honestly didn't think he'd demur if she just suggested they used someone else as a liaison between Skipper and herself. Brant didn't seem any more enthusiastic about his part in this crazy setup than she felt about hers. Whatever Jennifer had told him, he clearly thought she was going to do a hatchet job on his hero, Leopold Arnold. He was already bristling with indignation at the mere thought.

Kate needed someone more objective to help her. Investigative reporting required digging into areas that could be quite sensitive. Brant was too close to Skipper to see him clearly, or to want to see him as anything other than the successful magnanimous man of industry he appeared to be.

Jennifer said Brant had integrity, and Kate had no reason to doubt it. From the short conversation they'd just had, she knew he believed in speaking his mind, and she was inclined to accept her friend's assessment of his character. He might be prejudiced against reporters, but she didn't doubt for a moment that he truly believed in Skipper, and would do anything he could to stop her from printing another negative article about his friend. Kate wanted to know what was really going on, and he couldn't help but get in the way.

She tried to tell Jennifer as much when she next had the chance to speak with her. "You've got the wrong guy for this, honey. Brant hated me on sight."

"He didn't hate you. It's what you stand for," Jen said soothingly.

"I stand corrected," she answered snidely.

Jennifer nodded. "Uh-huh," she agreed distractedly.

Kate snapped her fingers under her friend's nose and spoke when she thought she had her attention. "Seriously,

Jen, I can't use him. He'll screw everything up," Kate insisted.

"He's the only person we can trust. You know how this business works," Jennifer argued. "One hand washes the other, everyone looks the other way. We need Brant. He's the only one who I know, for sure, will be up-front with you."

"I'm sure he's a very straightforward guy, but he's also completely biased toward Skipper, and equally prejudiced against me," Kate protested. "He doesn't like reporters. You heard him. He thinks the media is racist. And I'm guessing that includes Yours Truly. What makes you think he'll tell me anything?"

"He said he would," Jennifer responded. And that was that. She wouldn't be swayed. Short of going to the man and telling him herself that she didn't think he could do what she required of him, Kate was stuck with him as her contact in the industry.

Well, fine, she thought. *I'll just tell him he isn't right for the job.* When he asked her to dance, he gave her the perfect opportunity to carry out her plan.

They didn't talk at all at first. The orchestra was playing a classic by Duke Ellington, and Brant was a very good dancer. He guided her through the other couples and around the dance floor with a gentle, masterful touch. Kate hadn't danced this way in a long time . . . not since before her father's death. These days, when she went dancing, it was to a club where the music was contemporary, and she danced by herself, even when she had a partner. She enjoyed that, but this was something else. It was romantic. It made her feel nostalgic for her childhood when her dad taught her these steps. In those days, she still thought her daddy was the strongest, smartest, biggest man in the world. It was not the thing for a strong black woman in her thirties to admit, even to herself, but she felt young, innocent, sheltered, and secure in his arms. She was tempted to delay the unpleasant conversation she knew she must initiate with this man until the song was over.

But Brant took the initiative. "Kate," he murmured, "we should make an appointment for next week."

"Hmm? Oh, well, I don't think we should bother," she said softly.

"Why not?"

"It's clear to me that you don't feel comfortable—" she started to explain.

"I don't feel comfortable? I think you're the one who's uncomfortable."

"Wait a minute—" she protested.

"I may not be objective, but I can give you the information and introductions that you need to write this article on Skipper."

"May I speak now?" she asked.

"Of course," he said, just as if he hadn't been steamrolling over her objections.

"Do you think you can stand to work with someone you obviously disrespect?" she asked, going on the offensive.

"I don't know you well enough to have formed an opinion of you yet. It's your profession I don't care for," he claimed. "And I'd say we're equal on that score. You don't seem to think much of the construction business, either."

"Like you, I don't know enough about it to have formed an opinion," she contended.

"So, we'll learn," he said with a grim smile. "Monday morning, my office?"

"All right," Kate couldn't back out without appearing to be prejudiced against him and Skipper, and even though she knew herself to be exactly that, she refused to give him any reason to think so. It was a matter of pride.

"A matter of pride . . . and prejudice? You're kidding, right," Jennifer said, laughing, when Kate told her about the upcoming meeting.

Kate was not amused. "No, I'm not kidding. I'm a professional, a journalist," she said defensively. Jennifer let out another peal of laughter. "Professional pride and prejudice?" she finally managed to say as she continued chuckling.

"Funny, funny. A pun is the lowest form of humor, you know," she told Jennifer, but Kate couldn't help laughing a little. Unfortunately, Jen still would not take her seriously when Kate asked her to help come up with a diplomatic way to cancel her appointment with Brant.

"Just go," Jen urged. "What can it hurt?"

Four

The temporary construction elevator climbed steadily upward, gears churning smoothly, if not silently. Brant Fuller tried desperately not to think about the ever-widening gap between himself and the earth below. A fear of heights was definitely a detriment to a man in his line of work. Six square blocks of prime real estate in the center of midtown Manhattan spread out below him like a throbbing gray vortex that threatened to pull him from his perch. He wished he could enjoy the spectacular view. Unfortunately, he could barely breathe, let alone appreciate the silvery cityscape. A cable, a few floorboards, and the wire mesh walls of the Alamak were all that stood between him and a terrifying plummet down into the cement mixer.

The job was half-finished. The electricity and plumbing had already been installed, and the inspector had okayed the final stage of his contract, enclosing the pipes and wiring in the walls his firm was expert at constructing. Floors four through six were completely done. The interior design crew was already at work on them. But on seven, eight, nine and ten, there was still plenty of work for his men to do—on both the floors and the walls. Unfortunately, today he had to meet the drywall supplier and insurance agent all the way up on the top floor. No one else could take care of this for him—certainly not his belligerent crew chief who would just make things worse. Brant *had* to take this meeting. If the men he was going to meet chose to risk their lives climbing around buildings that didn't yet have proper flooring, walls, or even a ceiling, then Brant had to take that chance with them. It was all just part of the job.

He calculated the distance between himself and the ground as he came level with the fourth floor of the building. Sixty feet. If the elevator were to plunge to the ground from this height, he could survive it. People walked away from horrible accidents all the time. His mind filled with pictures of collapsed buildings and mangled cars. This wasn't helping. He tried to think of something positive and remembered an item he'd seen on the news: An infant had survived a fall from the fifth-story window of a burning building only a week ago. He had to relax, he thought. Like that baby. That was why it survived. It didn't even know it was falling. He rolled his head back in an effort to loosen his stiff neck and shoulder muscles, and tried to force his clenched jaw to unlock. He was only partially successful.

Construction could be dangerous, but Brant was successful enough that he could generally arrange to stay on the ground floor and hire other men to perch on skeletal steel beams putting in cement floors and walls and covering I-beams with drywall and plaster. No one knew about his phobia, and luckily, he was going up alone, so he didn't even have to talk, or make jokes, with any of his men. When he went up with them he forced himself to act naturally. That took a lot out of him. In comparison, this solo ride wasn't that big a deal, he told himself. His hold on the metal bar that controlled the elevator's ascent tightened as he passed the sixth floor, and came level with the seventh, which wasn't quite finished yet. He was perfectly safe. Alamaks held a maximum weight of six thousand pounds and the cable that pulled him upward was made of reinforced steel. He forced his eyes upward to his destination—the half-finished tenth floor.

He hadn't been needed "up top" since the day strong winds had started blowing the sheets of drywall around on the seventh floor. Overseeing the chore of getting the heavy materials secured while his crew chief kept the men working, and on their tight schedule, had been some job. Brant trembled like a leaf for the rest of the day.

He reminded himself that he'd seen guys tumble forty or fifty feet and walk away with barely a scratch. In the construction business, stories of near misses and narrow escapes was the basis for casual conversation. They circulated from one crew to another. Horrifying tales of accidents and the resulting injuries were related and embellished upon, by men perched on thin plywood slung across steel girders, their feet dangling over the edge of the unfinished framework that would form the bones of the tenth, or the twentieth, or the thirtieth floor of the building they were forging from metal, rock, and glass.

He had paid his dues, working his way through graduate school alongside the men who risked their lives erecting the apartment houses and office buildings he was dedicated to constructing. Then he got his structural engineering degree and started his own business. He made a name for himself, in a small way, by being thorough and honest and a little less expensive than other subcontractors who specialized in walling and flooring.

Brant didn't usually bid on contracts as big as this one, but it was for a church, and he liked the idea of working on a building that would house people and businesses and provide income to the church to whom this prime real estate had been bequeathed. If it hadn't been for friends of his who convinced the church board not to just sell the parcel of property but to build on it, this building wouldn't even exist, and he felt he had an obligation to support a project as worthwhile as this one. The job was less profitable than one this big should have been because he tried his hardest to keep costs down for the A.M.E.— including his own paycheck. It was worth it, though, because it made him feel like he was actually making a contribution to society. At least, Brant thought, he was risking his life for a good cause.

The elevator was moving so slowly, he felt like he was stuck in one of his own nightmares. *Think about something else,* he told himself. Instantly, he thought of the reporter he had met on Friday night, Kate Ramsey. She was not what he had expected. Somehow he had envisioned her as Jenny's alter ego because Jennifer Collier had a dispassionate, almost cynical view of the way the world worked, which seemed to him the perfect attitude for a newspaper reporter.

He *had* expected Kate Ramsey to be intelligent and observant, because she was a journalist, and so Brant had not been surprised by her quick eye and quicker tongue. What had thrown him for a loop was that she was absolutely *nothing* like Jenny. They were supposed to be the best of friends, so of course he thought they would be somewhat alike. There had been no reason, he realized after he met her, that she should be tall and willowy, or cool and detached.

Ms. Ramsey was none of those things. She was a fireball—candid, direct and disconcertingly open. Her personality just didn't fit with his preconceived notions of what a journalist should be.

The elevator jolted to a stop at ten. He had made it. This far. Whatever happened when he met Kate Ramsey on the following Monday, his association with her had already proven useful. He'd survived this ascent without succumbing to panic. Now all he had to do was get his insurance agent to back him up with the drywall guy, and he was in business.

Putting aside thoughts of the reporter, he stepped out of the elevator and braced himself for the open, unprotected, windy platform that would be this building's top floor when his men finished constructing the walls. Brant looked around. It should not have been hard to spot the men he was meeting. Suits were not exactly standard on a working construction site, let alone the latest from Brooks Brothers. Brant was surprised when it took him a moment to find Oliver Katz and George Pappados in the crowd.

In fact, it was George, his supplier, who wasn't wearing a suit, who saw him first. The dark-skinned, weather-beaten man was dressed in jeans and a flannel shirt that protected him from the wind, which was constant up this high. He waved, and Brant went toward him and Oliver Katz, who stood next to him. The accountant was tall, thin and pale, and next to George, he looked like an undeveloped adolescent although Brant knew him to be at least ten years older than the burly, second generation Greek. The two men were the only ones up here not hard at work. Neither of them appeared to have any problem with heights. They stood, sipping coffee, relaxed and at ease. Oliver actually looked like he was enjoying himself.

"This is quite a view," the insurance agent said, confirming Brant's suspicion. "I never get to see projects at this stage. I'm glad you asked me to meet you up here."

"I appreciate you coming," Brant replied. "But it was George's idea that we meet up here." Pappados had made it clear he had every intention of taking back his drywall, today, if he wasn't paid (and perhaps even if he were). A check to Brant's insurance company had bounced because of a bookkeeping snafu, and it was policy for the insurance company to contact his major suppliers in the event of a missed payment. It was his drywall supplier's policy to take back his materials when he thought he wasn't going to be paid. The meeting could only take place if Brant arranged for them all to be where the drywall was. Brant hoped his insurance agent could help him talk the supplier out of reclaiming his materials.

"I wanted to make sure you weren't having financial problems," George said. Brant was glad to see the men working, without interference from Pappados. "The job has proceeded very smoothly up until now," Brant assured him. "And I called Oliver so he could explain his company's policy. As I explained, they were never thinking of dropping my insurance. It was a mistake."

"Right," Oliver confirmed, nodding. He knew, as they all did, that if there was a problem with the insurance, the job could not be completed. At least not until after any such difficulties were cleared up. Brant couldn't afford a delay at this stage. His men were depending on this job, and he himself had gambled his career on it. Even after ten years, he was still young and new enough at this that every time he took on a contract, he put his future on the line. Any delay in the project ate away at the budget, and a long delay would definitely cut into his paycheck—which wasn't large to start with. He had taken on this job more for his gratification than for profit.

"So have you got my check?" Steve asked.

"Right here," Brant tapped his pocket lightly. "Certified, as you requested." He'd agreed to pay the month's bill two weeks early as a sign of good faith. It would be hell on the bookkeeper for the next two weeks, but he supposed that was poetic justice, since it was her mistake that caused this brouhaha.

"So, are we all clear?" he asked, before turning over the money. "Do you need to ask Oliver any questions?"

"No I believe it was just a clerical error." Brant breathed a sigh of relief. "Looks to me like your guys are doing a good job," Steve replied. "I'm sorry I was so tough on you, but construction can be a bad business. I can't take a chance on letting my invoices go unpaid because a contractor has problems getting paid on his end. If I did I'd have gone out of business long ago."

Brant nodded. Subcontractors, even general contractors he'd known, had been bankrupted that way. "It happens," he said philosophically.

He gave the check to Steve Landry and took Oliver aside for a moment. "I'm sorry I had to get you up here," he said. "I have to keep my suppliers happy, or I'm toast. I needed you to back up my story, just in case he didn't believe me. He has to know I've got insurance, or I won't get the materials I need. No drywall, no job."

"I know," Oliver mumbled sympathetically. "Like I said, this has been interesting. I'm usually stuck in my office this time of day. This sure beats that." Brant left him admiring the view.

Brant hated the money side of his business. It was complicated, often bordered on the corrupt, and the politics involved were too convoluted for his taste. Skipper Arnold was good at that stuff, but Brant never had been. If things got worse, Brant would call him for advice. He was a good friend. Brant hoped he could get Kate Ramsey to understand that.

Kate came to meet him at his office on Monday as they'd arranged at the party. He'd been working out of a trailer on the lot, overseeing the day-to-day operations of his crew. Thanks to the workmen's whistles and catcalls, he knew before she appeared at his door that a woman was approaching. The men always announced the entrance of any woman to the site in this manner, and when Brant heard the commotion, he knew immediately who it was. At that instant, he realized he'd been subconsciously awaiting her arrival.

He put aside the paperwork he'd been checking over and met her at the door of his temporary office. She was all business. Her outfit, a navy blue linen suit with a short, narrow skirt, was completely out of place in the cramped, inelegant trailer. He liked it, though, especially the high heels. She looked so cute, he almost forgot what a shrew she was. That was, until she spoke.

"That's some reception area you've got," she said acerbically. It wasn't just her complaint, but also her tone of voice that grated.

"We don't need video cameras," he responded flippantly.

"Am I supposed to feel flattered?" she asked.

"Pretty much," he answered honestly. "It's a compliment to your sex. At least they don't discriminate if that makes you feel any better. Every woman gets the same treatment: tall, short, skinny, fat. They love 'em all. But I have to say—in this instance, they show taste."

She didn't even crack a smile. "Well, as you seem to be acting as their spokesperson, may I act as the same for my own?" The woman was obviously trying hard to keep her tone light, but it was clear she felt she'd been insulted. Her eyes sparkled with emotion. She was indignant and trying not to show it. "We women, most of us, don't appreciate the compliment."

"Really?" he asked facetiously.

"Really," she said emphatically. "You can pass that along." She shrugged, still trying to appear calm and composed. "If you want to." Beneath that cool facade, he could tell that she was more than a little irritated, but as long as she wanted to pretend, he would play along.

"Sure thing," he replied. He sat back, folding his arms across his chest and watching her, trying to decide whether she was going to be real trouble, or just a minor annoyance.

He knew that her opinion of his mentor was not high, and he wanted to show her how wrong she was. He owed Skipper that much, and more. Much more. When he ran into complications on his first few projects, he could always count on his mentor to help him to extricate himself from the dilemma. The man was a virtuoso when it came to playing the system. But that did not make him crooked—no matter what Kate Ramsey thought. It meant only one thing in Brant's estimation. The old man was good at what he did. He was, in fact, the best, and he knew it. His arrogance had made him a target before—for the police, for the politicians, and for the press. But Skipper had beaten them every time. This time, Brant wanted to shield him from the ugliness if he could.

Kate Ramsey sat opposite him looking him over, measuring him up in just the same way he was evaluating her. Brant jumped right in, thinking the best defense was a good offense. "So what do you want to know about Leopold Arnold?"

"Do you mind if I record this interview?" She took a small tape recorder from her bag as she spoke and put it on the desk between them.

"No problem," Brant answered, although her simple action made him feel somewhat ill at ease.

Kate was totally in control again; the fire in her eyes had been banked and she was all business. It was as if someone had flicked a switch inside of her; Kate Ramsey was as detached and unemotional as her tape recorder itself. "You've worked with Mr. Arnold for years. How would you characterize your association with him?" She seemed completely relaxed. The she-cat who had walked into his office outraged by his men's chauvinistic reception had disappeared.

"He was my mentor, he has been my employer and partner, and he has always been a friend," Brant answered.

"How did you meet?"

"I was just out of college, at an alumni function, and he was a guest of one of the alumnus, who was another man he had mentored, by the way."

"What was he doing there?"

"Mingling, mostly," Brant said mockingly.

Kate acknowledged the joke with a perfunctory smile. "Why was he there?" she pushed. "He never went to college, so he couldn't be an alum, and with his money, I doubt he was there for the free drinks, so what was so enthralling about a group of CUNY students?"

"Did Jenny tell you I was a CUNY grad?" he asked, wondering if she'd done her research on him, too.

"I never reveal my sources. So?" she said dismissively.

"So, why was Skipper there?" he repeated her question, thinking. "He was there because Clive Bushner invited him to meet some of his friends." Kate scribbled something in the small notepad she'd taken out of her purse. Brant surmised that it was a note to herself to call Clive—now a rather well-known lawyer, and a budding politician. "I think Clive was showing off a little, if you want to know the truth. Mr. Arnold is an important man, and Clive was just starting to make it as a lawyer. And it worked. We were impressed."

"You admired Arnold?"

"Of course. He's a brilliant businessman, and a black man, and one of the most successful developers in this city, which means he's one of the most successful anywhere."

"And is that when he became your mentor?" she asked.

"We talked. He gave me some advice about how I could establish myself in the business. And he graciously offered to meet with me again. To give me more pointers."

"So, that is when he became your mentor?" she asked again.

"Yes, I guess so."

"Didn't you work for Powell at that time?"

"I was employed there for a few years," he answered, positive now that she had indeed been looking into his past. Brant felt strangely flattered, and a little bit wary.

"Wasn't his company, Leopold Engineering Operations, in competition with Powell Enterprises?" she inquired.

"Not for me. It's not like Skipper was trying to steal me away from the company or anything," he joked, curious as to where her questions were leading.

"Didn't Powell lose a couple of big contracts to L.E.O. that year?"

"Huh?" Brant started to get irritated as he realized that she was implying he had been approached by Skipper to spy on Powell. "L.E.O. and Powell were both major construction companies. Of course they were bidding on the same contracts. Don't you go after some of the same stories that your fellow journalists do?" he asked, taking offense at the implication.

"Sure," she said meaningfully. "That's why our sources are so important to us. When you're competing for a big story, it's your sources that are the determining factor in who gets more, and better, information."

"Sometimes you win, and sometimes you lose," he said, seething as he realized she actually thought he might have sold out his employer.

"Were you a source of information for Leopold Arnold?" she asked outright.

"You have some nerve, lady. Are you accusing me of

leaking our bids to the competition?" He was more than a little angry, but she just continued, seemingly unaffected by his barely suppressed rage.

"I'm not accusing you of anything. I'm just wondering if an important man like Skipper Arnold might have had an ulterior motive in cultivating the friendship of a young construction worker from a competitive firm. And you still haven't answered my question," she said coolly.

"It doesn't deserve an answer. But I'll tell you. For the record." He picked up the tape recorder from the desk between them and spoke directly into it, without ever taking his eyes from her face. "I did not, at any time, give Leopold Arnold any information on any bid made by Powell Construction while I worked there. He is a good man who has never, to my knowledge, done anything unethical or illegal in pursuit of a contract or construction deal." He put the recorder back down firmly but gently and glared at her challengingly.

The reporter didn't seem disturbed, or embarrassed, by his emotional outburst. From all outward signs, she was impervious to it and to him. She consulted her notepad again. "What do you think of the accusations that are currently being leveled at him that he employs racist practices in his hiring, specifically at the L.A.C. Parking Garage site on Ninth Avenue?"

"They are not true," he stated categorically. He didn't think he liked this woman anymore.

"You discount them as . . . what? Politically motivated, Or maybe it's a personal vendetta by a member, or certain members, of the union?"

"You mentioned this when we met," he said through gritted teeth. At the time, he thought she was kind of cute. Now that he knew that that kittenish exterior masked nerves of steel, he was annoyed with himself for falling into that old trap. Just because a woman was pretty and little and felt good in his arms, that did not mean she was as pliable as she might feel. He was going to have to be more careful with her than he thought. He agreed to meet with her to protect Skipper, but she wasn't going to just accept his opinion of the old man. Kate Ramsey was after a bigger story. "I can only say that this is a very complex issue, and I'm not directly involved in the dispute. You'll have to interview people who are," he continued. Brant thought that would be the end of it, but the witch was nothing if not tenacious.

"So whom do you think I should speak with?" she asked, her pen poised over her notepad.

"Specifically?"

"Yes. Even though you're not—as you say—directly involved, I'm guessing you know who the major players are. Whom would you recommend I call?"

"Well," he said, drawing the one syllable out as long as he could as he considered whom he should serve up to this wildcat next.

"Skipper, of course," he advised.

"I'm already set to interview him next week," she said.

"And, um, perhaps," he stammered, thinking hard. "It might be helpful for you to interview . . ." He cast about for a harmless, but helpful, pigeon he could steer her toward. Suddenly he thought of the perfect guy. ". . . Professor David at the Labor Relations Board. He's studied the history of the New York unions." *And he would love to expound on his favorite subject,* Brant thought, relieved at having thought of someone who would love to speak with the reporter about her article, and who would help her *without* hurting his old friend Skipper.

"Great!" the reporter responded. "And could you suggest anyone at the P.S.W.U.A. offices?"

"I haven't actually had many dealings with them. I'm

a subcontractor, not a general contractor. I don't employ the steelworkers."

"But you know who the important men are over there, don't you? The ones whose opinions count in matters like this?" she pressed.

"Jennifer could probably help you there," he suggested.

"She's in public relations. You're in the construction business. I would think you'd be better informed on who the real movers and shakers are, as a matter of self-preservation."

"As I said, the kind of work I do only rarely brings me into contact with the union."

"That's why Jen introduced us. She figured you would know who was a figurehead and who was a real leader. I don't want to waste any time chasing double-talk from some figurehead."

"Did Jenny tell you that?" he asked, hoping to distract her.

"She didn't have to," Kate answered wryly. "Why else do you think she suggested that I get your help?"

He had to admire her guts. She had turned the tables on him very neatly. In effect, she challenged him to answer his own question. *Fine,* Brant thought. *If you want to play, I'll play.* Her defiant gaze dared him to try to dance around the question.

"If I had to guess, I'd say Jenny introduced us because she knows I'm one of Skipper's good friends, and she wanted you to hear about what a great guy he is from a colleague rather than his public relations director. That is her job, you know. I'm guessing she tries to deflect members of the press who want to sully the reputation of her client. She is supposed to provide Skipper with testimonials as to his good character. And that's why she chose me." He smiled triumphantly at the newswoman, pleased with himself for coming up with that little speech.

His cocksure smile did not last long. Only until she provided an alternative to his theory. "You know Jen," Kate said laconically. "Don't you think she might be a little smarter than that? Don't you think she'd realize that, if she pawned me off on some obsequious yes-man after I asked her about the strike, it would be like waving a red flag at a bull? She knows my desire to get to the bottom of the matter would only grow stronger if I thought she was trying to divert my attention away from it."

"Uh-huh," Brant mumbled, defeated.

"So," Kate said implacably. "*Is* there anyone at the P.S.W.U.A. that you would recommend that I interview about this situation?" She was good. He had to give her that.

"I'll have to get back to you," he said to buy time. He had to think carefully about how to satisfy that request. Skipper was extremely unpopular with all the union leadership at the moment.

"And perhaps you could also suggest whom I might contact among the other developers concerning why this situation has arisen at this particular point in time."

"I think you know the answer to that," he said dryly. "He's been attacked because he's vulnerable. That's the law of the jungle."

She pounced on that. "In what way do you feel he's vulnerable?"

"He's a successful black man," Brant explained shortly.

"You're saying he's being persecuted solely because of his race? His decision to hire non-union labor has nothing to do with the firestorm of criticism?"

"He was asked to help the Hispanic welders. He did. Now he's being hounded by the same union that asked for his help, and by former friends, and by you—members of the press—because of it," Brant pointed out.

"I don't think the Hispanic community, or anyone else, expected him to take advantage of their request for his support," she argued, her clear-eyed gaze daring him to contradict her.

He was just as straightforward with her. "Face it, Ms. Ramsey, Skipper came up with a clever solution to a sticky problem."

"A little self-serving, don't you think, to choose to address the problem by cutting his own costs?" she countered.

"He refused to be used by either contingent of the union. He hired more Hispanics, but on his own terms."

"At the expense of those few who are in the union, like Julio Gonzalez."

"You have to admit, he did create equity in the workplace."

"Okay, I can see we're going to keep going around in circles on this one," Kate said. "I've got your comments on record—"

"You can quote me," he interjected before she could continue.

She ignored that. "Is there any other information you feel I should have? Besides those names you're going to give me later?" she asked.

Brant smiled. "Not that I can think of, offhand," he responded.

"Well then, thank you for your help." She closed her notepad and reached for the tape recorder. "I'll be in touch," she promised.

"I'll be waiting," he said wryly, standing as she rose out of her chair. He showed her out of the office and breathed a sigh of relief as he closed the door behind her.

That had gone as well as could be expected, he supposed, but he wished they had been able to agree on more than their differences. Still, he had a feeling Kate didn't completely disagree with him. It might have been wishful thinking on his part, but he thought she'd ended the session when she had because he was actually starting to sway her opinion. He hoped he had had an affect on her. He was pretty sure he would have another opportunity. He had a feeling he had not seen the last of Kate Ramsey.

There was something so appealing about the little witch. She was so quick to challenge him—on the offensive from the moment she sensed his disapproval. He did not doubt her ability to face up to anyone. But she lacked finesse. He did not think she was the type to accommodate her bosses at the newspaper when they asked her to back off from a story that might embarrass one of their major advertisers. Nor could he imagine the lady compromising with the powers that be should they request her cooperation in printing some little slob's sensational story just to sell their rag. Then again, he could be wrong about her. He really didn't know anything about her, except that he looked forward to seeing her again.

Five

It was a start, Kate thought. Even if Brant didn't come around, she thought she had enough material to sell an article on Skipper, if she was able to interview Skipper Arnold as effectively as she had his friend. And Jen was sure Mr. Sensitive would cool off, and take his calls. Kate told her how angry Brant was, but was reassured that he wasn't the kind to hold a grudge. Although he had a temper, Jen said, Brant Fuller always chilled out as quickly as he blew up. Kate was tempted to ask how extensive Jen's knowledge of the subcontractor actually was, but she didn't have the nerve. She could only hope her old friend was right. The story would be better if she could get his input, no matter what she found out, or which way it went.

Besides the meeting with Charles at her own paper, the *New Amsterdam Press,* she had spoken with a friend at the *Village Voice* whom she wrote for occasionally, as well as a couple of other editors, about the piece. She also activated her network of spies, informants and gossips for any tidbits on the grapevine. New York was actually a much smaller town than it appeared. Someone always knew something. It was not easy to keep a secret, especially if it was a juicy one.

With her tentacles spread all over town, her contacts

alerted to the possibility of a big story, Kate went out dancing that night. About once a month, Kate released pent-up tension at Body and Soul, the drug-free, intelligent, adult version of the raves she attended as a teenager. It wasn't a place for the beautiful people, or even the bridge-and-tunnel crowd to see and be seen. Usually Jennifer disdained the unpretentious nightclub, but for a change she had decided to meet Kate there.

During the cold winter months, it was a pleasure entering the steamy basement where her fellow enthusiasts gathered to dance to World Music in a cacophony of rhythms and voices from around the globe. However, after the warm weather of the last few weeks, the heat that rose to envelop her on the stairs as she descended gave her pause. Kate had forgotten how overheated the space could get. It didn't deter her, though. She had come for one reason and one reason only. She wanted to dance.

She came alone, but some of her crowd was already there. Marie, David, and Tanikwa were all on the floor, and they shouted greetings over the music when they saw her. She shucked off the cashmere sweater she wore over her thin cotton dress and joined them.

"Hey, girlfriend, long time no see," Tanikwa yelled.

"I know. I'm sorry. I've been working day and night. Not that you would know anything about that." Tanikwa worked when she felt like it. Sometimes that meant she had to crank out advertising copy until three in the morning, but more often she worked when she was inspired. She was an absolutely brilliant copywriter. Her office was like a playroom, and she was Kate's kookiest and most creative friend.

As usual, the sister wore an outrageous outfit. It looked like chain mail over spandex, and it probably was. It was also more than likely to appear on the cover of *Vogue* in the next few months. Tanikwa was always just a step ahead of the latest fashions. She could carry off the clothes, too. She was six-foot-one, and had a long slim torso and even longer lanky legs. Tonight, with a straight blond wig covering her smoothly shaven scalp, she really did look like a high-fashion model. The contrast of blond hair against café au lait skin was striking.

"It's a rat race, love," Marie said, her British accent still audible after ten years in the States, even over the music. In her late thirties, with her pale skin and dark hair, she reminded Kate of the actress on *Frasier,* which inspired her nickname, Ms. Moon.

"Not for me," Tanikwa said, twirling into David's arms, catching him unaware. He managed to catch her. The sweet, middle-aged businessman had fallen in love with Tanikwa at first sight, and no matter how often, or how drastically, she changed her appearance, he never faltered in his single-minded devotion.

"Don't get too cocky, *ma cherie,*" he warned. "You never know what could happen."

"I know I'll always get what I want," Tanikwa said, ignoring his advice. "No one can resist my charms. Least of all, you."

"Perhaps he can't, but Kate and I can," Marie warned. "In fact, when you talk like that, what we can't resist is the urge to take you down a peg or two."

"Go ahead and try it," Tanikwa dared her.

"I don't have the energy to think up some devious plan at the moment," Kate said. "That's why I came tonight. I need to recharge my batteries."

"Later, then," Marie said, with her characteristic British calm.

"Possibly," Kate said, starting to dance.

Hips swaying, feet stomping, arms waving, they all moved to the music. They danced as a unit and as individuals in that unique manner she'd only seen in big-city nightclubs. The music throbbed as West African drummers pounded on a variety of drums of different sizes, widths and depths. The band created a beat that seeped into her skin and bones, and made her blood pump faster. Her heart slammed into her chest with each deep thrum of the lead drummer's gigantic tabla. Kate lost herself in the music; her mind vanished and her body took over until she was drenched with perspiration and breathless from the exertion. Let others jog in the park; she loved to dance.

Jennifer was waiting at the bar when Kate went over to buy a club soda. "This is Raffael." She introduced Kate to the tall, handsome man beside her.

"Your date?" Kate asked, though she hadn't heard her friend mention the name before.

"We just met. He's from Rome. Visiting relatives for a couple of weeks," Jen clarified, winking. Kate marveled at the beautiful, golden-skinned young man. He couldn't have been more than twenty-four, but it hardly mattered in a place like this. There were no rules at Body and Soul. It wasn't the usual pick-up scene. While far from unheard of, hook-ups were rare since the crowd was comprised of an eclectic gathering of nationalities, races and professions: some émigrés, some tourists, and a smattering of native New Yorkers. Haitian cabdrivers mixed with top record producers while aspiring young actors danced with computer programmers.

The rules of New York society were abandoned in this atypical nightspot—which was why she liked it so much. The atmosphere imbued Kate with a feeling of freedom. However, starting a relationship with anybody one met in these circumstances was asking for trouble upon return to the world outside. Through the door at the top of the stairs was Greenwich Village. It was miles apart from its counterpart, the East Village, though all that separated them, geographically, was Broadway. The city, though small, was split into clearly defined neighborhoods, its huge population was even more fragmented.

The best and the brightest migrated to the city to prove their mettle. Actors starved, waiting for that one-in-a-million shot at working on Broadway. Bankers and brokers headed for the Mecca of finance—Wall Street. Designers poured their hearts and souls into earning recognition on Sixth Avenue, and Madison Avenue was the center of the universe for anyone working in advertising. In her own profession, Kate had heard and seen her colleagues scoff at journalists who sacrificed a chance at a hot story in order to keep an important date and at editors who chose to invest time and energy in their community over accepting promotions that involved uprooting their families. It was probably right that if you could make it here, you could make it anywhere. In the Big Apple, complete and utter devotion to one's chosen profession, art or avocation were required. Success required almost fanatical dedication on one's part as well as fantastic luck, which could only be achieved by networking. That made it very difficult to pursue a relationship with anyone from outside of one's small social circle.

Jennifer Collier, however, did not discard her personal rulebook just because no one of importance was watching. She did not dance with balding French bankers, Amazonian copywriters, or her best friend—at least not since she had graduated college. When she went to a nightclub, any nightclub, she danced with a handsome man, preferably one from her list of acceptable escorts. She might break with tradition a tiny bit by dancing with a young Italian tourist, but only if he was incredibly beautiful, and already smitten with her exotic good looks. Kate could tell at a glance that Raffael fit the criteria. She had seen it before. He was entranced by her old college roommate.

Kate shouldn't have been surprised. Through sheer willpower, Jen was able to snag a dance partner she considered suitable for the evening. She had done it before.

They danced for a couple of hours. Raffael seemed charming. Though he spoke little English, he was welcomed by "the gang." Kate knew well that Jennifer would use him as a buffer against the crowd for the evening and leave him without a backward glance when she went home. He might be acceptable, barely, as her companion for an evening of dancing in this setting, but Jen thought of him as a convenience. Her philosophy was simple. A dance partner was a necessity in a place where one danced. Kate forbore to comment on any of Jen's romantic adventures. She didn't want her own dating practices to be judged, and so she was not judgmental of Jennifer's behavior when it came to men. In fact, neither woman ever interfered with the other's love life. But, later that night, as they visited a coffee shop before heading home, Kate was sorely tempted to ask if Brant was one of Jennifer's past conquests The urge had nearly overwhelmed her before, and she tamped it down again now, as she had then.

Kate told herself that it didn't matter one way or the other, since she was only interested in Brant as a source of information. However, she did look forward to seeing him again, Kate admitted to herself. For all his prejudice against "her kind," she sensed that Jennifer was correct in her assessment of the man. Kate thought Brant Fuller really might be frank and honest as her friend proclaimed. He had impressed the hell out of her during their interview, not only with his loyalty to Skipper, but also with his unflinching responses to her questions about his own activities. He didn't try to pussyfoot around the issues, or soft-soap her. He came straight out and immediately refuted any implication of impropriety. You didn't meet men like that every day. You didn't even meet many women like that anymore. Everyone was too political.

She couldn't help wondering where Brant came from, and how he got where he was. If Skipper Arnold had something to do with the subcontractor's success, the developer had done at least one thing right.

Over coffee, Kate gently probed the publicist for her opinion of the relationship between the two men. "I may have my doubts about Skipper," Jennifer said. "But I believe he respects Brant. That's one of the reasons I introduced you two. Brant, I'd be willing to bet, is incorruptible. And Skipper knows it. Just like I do. Just like you do."

"I don't *know* anything about the man," Kate disputed. "I only interviewed him once."

"Trust your instincts," Jennifer advised. "Trust him."

Kate wasn't sure she was ready to go that far. He was a virtual stranger to her. But she did want to talk with Brant again.

She told herself there was only one way to know if Miss Collier was right about him, and his temper, and she called him the next day. She surprised herself by asking him to meet her that night for cocktails and was thrilled when he agreed. Kate didn't examine her motives for arranging to see Brant in person. She didn't have a good reason: none anyway that would stand up to close scrutiny. As she left her apartment to meet him, she told herself that she was just testing Jen's theory.

Sure enough, when she saw him again, he didn't seem to be angry anymore. They met at Rosie O'Grady's, a midtown restaurant frequented by low-level executives and the few tourists who worked their way up from Times Square to the quiet wood-paneled bar and grill at Fifty-second Street and Broadway. It was always pretty busy during the cocktail hour, because it was a convenient place for commuters to meet on their way home from midtown offices to Penn Station and Grand Central Station and the commuter train home. Kate liked it because it had a relaxed atmosphere. It was located only a few blocks from the construction site where Brant was working, and even though he said he'd never been there before, when she suggested the place, she knew he'd have no difficulty finding it.

She led him to a small round table across from the bar, just far enough from the regular patrons who sat on their bar stools, and the transients who stood with one foot up on the brass rail that ran the length of the oak bar while they downed a quick drink or two on their way to someplace else. "If you want a bite to eat, there's a bar menu. Just burgers and appetizers," Kate explained.

"Thanks. I'll just have a beer," Brant answered. "If that's allowed?"

"Why wouldn't it be?" she asked.

"I assume we're here for another interrogation session, and I wouldn't want you to think I was under the influence or anything." His easy smile made it clear that he hadn't intended to sting her with the flip remark.

That smile was something else again. Sexy, playful, and completely unexpected, it made her pulse jump. Kate was pretty sure there was an appreciative glint in his eye as he looked across the table at her, too. She cleared her throat nervously. He certainly didn't seem to be harboring a grudge against her because of that first interview. In fact, his mood seemed good. Kate felt a twinge of disappointment that this meeting was purely professional in nature. But he was, to all intents and purposes, just another source, and she needed him.

Their waiter came to the table and took their order. Kate wanted until his beer and her wine were served before she began. "Thanks for meeting me. I'm afraid we got off to a bad start yesterday. Today, I promise to be totally inoffensive. Okay?"

"Sounds good to me," he said, but, despite his apparent good humor, he didn't sound completely convinced.

I can work with that, Kate thought, satisfied. She truly didn't plan to offend him. She hadn't meant to attack Brant the last time. But she had to ask what she did. Otherwise she wouldn't be doing her job. "I just have a few simple questions. No tricks. Nothing up my sleeve."

Brant smiled. "Shoot," he urged.

"I'll be gentle," she promised.

He took a swig of beer. "That'll be different," he joked.

"I'm not out to smear anyone here," she assured him. "And I'm not accusing you of anything."

"But Skipper is fair game?"

"He's a public figure. I have the right to do a story on him," Kate answered. "I just hope you'll keep an open mind about me, and my motives. That's all."

"I will if you will." He wore a bland expression, but he sounded less skeptical. "What can I tell you?"

"Do you know anything about how Skipper got started in the business?"

Brant visibly relaxed. Kate guessed he hadn't been expecting such a normal, seemingly harmless, question. "Not really. I mean, I've heard all the usual rumors. He was born and raised in the islands. A poor family. He came to the States in the fifties and worked his way up the ladder to where he is today."

As much as she wanted to appease Brant, she had to dig deep below the surface. "I was able to discover that his family lives in St. Thomas, but I can't find any trace of his trip to this country." She wasn't planning to do a puff piece—not on a man who had gotten to the place Leopold Arnold had. He was a powerhouse in a cutthroat business. And men, especially black men, didn't have that kind of success handed to them on a silver platter.

He wasn't so nonchalant anymore. "What possible relevance could this have? It was over forty years ago."

Kate finished her drink. "No one seems to know how a poor, uneducated, black kid from St. Thomas managed to pay his airfare to the States, let alone afford what he lived in when he got here, or how he arranged the paperwork so he could get a job. It's a British Isle, as you know, so we don't exactly throw out the red carpet for common laborers from the islands. Back then it was easier, but still you can understand my curiosity."

"There are a lot of immigrants in this city who can't account for how they got here," Brant asserted. "Isn't that sort of the history of this country?"

Kate let it go. She had more difficult questions to ask. But, first, she needed another glass of wine. And, she decided, something to eat. "Do you mind if I order a burger? I haven't eaten all day."

"No, no," he replied. "Are they good here?"

"They're big," she told him. "Other than that, I don't know what to tell you. All hamburgers look alike to me." She waved the waiter over and ordered another round of drinks and a bacon burger.

"I'll have one, too," Brant added. "With mozzarella."

Kate would have loved to take a breather, but she figured she might as well get the unpleasantness over with as soon as possible, so she jumped right in. "Were you aware of his record?"

"What record?" he asked, confused.

"His criminal record. Leopold Arnold was convicted of a felony. In 1957. He and some friends stole a truckload of building supplies from a man they felt had cheated them out of their pay."

"No, I didn't know that. What does it have to do with anything?"

"He's a hero of yours, right? Don't you want to know if he deserves to be?"

"Nothing you tell me will make me admire his achievements any less. He's got a great mind, he's a good, ethical man, and he's a friend. Some trumped-up burglary charge from when he was a teenager isn't going to change that."

"What about the fact that he was investigated by the Feds last year on a bribery charge? Would that change your opinion at all?" She pushed on.

"I don't think so. He's black. I've never known a black man to rise without being hounded to death by the law as well as the press." He shrugged. "Apparently, the investigation didn't lead anywhere, or he would have been charged."

Kate didn't want to ruin his dinner, but Brant had to face the truth if they were going to work together. "You know that it doesn't always work that way. He could be as guilty as sin, and still conduct business as usual."

Their drinks arrived. *Just in time,* Kate thought as she continued. "This is a business where known criminals prosper. Such as the contractor who was hired to build a high-rise while serving time for bribery at Rikers."

"I don't think I know that story," he said.

"I'm surprised. It was in the *Times.* He's a rather well-known general contractor. And apparently, despite his criminal tendencies—or perhaps because of them—it was arranged that while he was serving his time, he could work on the project through Riker's work-furlough program. I believe the developers justified hiring him because, in their words, he was 'the only one who could get the job done.' The bribery conviction was incurred as the result of his work on his previous construction project."

Brant was intransigent. "Skipper isn't a criminal. Why are you so determined to make him one? He isn't in jail, despite allegations and investigations and repeated attacks by the media. Is this all you wanted to talk about? I thought you were interested in the real story."

"My focus is the strike that's going on at the L.A.C. Parking Garage construction site. But I'm trying to get a feel for the kind of man he is. From you."

"I don't think you are," Brant disagreed, but there was no heat in his voice as he continued. "I think you're just trying to get a story, a sensational story. Because that's what you're supposed to do. That's your job. Construction may be a cutthroat business, but journalism is at least as bad."

"The media isn't like other corporate enterprises. Their goals are very different. Selling shoes and informing the public are not comparable," she said.

"Only in that when you people destroy a man's business, it's not only expected, it's rewarded. It's *good* reporting. When Skipper crosses the line from good old boy to serious contender, he becomes a pariah. A little rugged American individualism is fine, until he puts his competition out of business. Then they say he's corrupt, even criminal. Without a shred of evidence, by the way. And the media jumps right on the bandwagon."

"Skipper's story aside, you must agree that the media serves an important function in a free society. It enlightens. It guards our beliefs and freedoms."

"And in construction, we create homes, offices, schools, et cetera. You don't think we serve just as important a function as builders?"

"Sure, but can't that be done without someone getting screwed?"

"You are not that naive," he said, looking at her knowingly. "You know what's at stake here."

"Money," Kate said. "Only money."

"The more, the better," he replied flippantly. "Same as in your business."

"Look, I'm not going to try and tell you that we don't have to make money. Of course we do. One thing that distinguishes the European press from the American one is that most of their revenues are subscriptions. Ours is determined by advertising, so actually what's in the news is what the advertisers think people want to read."

"And you put down what I do," he said, shaking his head. "You exploit people's misfortune in order to make a buck."

"It is human nature for some people to exploit the misery of others, and human beings do work in the media, but journalism doesn't have to be that way. 'No government ought to be without censors, and where the press is free, no one ever will.' Thomas Jefferson wrote that in a letter to George Washington. You are an intelligent, educated, well-read guy—you know the importance of the Fourth Estate."

"That's true, but I don't have to like it."

The waiter brought them their hamburgers. The crowd was starting to thin out and the noise level dropped. Soon the theatergoers would be leaving for Broadway where the curtains would go up at eight o'clock. Brant leaned toward her, making her feel as though this were an intimate dinner rather than business. But the conversation, while not directly related to the interview, made her feel less like she was out on a date. It was reminiscent of a dinner she had had with Jennifer. An exchange of ideas with a friend—an equal—not a *source*.

"You know how vital it is to monitor the government,

business, the powers-that-be. How would you suggest we do that if not with a free press?"

"You don't think the media is controlled by the powers-that-be?" he asked in disbelief, his sandwich suspended in midair, halfway between the plate and his gaping mouth.

"Oh, no," Kate said, rolling her eyes. "Don't tell me you're one of them!"

"One of who?" he asked warily, putting his burger back down, untouched.

"One of those people who believe the media has been taken over by the left, or the right, whichever side you're not on?"

"I think big money has a lot of power. Yes," he replied. He got back to his burger, taking a bite before he went on. "You've got to admit, they've got the most resources, the most to lose, and the most to gain by manipulating the press. A small minority controls the media that you are so busy defending."

"I didn't realize you were a conspiracy theorist. I thought we were just talking about our respective businesses," she said dolefully.

"We were. We are," Brant said. "And I don't think I'm particularly conspiracy-minded. But there are certain facts that can't be ignored. One of them is that money talks."

"Sure, but it's not just about money," she argued. "There are other factors involved."

"Money is the main one though, isn't it?" he said snidely. "You said yourself that you rely on advertisers to pay your salaries."

"I said we have to rely on advertising dollars to make a profit, not pay our salaries."

His dinner finished, Brant pushed the plate aside and concentrated his full attention on her. "But you didn't disagree. Because you can't. Can you?" he pressed. "You

just said that your advertisers determine what's published
in the newspapers. Why them? Why not you? You're the
one who studied journalism, not the advertising executives, or their clients, or your audience. Why don't reporters tell the readers what's important? Isn't that your
job?" Despite his obvious frustration, she was fascinated
by his eyes, his lips. She couldn't stop staring at his
mouth.

"Unfortunately, our readers don't all agree on what's
important." Kate looked at the remaining food on her
plate and, though she was full, she contemplated taking
another bite, just for something to distract her from her
dinner companion. She had to stay unaffected. A good
reporter did not let her subject get to her. She controlled
the story, it didn't control her.

"They don't know!" he barked. "They don't have news
services informing them of everything happening in the
world. You have access to that information. Why doesn't
the press educate the public instead of pandering to
them?"

She gave up on the remaining half of her oversize burger and gave in to the urge to set Brant straight. "Because
this is a business. It's not just informing people, it's selling people the paper. And people don't seem to want to
buy dry, boring stories. They like their news exciting.
Sensational—as you call it." Kate had no intention of
apologizing to him for believing in what she did.

"So you feed their prejudices with stories about men
like Skipper?"

"When he does something that's newsworthy, yes. But
you seem to be forgetting that the companies that we sell
our advertising space to need the subscribers, or their dollar isn't worth a thing. Our readers do have the final
word."

"Not over you, though. You answer to a higher authority." She would have sworn he was baiting her. But why? He had to know that, as absorbing as this philosophical discussion might be, they were going to have to get back to the subject she had come to talk about—his friend Skipper Arnold.

"I'm not the issue here," Kate declared.

"You are very much the issue," he insisted. "You are the press."

"And I try to write stories my readers will be interested in."

"And how do you know what they're interested in?" he argued.

"When they buy what we sell," she stated. "I wish it were different. I really do. I'd love to write about . . . oh . . . the famine in Africa, the genocide in East Timor, and a lot of other stories that don't seem to interest our audience enough."

"I'd be more interested in reading those articles than most of what's published," he claimed.

"You're not the typical reader. You're in the minority— no pun intended," she joked. "We can't customize each newspaper to fit individual tastes. We have to write for the majority of our readers. The simple truth is people buy the paper when they see certain things on the front page. For example, who would have thought people would have bought all the papers that featured Princess Diana before and after her death? But whether I think they should be interested in the subject or not, I have to write *for* them."

"I don't believe it," he said.

"Of course not," Kate retorted. "You'd rather believe it's all a big conspiracy."

"Is this how you conduct all your interviews?" he asked mildly.

"No," she said decisively. "It may surprise you to learn

that I rarely debate the merits of the newspaper business with my subjects. But you are not, strictly speaking, the subject. Leopold Arnold is. And, speaking of the subject, you keep getting off it."

"*I* keep getting off the subject?" he repeated incredulously.

"*We* keep . . . getting distracted," Kate corrected herself. It was true. When she was working, she was usually calm and controlled. Perhaps every once in a while, she became overly passionate about her articles, but usually, she was a consummate professional. Brant got under her skin, somehow. Maybe it was his attitude. She wasn't accustomed to being attacked because of her profession. However, she had to put a stop to this incessant quarreling. Kate promised herself she would keep the interview on track from that moment on.

"I think you're a hell of a lot more interested in selling newspapers than you are in how Skipper got to this country," Brant accused. He was definitely trying to provoke her. Was it loyalty to Skipper that made him so contentious, or was it something about her?

True to her promise to herself, she refused to let him divert her from her object. "So change my mind. Convince me I'm on the wrong track. Tell me more about Skipper," she requested.

"What else do you want to know?" he asked. "I don't know how he got here, and I don't believe he's crooked."

"You seem so sure," Kate said. "But you yourself said this was"—she referred to her notes—"a cutthroat business. Why are you so sure he hasn't taken any shortcuts?"

"I know the man. That's why," he proclaimed.

"Okay, but—" she began.

He interrupted. "No buts."

"But—"

"There are no buts. He's a straightforward, honest,

hardworking businessman, and everyone who knows him admires him." *Not everyone,* Kate thought. Jennifer Collier had a lot of doubts. "You're barking up the wrong tree, lady," he said firmly.

But Kate trusted Jen's instincts. Her old friend might not be the most reliable source, but when it came to self-preservation, Jennifer was extremely motivated. "I'd still like to talk to some of the people involved in the strike," she persisted.

"I've been working on that," he said.

"You have?" she asked, astonished.

"I want to be there when you find out how wrong you are about Skipper," he said, taking his cell phone from his pocket. He punched in a phone number. "Actually, I am expecting someone to call me back tonight."

Great, Kate thought. *He's going to put me in touch with another member of the Skipper Arnold fan club.* She took a sip of her drink. The food had cleared her head. Kate figured that was probably a good thing. She needed to keep her wits about her with this guy.

"We're all set. He can meet us on Friday at two o'clock," Brant told her after listening to his messages.

"Okay," Kate agreed. If he thought she was going to drop her investigation if his friend confirmed his story, he was going to be very disappointed. Kate couldn't decide what would upset him more: having his friend confirm his opinion and then finding out she was not giving up on the story, or finding out his friend didn't share his opinion of Skipper. Kate knew which scenario she was hoping for.

Either way, the interview was bound to lead to further controversy between the two of them. She was . . . almost . . . looking forward to it.

Six

Kate thought about the interview with Brant quite often during the next two days. Even though it had gotten off-track, it had been stimulating. She loved a good fight. As a reporter, as she had told Brant, she had to look at all sides of an issue, because it was the only way to tell the whole story. Her personal motto was: the truth, the whole truth, and nothing but the truth. It wasn't original, but it suited her temperament perfectly. In conversations with her friends and colleagues, she often played devil's advocate. She didn't find it very arduous to argue either side of a question, because both were usually interesting, and each always held elements of the truth.

Her battles with Brant, while somewhat heated because of the passion she felt about her vocation, were minor skirmishes compared to some of the years-long debates that went on between herself and her friends. But the contractor was an intriguing puzzle. Kate was definitely attracted to him, little as she wanted to admit it. It was totally natural. He was more than pleasant to look at, obviously intelligent, and quite charming when he chose to be. He was a potent, self-assured man, and she was drawn to that.

She worried that she was getting a bit too preoccupied with planning what she would wear during their next meeting when Kate was quite effectively diverted by a more serious problem. She opened her weekly newspaper Friday morning to find that Jeremy Hallston had stolen *her* story on the hotels that catered to the homeless. Kate was livid. She called Jennifer and raved at her about the little weasel's latest stunt until she thought she'd gotten the worst of it out of her system. Then she called Charles. Either he really wasn't in, as his wife insisted, or he was not going to take her call at this hour of the morning. So she telephoned Miranda. Even then, Kate's wrath was not expended. She called Jeremy.

She knew it was a mistake before she did it. She knew it was going to be a huge blunder if she said to him what she was thinking about him. But she felt compelled to do it. At six o'clock in the morning.

She woke him up. "You scum-sucking, back-stabbing weasel," she spat fiercely into the phone. "You dirtbag. How could you be such a jerk?"

"Iris?" he said, sounding dazed.

"Iris? Who's Iris? Actually, don't answer that. I don't care. It's me, Kate. I don't believe this. I can't believe I was surprised by this. This is typical, Jeremy."

"Kate? Calm down, Kate," he said sleepily. "S'up?"

"How stupid can you be? How could you screw two women in the same week? That takes talent, maybe even a little brains, and you don't have either."

"Ouch," he said, but she could tell from his voice that he wasn't particularly upset, or nervous. He was laughing at her.

"Why did you do it? Huh?" she pushed when he didn't answer right away.

"It was a good story, that's all," he said without remorse.

"It was *my* story. You stole it. Have you ever heard of a little thing called ethics? Of course you haven't. You probably blocked it out of your memory five minutes after graduate school, if your behavior is any clue."

"Look, Kate—"

"Don't 'Look, Kate' me," she fumed. "If you value your life, you'll make sure I don't see you for a while, if ever." She spoke quietly, but with force. It was no idle threat. She was angry enough to cause him actual bodily harm. If she'd been in the same room with him, Kate thought she might have beaten him to death. Not just because of the story, but because it was the second time he'd slipped one past her. Even though she couldn't have predicted that he would actually do something so stupid, and so wrong, she couldn't deny that there had been clues: namely, their little walk down the hall together the previous week. She was as angry with herself as anything else, which irked her even more.

"Jeremy, don't be in the office when I'm there," she warned. Then she slammed the handset back down on the receiver.

After a morning of fretting and fussing, to herself and anyone else who was unfortunate enough to come within the sound of her voice, Kate wasn't in the best frame of mind for a meeting with a man as aggravating as Brant Fuller. In her foul mood, Mother Theresa would have probably annoyed her today. She tried to prepare herself for the encounter with Brant Fuller by using a meditation technique she'd learned at a stress-reduction seminar. She sat completely still, breathing deeply, and visualizing a peaceful blue mountain lake. She practiced the relaxation technique for nearly half an hour before she left for her appointment, and her roiling emotions were under control when she arrived at Brant's office.

"Hi, there," she said cheerfully when she saw him. He looked incredibly handsome. His square shoulders filled out his suit coat so well that Kate couldn't help picturing the musculature concealed beneath the gray gabardine. *Yup,* she thought. *Brant Fuller is just what the doctor ordered.* After a morning spent obsessing on how to punish Jeremy Hallston, Brant's beautiful dark eyes were balm to her shattered spirit.

I'm going to fantasize about him, she thought, unabashed. *And I'm going to enjoy it.* There was no rule against that. At least, none that was enforceable anyway.

"Hello, Ms. Ramsey," he greeted her warmly, winking as if his use of her name was some private joke just between them. At that moment, she wished it were. Kate desperately longed to kiss him . . . to know for sure the masculine landscape beneath that Armani jacket was as spectacular as she imagined.

"We're going to meet Andy at the site he's working on. Okay?"

"Great," she agreed, still not sure that it would be of any use to interview his buddy. Brant was too eager to have her talk to this guy.

"I don't think you'll be disappointed," he said.

"I appreciate your setting up this interview," Kate murmured. "Whatever the result."

"Andy and Skipper have an . . . interesting relationship," Brant declared.

Kate's ears perked up. Did she detect a hint of controversy here? "Interesting, huh? I find that very intriguing," she commented.

"Just trying to keep the customers happy," he responded in the same light tone. "If you're happy, I'm happy."

"I doubt that," Kate mumbled. While she didn't want her next interview to consist of character assassination, she definitely didn't want to hear another ode to Leopold Arnold, and she suspected that was all that Brant Fuller wanted to hear.

"Whatever happens, happens," he stated philosophically. "Just don't forget that I kept my part of the deal. I'm keeping my mind wide open."

"Me, too," Kate replied. They strolled along silently for a moment. "You really don't know what this guy is going to say? Isn't he a friend of yours?" she asked.

"Yes. He knows Skipper well, but he doesn't talk about him to me. I'm not sure why. So, why are *you* going after Skipper so hard?" he blurted out a moment later.

"The strike," Kate answered. "There's something odd about the whole situation."

"I understand that you have questions, but what makes it newsworthy?" he pressed.

"You said it. Big money. Not only does the green stuff talk, but people are always interested in who's making what. And how they're earning it," she said glibly. Kate wasn't really in the mood for another debate about journalistic ethics, although she was sure it would come up again in the course of her acquaintance with this maddening man.

Kate wondered briefly if she could go so far as to call what they had a relationship. In some ways, it wasn't a bad one. Especially compared to some others she'd had. So far, she and Brant had danced together, had cocktails together, and shared some lively philosophical debate. Not once had she had that sinking feeling that he was only waiting for her to stop speaking so he could talk, or worse, so he could get her into bed. He actually listened to her. Despite his obvious disagreement with much of what she had to say, he didn't discount her opinion like so many of his sex. Her old friends, male and female, had been drawn to her, and she to them, largely because they shared her enjoyment of a good, intellectual discussion. She'd bonded with her current circle of good friends during late-night discussions about issues ranging from abortion to the death penalty. But she hadn't made any new friends in a while, in part because most people she met these days seemed to prefer harmless small talk—about movies, or sports, or occasionally books—more than the long, lively discussions she so enjoyed. Especially the men she dated.

Technically, this relationship was going more smoothly than the last two, or three, she'd been involved in. She thought back. Maybe even four or five, she amended.

Brant walked beside her, silent, while she mulled over this revelation. Apparently, his thoughts had traveled along quite different lines. "Do you really think you'd be writing this story if Leopold Arnold were white?" he asked, still caught up in the subject he'd raised earlier.

"Sure." Kate might have taken offense at the implied insult, but if she lost her temper now, with Brant, she was afraid she wouldn't be able to get it back under control and effectively interview his friend. She was still on edge because of the morning she had had. There was time enough to refute the offensive statement later.

"I don't think your audience would question a white developer if this situation came up on one of his projects. Your readers wouldn't care about him using a union that underrepresented Hispanic welders. It's been going on for years. It's only because the boss on this site is a minority member that makes you think this story would sell newspapers," he contended.

"That's not true." She tried not to grit her teeth as she answered him. "It does add a touch of irony to the story, but I believe it would be a good article without the element of race."

"There is no article without that element. Not in this day and age," he maintained.

Kate did not want this conversation to go any further in this direction. She could not continue to be calm and reasonable for much longer. Though she'd recovered somewhat, her nerves were frazzled from the shock of finding Jeremy, that snake, had appropriated her story. She kept a tight rein on her roiling emotions. "This isn't about Skipper's race," she reiterated.

"Of course it is. We live in a racist society, which has created institutions that are, by necessity, also racist, such as its newspapers. And the reporters who work for them."

Perhaps she should have rescheduled this appointment. Meditation was all well and good, but when she left her apartment to meet him, Kate knew she was on the verge and that it wouldn't take much to push her over the edge. But she was doing all right, until he called her a racist. He had gone too far. She stopped dead in her tracks and turned to him. "Look, I know you think I'm some tool of the devil, and my press pass is just a license to maim and destroy nice, honest guys like you and Skipper Arnold," she spat at him. "But I happen to believe that what I'm doing is worthwhile. Even important. So would you let me do my job? Please? Without the advice from the peanut gallery."

"I thought that was what I was here for," he said, undisturbed. "To advise and help you investigate your story."

"That was the plan." She was past trying to hide her clenched jaw. So what if the man saw that she was frustrated? Maybe it would stop him from making any more asinine comments. "Let's go, then, shall we?" The words were pleasant enough, but the tone of her voice was harsh, even to her own ears. "Okay?" That was better. She sounded almost like her normal self. Inside, she was still seething. He had no right to judge her.

They walked in silence the last two blocks to the address his friend had given them. It was a building under construction, like so many in New York. It rose straight up into the sky. Men were scurrying about on the ground level but the real action was high overhead. A massive steel girder swung through the air above them, held by steel cables extending from the arm of a gigantic crane. From this distance, the girder looked like a piece of an erector set, the cables like thin strings. The top of the tower crane also looked much smaller and insubstantial than the mammoth body and wheels, which took up a large section of the lot in which they stood. Kate thought it looked like the enormous, earth-moving machine had been miniaturized on its way up to the top of the skyscraper. A shiver ran down her spine. If that steel beam were to fall on them, it would crush them as if they were insects.

"How many stories do you think it is?" Kate asked Brant, her exasperation fading in the presence of the magnificent structure that was being constructed in front of her eyes. She couldn't stop staring at the bustling activity of which from their lowly vantage point they could only catch a glimpse. "Do you think they'd let me go up there?"

"He's not supposed to, but he might, anyway. It you're nice to him" Brant teased. He didn't look like he thought much of her chances. "Want to give it a try?"

Kate didn't rise to the bait for once. "I can be nice," she said, trying to match his flippant tone.

He looked at her skeptically, but he didn't argue. Instead he led the way across the lot to a trailer that stood a little away from the piles of gravel, metal, and dirt that dotted the construction site like oversize anthills. It looked exactly like the one Brant used as his office. But this trailer was locked and no one answered when he knocked.

"He must be up there." He jerked his head toward the building under construction—without looking up.

Kate thought it was a little strange that Brant wasn't

more eager to test her mettle on his home ground. Then she realized that, so far, he hadn't seemed to feel the need to brag about his work, or do any of that macho nonsense. Maybe the petty thought that he could show off for her here, on a construction site, hadn't even entered his mind.

"Hey, where's the boss?" he called to one of the hard hats.

"Up top," the man answered.

Brant seemed unduly displeased by this turn of events. *Of course,* Kate thought. *For me, this is an unexpected bonus. For him, it's just another delay.* Kate was dying to see what it was like at the top of the building. But for Brant there was no novelty in that experience. He did it every day.

She was thrilled at the idea of conducting her interview at five hundred feet above street level, in an unfinished building

"Let's go!" she urged.

"We're early, and he's probably running a little late. I'm sure he'll be here in a few minutes."

"Hurry up, then! We've got to get up there before he comes down." She trotted toward the building, without waiting to see if Brant followed. When she turned around he had disappeared.

"Brant?" she called, impatient to ride in the steel cage that would carry her up into a new world—a New York she'd only seen in photographs. Fascinating as it was, the view from the Twin Towers would never be like this.

He reappeared, wearing one hard hat and carrying another. He looked distinctly unenthusiastic.

"You don't look happy," Kate said, thinking he didn't approve of her intentions. She tried to appease him. "If Andy says it's a no-go, I'll come right back down, I promise."

Reluctantly, he handed her the protective helmet dangling from his fingers. "Put this on."

She quickly complied. It couldn't be their argument, she thought, that turned him into this dour, forbidding figure. He didn't stiffen up like this during even their most heated exchanges. In fact, Kate would have sworn that he did not let their little squabbles get to him. He wasn't like her. Brant was even-tempered and steady. She was the one who had been really upset earlier. He had seemed unperturbed. She couldn't figure out what had changed. But Kate didn't dwell on it. She was too busy figuring out how the mechanism that drove the elevator worked.

"Forward, up. Middle, stop. Pull toward you, down." Brant issued instructions in an aggravated tone.

"Okay, okay." she acknowledged. "Just give me a second. I'll get it." Kate was surprised he didn't take over, given his obvious annoyance with her inept attempts.

As the elevator started to rise, she turned to smile at him triumphantly, only to find him gazing blankly out at the buildings they were quickly rising above. Brant's eyes were unfocused, his jaw tight. His stance was rigid, and his arms were crossed over his chest in a seemingly casually pose, but his knuckles were white where his hands gripped his arms. That was when she knew. His desire to wait for Andy's return and his reluctance to bring her up in the elevator, and his stillness all suddenly made sense. He was afraid.

"My God!" she blurted. "How can you work construction?"

"Huh?" He turned his head toward her slowly, blinking rapidly as if he had just awakened from a deep sleep.

"I—" he started, whether in explanation or protest she didn't know as he didn't finish the sentence. His hands came apart in a whirl, fluttered and settled on the steel mesh that made up the walls of the cage, fingertips gripping the wire tightly.

Kate brought the elevator to a stop. They were between floors, some fifty feet below the top where, presumably, Andy waited for them. She didn't care. This was too bizarre.

"Get it going!" he ordered, but desperation colored the demand.

"You're really scared, aren't you? I must say, you hide it very well."

A low rumbling noise, like a muted roar, started somewhere deep in his throat, and came out. "Go!"

"Okay, okay," she agreed, and turned back to the control box. She didn't purposely push the lever forward. Her hand brushed against the sleek metal and they dropped a few inches—a foot at most—but she heard the sharp intake of breath from behind her and took more care the next time. In a second, they were moving steadily upward again.

"I don't get it," she said, shaking her head. She looked out at the rooftops around them and then back at Brant, backed into the corner of the lift like a wounded animal, his eyes closed. "It's beautiful up here. Have you tried therapy?" He didn't respond.

They reached the top floor where men scurried about, working on mysterious, presumably dangerous, tasks.

"Now what?" she asked.

"Out," he said through gritted teeth.

Brant followed closely behind her, as she walked forward onto the half-finished thirty-second floor and approached the nearest hard hat.

"Excuse me. Is Andy Ross here? I was supposed to meet him for an interview" Kate asked.

The man barely glanced at her. Apparently, construction workers saved their leers and comments for the ground floor. "He's over there." He pointed to a group of men clustered around a makeshift table comprised of two saw-horses with a plank balanced across them. They were examining papers of some kind. Kate headed for the group. She noticed as she came closer that they were bent over a large diagram—architectural plans, perhaps. They were so intent on their discussion that they didn't notice her approach.

"Hi, guys," she said as she drew near.

They all looked up immediately. She assumed they were surprised to hear a woman's voice. She hadn't seen any women working here.

Andy's confused expression cleared as he saw Brant behind her. "Hey, Brant, you made it." He acknowledged her next. "You must be the reporter."

She introduced herself. "Kate Ramsey." She carefully avoided looking over her shoulder at the man behind her.

"You know what to do, here," Andy said to the men with whom he had been speaking, before he excused himself politely. "I've got to talk to these folks." He came toward them. "Shall we go back down to my office?"

Kate hated to lose this chance to see this unique view, but she fell into step beside him as he started back to the elevator. "This is incredible. I've never seen anything like it," she said.

"It is great," Andy answered, smiling. "Do you want to look around a little?"

Kate hesitated, tempted. But she felt Brant stiffen beside her and couldn't bring herself to torture him further. "I'll probably be able to concentrate better in your office," she answered.

If she had known how it would effect Brant, she wouldn't have brought him up here in the first place. She refused to feel guilty about it, though. It was his own fault that he'd been made uncomfortable. All he had to do was tell her that he was afraid of heights. She would have understood.

Kate had to admit she was sort of glad she hadn't known. Unintentional, though it was, she couldn't help feeling a slight twinge of satisfaction at having made him suffer a little after he had the gall to accuse her of being racist. It was difficult enough to be a black woman at a major metropolitan newspaper without one of her own accusing her of being a traitor to her race. She didn't need Brant to give her any more grief.

She would never use it against him, but now that she knew his weakness, Kate felt better equipped to deal with him. He had learned quickly how to get a rise out of her because she was so easily provoked. Now, even if she never mentioned his phobia, she had a button of her own to push. They were even.

Seven

The door of Andy Ross's office had barely closed behind them when Brant asked, "What was all that about the union?"

"So you were listening?" Kate said sharply.

"I thought you wanted to know about Skipper."

"I do." Kate turned to walk back uptown, toward Brant's office.

He fell into step beside her. "So why all the leading questions?" he asked her petulantly.

She didn't take offense. "I wasn't leading him anywhere." Brant was not really angry about the interview. Her questions couldn't have come as any surprise to him. He was probably taking his annoyance out on her for finding out his little secret. "I knew you weren't really paying very close attention. It makes perfect sense. You were distracted," she said placatingly.

"I heard every word you said," he demurred.

"So you heard what he said, too? He thinks your friend Skipper should take a stand."

"And you heard Andy say he wasn't sure what he would do if he were in Skipper's position."

"I did. I just thought it was interesting."

He reached out and grasped her arm above the elbow, stopping her and turning her toward him. "Was it interesting, or was it what you wanted to hear? Have you got a good quote now, for your article?" He stared into her eyes as if he would find an answer there, rather than in what she said.

Kate held her head high and returned his gaze. "I have a lot of quotes, from you, and from Andy and from others I've spoken to. But what I'd like to get is the truth."

He searched her face forever but whatever he found there didn't seem to satisfy him. "What truth? What is this?"

"Investigative reporting. I'm sure you've heard of it." She let a hint of sarcasm enter her voice. She understood that he was upset that she'd seen his weakness, but this confrontation was too much like the others he'd forced upon her. Kate wasn't going to back down, not from him, not from anyone. This was what she did, and she was good at it. Nothing Brant Fuller said was going to deter her. "I am going to continue this investigation until I find out what I want to know."

"You already know what you're going to write, don't you?" he accused.

"Not at all. I have questions, that's all. What I write is going to depend on the answers."

She didn't know when he'd released her arm, but she realized suddenly that she was free, and she started toward the curb. "I'll grab a taxi home," she told him, suddenly tired of this struggle to win his confidence. "Thanks for setting up the interview, anyway. I won't bother you again." She held her arm up to signal a taxi.

"You don't bother me. You can call me . . . if you have any questions."

She had to smile. "Come again?"

"I'd rather see that you get the real story on Skipper with my help than have you wander around clueless."

"I don't wander around clueless," she objected. "I'm a professional."

"I know you are. But you said yourself it was hard to get the inside dope from the old-boy network."

"I'll manage."

"I'm sure you will, but I *can* open doors for you." His smile was disarming.

"Why the sudden change?" she asked. "You didn't like me much to start with, and after today, I figured—"

"You figured wrong," he broke in. "I like you fine."

"You do?" She started walking again, and he did, too. Kate wasn't thinking about where they were headed. She was too intrigued by his last statement. *He likes me? When did that happen?*

"We can do this," he stated securely. "As long as you promise to be fair."

She bridled, but she refused to let him goad her. "I always am." She knew he was right, she'd get further with his help. "I don't let my personal feelings . . . about anyone . . . influence my work."

"You have personal feelings?" he said in feigned disbelief. She hoped his glib remark signified that he had forgiven her for his earlier discomfiture.

She matched his light tone as she teased, "If you're worried that I'll write about your little phobia, don't. I can be discreet."

He grimaced. "Discreet, right," he said sardonically. "That's why you pulled that little stunt."

"What little stunt?" she pretended ignorance.

"Stopping the elevator. Up there."

"I was just so shocked. . . ." She started to excuse herself, but he shook his head at her. He wasn't buying it. "All right, I was mad at you because of what you said to me about working for a racist institution, and I couldn't resist torturing you a little. The temptation was just too great. I'm sorry."

"When it comes to Skipper's story, I'll help you resist the temptation to . . . elaborate," he said complacently.

Kate wanted to puncture that inflated ego, but when she looked up into his face he didn't look as smug as he sounded. The complacency she thought she heard in his voice could have been her imagination. She decided to give him the benefit of the doubt.

But that didn't stop her from questioning his sudden change of attitude. "You like me?" she asked.

"What?" he asked, confused.

"You said I don't bother you. Before," she clarified.

"You're annoying, of course, but I'm sure other people have already told you that."

"Actually, they haven't," she lied. "I tend to get along really well with people."

"Hmmm," he murmured noncommittally.

"It must be something about you," she continued.

"I'm considered a pretty easygoing guy," he replied. "But maybe we just rub each other the wrong way."

"I thought you said you weren't bugged," she challenged him.

"I'm not really. You're not that big a pest," he said. "I've known worse. By far."

"Not me," she said. "You are definitely the worst pest I've ever known." He laughed out loud.

They had reached his job site, the lot where his trailer was parked. Kate stopped at the entrance. She couldn't think of any reason to go into his office, although she would not have minded continuing this nonsensical conversation. It was the most fun she'd had all day. In fact, if someone had asked her that morning if she thought she could end the day like this, she'd have told them it wasn't possible. The man might frustrate and irritate her, but he did take her mind off things, such as stolen stories.

He looked up at the building his men were working on, and Kate marveled at how calm he looked. How did an acrophobe work construction? The question was on the tip of her tongue, but she restrained herself. She preferred to enjoy the view, rather than to bring up a subject that might set them off again. She didn't want to fight. He looked too good. She licked her lips. Brant caught her staring at him, and he smiled. His dark eyes twinkled with suppressed humor, and his sensuous lips curled up at the edges.

His knowing expression should have made her uncomfortable. Kate chose to ignore it. "Did I thank you? For setting up the interview today?" she finally asked.

He grinned. "Not enough." Was he flirting with her? Kate tried to think of a cute comeback, but before she could think of one, he was asking, "Does this mean you're going to call me again?" Now she was sure there was definitely a flirtatious tone to his voice.

"You can always call me." She said it with just the right inflection. Not too soft, but definitely congenial. Kate couldn't resist the urge to flirt back. It wasn't just his negative attitude about the article that got under her skin. The attraction she felt toward him was a considerable part of the reason for her bad behavior.

"I do have your number," he said with a wide smile.

Kate forced her gaze up from his lips, and was caught by the intent in his deep brown eyes. She couldn't make herself move either toward him, or away. They stood like statues in the middle of a busy sidewalk at rush hour. The streets were full, teeming with traffic that moved slowly but noisily along, and with commuters who were hurrying home. Pedestrians streamed around them and darted past them.

This was midtown Manhattan—a vibrant, raucous tumult: a sea of office workers in their suits, punctuated by cops in blue and traffic cops in brown, and workmen in green and tan, and children of all colors, ages, and sizes, as well as cabs, trucks, limos, and private cars all creating heat and noise.

It all came to an abrupt halt within inches of their frozen bodies. They stood in the center of a whirlwind of motion and sound and Kate could not move an inch. Brant was as still as she was. She wanted him to reach out and touch her. He was close enough. But he just stood there, looking down at her.

Kate was an intelligent, ambitious, goal-oriented woman. She didn't wait for the man to make the first move. She should just step toward him. He was only eighteen inches away. But Brant was . . . different from other men she'd known. She couldn't bring herself to reach out and touch him. He already thought she was too assertive. Pushy, even. And she was. She knew she was. Usually that was an asset. In her career, even in her personal life, it was generally a good thing. But not today. Not standing here. She was a foot and a half away from the man with the most heavenly mouth she'd ever seen. She wanted to taste it.

"So I'll call you," he said.

"Good idea." Kate tried to keep her tone light but she failed dismally. She still couldn't tear her gaze from his face.

"Thank you," he murmured.

"For what?"

He chuckled, breaking the spell. "Damned if I know."

She held out her hand. He took it and turned it over in his own, examining it closely. She watched, mesmerized, and felt the heat from his palm permeate her skin.

She stepped closer and stretched up to kiss him lightly on the cheek.

His skin was smooth, his strong jaw hard beneath her lips. She drew back slowly, but the spring breeze drew the warmth of his cheek from her lips. She wished she could savor that first small taste of him and the faint scent of his soap. But they were standing on the street, completely exposed. It wasn't the time or the place for kisses, sweet and chaste or hot and wet. She had work to do.

Kate pivoted on her heel and walked briskly across the wide gray expanse of the sidewalk to the curb. There she raised her hand to hail a taxi. Fortunately, a cab pulled up in front of her after only a second. Usually Kate's luck was not that good, but it seemed that she was going to be able to make a graceful exit, for once. Kate resisted the urge to turn and see if he was watching her go.

Kate gave herself the entire weekend to calm down and then called Charles on Monday about Jeremy's theft of her article. This time her editor took her call, to tell her that the story they had printed barely intersected with her own proposed piece on the homeless.

"You're writing about single-room occupancy hotels. Hallston's piece was about a man who was killed for his coat. He happened to be homeless, and he happened to be killed in an SRO, but it's only peripherally related to your story—the only crossover in Jeremy's article was that he mentioned how lax security was in the hotel. I expect you to get the dope on how these hotels make money off of these street people. Hallston didn't even scratch the surface. It was a completely different story."

Kate was somewhat mollified, but she wasn't completely satisfied. "You said the story was mine, Charles.

You implied you weren't going to let him write his piece."

"I never said that," her editor argued. "I told you not to worry about it, and I meant it. I'm still planning to print your item . . . if you ever deliver."

"I will," she promised. "After I finish the Skipper Arnold piece."

"How's that going?" he asked.

"Fine, fine," Kate assured him. "I've got some great leads." But she knew he wasn't going to be too pleased with what she had found out so far. He would expect her to make allegations of criminal activity in her exposé. If the police or the Feds weren't either currently investigating Leopold Arnold, or planning to investigate him, Charles might very well pull the story.

Her contact at the *Voice* was not as hard-nosed about the Leopold Arnold story as Charles Grover was. She thought that a story on the developer's decision to use nonunion labor, and the resultant uproar was enough to get approval on the article, especially since the near riot caused by police presence at the last big demonstration at the construction site had been so well covered by the television news. She didn't need an arrest to go ahead with the piece. But a little mob involvement might spice things up.

Kate went back to the police for any further information on Julio Gonzalez's death, but she hit a dead end there. Her contacts in New York told her Julio's accident was outside their jurisdiction, but as far as they knew, it had been ruled an accidental death. She tried to contact the proper authorities in Westchester, but was out of luck. They weren't releasing any information to the press. She was going to have to talk to the family. Kate did not look forward to that. Speaking to a grieving widow about her husband's death was not high on her list of favorite things to do.

She was going to have to go it alone. She was able to obtain the woman's address by masquerading as an insurance agent at the hospital where Julio was declared dead, but she didn't dare use that identity with Señora Gonzalez. The ruse was too easy to detect; there were documents, and identification numbers she did not have access to, and one slip could lead to the phone call that would expose her as a fake. She decided to undertake a less risky impersonation and pose as a friend of the deceased come to pay her respects. His wife couldn't possibly know all of his friends. Or so Kate hoped.

She wore a simple black dress, hose and heels, and even found a little hat in her closet that she'd worn to a hat party a couple of years back. It had a veil, which helped her get in the spirit of the character. Kate wasn't an actor. She had a number of friends who were in that profession, living, as she did, in their Mecca, but she had never been very interested in pretending to be anyone other than herself. She didn't feel she had any talent for it. As a reporter, she had hustled to get some of her stories, and her efforts had produced adequate results, but it made her nervous to create a false persona.

Kate used public transportation to get to the small suburban town where the Gonzalez family lived. Living in the city, she didn't need a car, and didn't own one. From the commuter train station she was able to walk to the house, and she used the time to prepare herself for the difficult interview ahead. Nevertheless she was awfully tense as she walked up the front walk to the small gray shingled house with white shutters. She squared her shoulders and knocked on the door, firmly but gently. The lady of the house responded promptly to the summons.

"Hello. May I help you?" Julio's wife was a pretty woman in her mid-forties with fair skin, dark hair, and sad eyes. Her voluptuous figure was complemented by the black dress she wore.

"I am Linda Florentina," Kate lied. "I've come to speak with you about your husband."

"Come in, please," the woman said, stepping back and inviting her inside.

A twinge of guilt assailed her, but Kate still stepped eagerly over the threshold and followed the attractive woman into the homey living room. This was a room where the family must have gathered often. The furniture wasn't old, or shabby; it just had that well-worn, comfortable look.

"I'm so sorry for your loss," Kate said.

"Thank you."

His wife sat on the other end of the couch, and settled back for a chat, openly curious about Kate's presence, but not at all suspicious. "How did you know my Julio?" she asked.

This was the tricky part. Kate had been half expecting to have to supply the answer to that question before she was allowed into the house. "I am a secretary at union headquarters," she explained. "Julio asked me to do some typing for him, once or twice, and I worked with him on some letters he wanted to send to the newspapers." She had found some letters to the editor that the dead man had sent to the newspaper, so it was a background story she could expand upon if necessary. But without hesitation, her audience of one seemed to accept the tale she'd concocted.

She nodded her understanding. "Julio could speak nicely, but his writing needed some work. English was not his first language." Her own accent was a little more pronounced than her husband's had been.

"He had a lot to say," Kate prompted.

"He very much believed in what he was doing," Señora Gonzalez agreed. "He didn't say anything he didn't mean." Whatever Jennifer and others thought of Julio, his wife was clearly proud of him.

"I helped him with this letter." Kate took an envelope from her pocketbook and held it out to the woman without taking out the sheet of paper inside. "He never got to send it to the *Times*. It's about Leopold Arnold and the L.A.C. Parking Garage construction." She'd faked a pretty good imitation of Julio's published letter to the editor, but she hoped that his wife wouldn't read it.

The woman sitting opposite her had no apparent interest in looking at the phony document. "Julio was very strong. He had his opinions. They were published in the newspaper. See here." She took a scrapbook from the coffeetable, and opened it to clippings about her late husband. It was clear Julio had been a very vocal, very political union man.

He probably, Kate thought cynically, *learned the importance of being quotable. Reporters were always looking for sound bites from men like him.* Aloud she just murmured, "He'll be missed." She took the scrapbook and looked at some of the pages. She had seen a number of the articles before when she'd first researched Julio, but some of the quotes were in articles unrelated to the construction site, and she hadn't seen them.

"Julio was very proud to be in the newspaper. It showed he was an expert."

"Why was that important?"

"To be an expert is good for work, for position. Also more people will listen. The newspapers, the TV people. Also, more people could know what he was trying to do."

"What did you think of the strike he started?" Kate asked.

"Julio didn't start that. He supported it, but he was just one of the members. It's hard to know what to do."

Kate sensed some regret in the way she said it "You didn't think it was the right thing to do?"

"He paid his dues, he didn't have to fight for those others. But I thought it was right. He wasn't sure the strike was the right way. But he had to stand up for other Hispanics. Make it easier, more fair, more equal. Maybe it wouldn't be my first choice to sacrifice, but Julio had to do it."

"Did he tell you he *had* to do it? He didn't want to?"

"No, por supuesto, of course not. You knew Julio. Like he says in the letters he wrote to the newspapers, he thought the union all had to stand behind the Hispanics. Everyone together." Kate quickly nodded, and murmured her agreement. Her skin grew warm at the thought that she'd almost forgotten the fiction she'd created. She was so engrossed in interviewing this woman, she had slipped into journalist mode.

It took her a moment to recover and say, "I knew that." If Julio had been bribed or threatened by Skipper Arnold, or anyone else, she did not think his wife knew about it.

"Are you going to send this letter to the newspapers?" the woman asked.

"No, no." Kate folded the phony document and inserted it back in the envelope. "It's not finished, I'm afraid. But Julio's opinions are already a matter of public record. I'm sure they won't be forgotten by his friends at the union."

"I think you are right. Everyone has been so kind."

They didn't talk for much longer. Kate couldn't very well ask this woman if she thought her husband's death might not have been accidental. It was clear that Señora

Gonzalez had no such suspicions. Kate just wanted to get out of there, and let the grieving widow get on with her life.

The death certificate listed the cause of death as accidental, and the police report was clear. On the night he died, Julio had a blood alcohol level well over the legal limit for driving a car, and the local authorities apparently felt that was all the evidence that was needed to explain his death and close the case. She was grasping for straws, and it was all Jennifer Collier's fault. During the train ride home, she decided her next meeting was definitely going to be with her former roommate.

Before she met with her old friend, she wrote up all the pertinent facts she'd collected on Skipper Arnold and played with different approaches to the story. She had an interview with the hard-to-get Mr. Arnold scheduled for the following week. She had to make it count.

Eight

Jennifer agreed to a meeting immediately, and when Kate arrived at her house on Long Island, she was waiting with wine, cheese, and crackers. Acquiring a little house in the suburbs had been her college roommate's primary goal when she left school. Kate thought Jen obsessed over owning her own home to compensate for the rootlessness she felt having been raised by an alcoholic mother and without any father. The sophisticated, urbane woman had planned her entire life around buying, creating, and maintaining her own little place. Kate suspected it was the reason she was still single. Jen spent every spare moment, and dollar, on her place. No mere man could compete with her stylish little three bedroom house.

As receptive as she was, it was soon clear that she was hoping to get a very different status report than the one Kate had to give her. "What have you got on the old man?" she asked, almost before she seated Kate on the sofa.

"Nothing to connect him to Julio's accident, for one thing. If there's anything there, I don't think I'm going to be able to prove it," Kate announced. "But I may be able to use the material I've got for an in-depth article on the struggle going on within the union, and between the union and the development company. Skipper's company.

"Oh," Jen said, deflated. "What would you write about him then?"

"Well, I'm not sure what I think yet. I still have to interview Skipper . . . but you know this story. It's certainly not a new one. When a black man becomes a success in the business world, or the art world, or anywhere in the modern world, he's measured by a different yardstick than a white man. Not only does he have to constantly prove himself to the powers that be, but to his own, as well. One question is asked of him repeatedly—not by his competitors or enemies, but by his supposed supporters, and friends . . . his brothers. They want to know only one thing. Does he help his own? No one asks Wolfgang Peterson why he hires the people he hires to work for him, but Spike Lee—forget it. Everyone knows nepotism is rampant in Hollywood, but when Spike hires a friend, every critic on both coasts speculates on the wisdom of his decision, and comments on his lack of professionalism."

"I know," Jen acknowledged grudgingly. "Doesn't it annoy you?"

"Of course nepotism annoys me—especially since I can't take advantage of it," Kate joked lamely. Her friend did not crack a smile. "But we were talking about Skipper. He's caught in a squeeze but good. If he supports the union management, he's a bigot. If he supports the Hispanic contingent, he's a traitor, and if he does nothing, he's condemned as a money-grubbing, profit-mongering whore."

"Unions are funny things," Jen added. "They can screw you up or save you, or both, and in the construction business, it's usually both." She poured more wine into her glass, which was empty, and Kate's, which was still half full. "Contractors and developers are as dependent upon union labor as unions are on them for work. You'd think that would even things out."

"But Skipper hired a nonunion outfit. He had to know they would try to crucify him," Kate observed.

Jennifer dismissed the possibility with a wave of her hand. "It's not like this is the first time that's been done. What's unique about the situation is the lack of support from Uncle Skip's friends. Usually these guys love to see something like this happen—especially if their butts aren't on the line. They may not publicly support a move like the one Skipper made, but in private . . . they'd be right there with him, cheering him on."

"So why not now?" Kate asked.

"One guess," Jen said sardonically. She took a healthy swig of wine and refilled her glass yet again.

"And we're back to the race issue," Kate announced. "By the way, Brant thinks this whole thing could be a conspiracy to bring Skipper down."

"It's not that personal. Skipper should have been born white, that's all. The unions have been predominantly white since their inception. Blacks have only been admitted to the P.S.W.U.A. for the past thirty years or so. They've worked their way up and eaten a lot of garbage doing it."

"So there goes any support from our community."

"It's hard enough to find a sponsor if you're black. The Hispanics have even less membership, and so less of a chance to apprentice."

"But your sponsor doesn't have to be the same race you are," Kate interjected.

"Of course not, but you know how things work, Katie," Jen said.

"I know. No matter how many right-minded white folks there are, or how many affirmative-action programs exist, most people still support their own. Everybody does it: white, black, Hispanic, and Asian. Solidarity, or whatever. It can screw us up just as badly as discrimination. It can also be just as divisive."

"And when it comes up in the context of politics and big business, taking sides becomes a matter of survival rather than morality."

"So you do see Skipper's dilemma?" Kate asked, surprised to find Jennifer at all sympathetic to her adopted uncle.

"I see his motive," Jen answered with stoic indifference. It was a cynical viewpoint. But then, Jennifer Collier had never been one to let her emotions overrule her good sense. In this instance she was clearly intent on getting all the facts before she chose a course of action.

Kate wasn't able to give her the information she needed to make any decision about what to do next. "Maybe after I interview Skipper himself," she told her friend.

She called a taxi to take her to the train station, and left a slightly sloshed Jennifer Collier in her precious little house. On the train ride home, she tried to interpret her friend's behavior. Kate acknowledged that, much as she sympathized with her college roommate, she had never understood her. It didn't help. Jennifer's most recent exploits were odd enough to defy explanation. Kate loved her, and supported her, and wasn't going to give up on the story Jen was so insistent that she write, but she just couldn't figure out why she was being asked to do it. Kate thought maybe she could have discerned Jennifer's motives in pursuing this investigation if she could have spoken with the woman's mother. She had never met Mrs. Collier—for reasons that were much easier to comprehend than the current mystery.

She and her college roommate had had one very important thing in common: they were both raised by single parents who were alcoholics. It might even have been what drew them together. Unlike Jennifer's mother, though, Kate's father had been a sweet, loving guy. And her mother hadn't deserted her, as Jen's father had. Elizabeth Ramsey died when she was a little girl, and Ben Ramsey never recovered from the loss, but he loved his daughter, and she knew it. He spoke with love for the mother Kate didn't remember and, despite his addiction, he tried to make up for his wife's absence. Mrs. Eugenia Collier, on the other hand, blamed her daughter for her husband's desertion, and she let Jen know it.

Kate knew how hard it was to introduce an alcoholic parent to a friend. She herself had been ashamed of her father. So she could certainly understand why Jennifer had never introduced her to Eugenia. At the moment, though, she wished she could have met the lady. It might shed some light on her old friend's unusual behavior. Jennifer Collier didn't often drink to excess. And she certainly didn't create murder plots out of run-of-the-mill car accidents. There had to be something Kate wasn't seeing. The Leopold Arnold story had become a riddle she felt compelled to solve.

Whatever Skipper had to say during their interview, Kate was pretty sure she would be able to get an article out of it. But if it was the story of a man who deceived the people who trusted him, then she wouldn't be able to use Brant's name or his contacts. He probably wouldn't know anyone who could help her anyway, but in the unlikely event that he did, he'd never forgive her for discovering Skipper's betrayal. Kate didn't want to think about why Brant's opinion of her was so important. She just wanted to figure out how she was going to proceed.

She had researched Skipper's background as thoroughly

as possible through the Internet. And she was going to interview the developer himself. But what if she couldn't get the answers she wanted? What if the only story there was was about a hardworking, upright guy who had not been able to see a good way out of a tight spot and had chosen the ill-advised course of bypassing the union. Skipper Arnold could, after all, be everything that Brant said he was.

She needed to talk this out with someone she could trust. When she arrived home, she called Miranda and made a date for lunch the next day at an old hangout of theirs, the Carnegie Delicatessen, telling the editor that she needed to use her as a sounding board.

"So, why am I here?" Miranda asked patiently. Kate knew that Miranda wasn't questioning her choice of restaurants when she asked, "Why are we here?" They were already seated, in the back room, having met at the front door. "Not that I'm complaining. I'm starving," Miranda added, confirming it.

"Let's order first, and get that out of the way," Kate suggested. "I find it easier to concentrate when I'm stuffing my face." Like that of the competition, the Stage Deli—just two or three doors down the street—the fare was traditional Jewish food, and lots of it. Chicken broth, knishes, tongue and corned beef were old standards, lettuce and tomato were not automatically added, and real New Yorkers never ordered French fries, or Coke. Small silver bowls of spicy mustard and pickles were on every table, and the favorite soda choice was Dr. Brown's old-fashioned cream soda or black cherry. The only concession to the current decade was the addition of diet Dr. Brown's sodas to the beverage selection. The Stage Deli's gimmick of mixing and matching meats and cheeses and

naming the sandwiches after celebrities was eschewed by
this restaurant's very traditional management. Kate didn't
suppose anything had been changed on the menu or in
the sturdy, unpretentious decor in forty years or more.
The small tables were still crammed together, the seats
were probably still covered with the original Naugahyde.
Unlike most of New York's famous eateries, the waiters
were not young and beautiful, but older and very effi-
cient. One served them almost immediately.

"Remember the story I told you about?" she began,
when she and Miranda had decided which of the delicatessen's overstuffed sandwiches to share and ordered their
lunch and egg creams.

"Sure," Miranda said. "Leopold Arnold, right? The
strikers were on the news again the other day. I thought
of you. Have you met the man yet?"

"No. But I interview him soon. What I've discovered
about him could be interpreted in any way you choose.
He was born on St. Thomas, but doesn't seem to have
any living relatives there. He appeared in New York out
of nowhere as a teenager and started working in construction right away—and got arrested and did time for steal-
ing building supplies."

"So far, that last part of the story is the only part
that's news to me. I've read about him over the years. . . .
Who hasn't? It seemed like he was a pretty classy guy
for a self-made man, and a multimillionaire at that."

"I know. I was surprised to find all this out, too. But
I had read all about the strike. My friend, Jennifer, works
for him, and she's known him all her life, so I've been
aware of him since I met her in college. I sort of followed
his career. She didn't ever say anything specific, but she
implied that his success was . . . hard earned, so I half
expected to read a headline that was less than flattering

one of these days. I didn't expect to be the one who would write it."

"And now you do?"

"Maybe." The waitress arrived with their lunch, and Kate waited until the woman left before she continued. "There's the background I dug up," Kate reported, trying to take a bite of her half of the huge turkey sandwich without losing any of the toppings. "I also have Jennifer's impression that something is not kosher." She ticked off her second point, and kept on. "But the contact she hooked me up with is a subcontractor who has worked with Skipper before, and he does not agree with Jennifer. In fact, he thinks the opposite. That may be why she chose him—I don't know. Anyway, he thinks Skipper is some kind of a hero. His friends, so far, don't exactly say they think so, too, but they tend to excuse his action in hiring nonunion rather than condemn it. Besides, Brant—that's the subcontractor—isn't really connected to this particular union, or the management."

"So your story is about the fight Skipper is having with the welders' union?" Miranda inquired.

"That's the story that's in the news right now," Kate answered glibly.

"And what are you going to write that hasn't been on television?" Miranda asked in her best editor voice.

"I've got an interview with the man himself. He's been saying 'no comment' since this debacle started. And on top of that, I thought I might do something more in-depth. In fact, I might be able to find out exactly how Leopold does business. That hasn't been done." Since there didn't seem to be any evidence connecting Arnold to Julio's death, Kate thought she'd better keep Jennifer's suspicions to herself for the moment. Besides, Miranda was the one woman among her girlfriends who had never really warmed up to Jen.

"It doesn't sound to me like you've got enough to go on. Even if, by some chance, you do stumble across evidence that he's crooked, how do you plan to confirm it? It doesn't sound like your inside guy is really inside, if he just freelances for him. And you may have an interview with Mr. Arnold, but I don't think he's going to confirm any criminal activity."

"Brant can . . ." Kate started, but didn't know how to finish the sentence. She'd been assuming that, if she could prove Brant was wrong about his friend, he'd help her nail the developer. But she didn't really know if that was true. Miranda had made a good point. Brant knew some of the men Skipper worked with, but that was all. He wasn't on the inside. Besides, Kate didn't know for sure if he'd be inclined to help her. So far, whenever she brought up the subject, he took offense on Skipper's behalf. Other than that first night's utterances, she wasn't even certain what he thought about the strike, or how strongly he felt about it.

Perhaps it was time to find out. Luckily, he had kept his promise to call. When she arrived at home after lunch, there was a message from him on her answering machine. Although she wanted to talk to him, Kate put off returning his call. She couldn't think of him without picturing him as he had been when she walked away from him on Friday: standing on the sidewalk in front of the construction site. She suspected that the next time she saw him, the memory of that brief kiss they had shared would distract her from the subject she really needed to speak with him about—his loyalty to Skipper Arnold. She had questions about both. And she didn't want to confront him about either.

She called him at his work number, right before five o'clock. She almost waited to call after five, so she could just leave a message on the machine, rather than talk to him, but that would just delay the inevitable. She had to talk to him sometime. And she needed to talk to him. She just didn't know what she was going to say.

He answered the phone on the second ring. "Hello?"

"Hi. It's umm . . . Kate," she said inanely.

"Hi, Kate. How are you doing?"

"Fine thanks. And you?"

"Fine, fine," he answered.

This conversation was ludicrous. She was acting like some teenager with a crush. This was business. "I called because I was hoping we could get together."

"Great," he said. "I was hoping for the same thing."

"Not on a date," she announced. "I mean, I didn't call for a date, I called because I need to discuss the story with you." She felt asinine, absurd.

"Oh." He sounded disappointed.

"Not that I wouldn't," she started to explain. "Didn't," she corrected quickly. "Don't . . ." Kate sighed. "I don't mean I don't want to go on a date with you. At some point. It's just that this call is about business."

"Got it," he said. Now he sounded dispassionate. Maybe she was making a fuss about nothing. He was a grown man. He had to understand that business came first.

"I didn't mean to imply that you were only calling to . . . to . . ."

"It's fine," he said shortly. "When would you like to meet?"

"Whenever you want," she answered. "At your convenience."

"Okay." He was silent for a moment. Kate fussed with the paperwork on the table in front of her while she waited. "Are you busy tonight?"

"Tonight? Sure. I mean, no," she faltered. "I'm not busy. Tonight would be good." She'd be glad to have this over and done with, she thought. "Do you want to meet at Rosie O'Grady's again?"

"Would it be breaking the rules if we had dinner?" he asked. "I'd like to get this out of the way." He unconsciously echoed her own thought. "And I missed lunch today," he explained.

"Dinner is fine. No problem. We can eat and talk," Kate said eagerly. Too eagerly. To her own ears, she sounded desperate. She couldn't imagine what he must be thinking. Normally she was good on the phone, but at the moment, she sounded like some cretin.

If Brant thought she sounded idiotic, there was no sign of it in his voice. "Do you know Julian's? It's a little Italian place on Ninth Avenue in the fifties."

"I've been there," Kate said. It was only a few doors away from the strike site. She wondered if he chose that particular restaurant for that reason. Perhaps he would tell her that when they met. "Six? Six-thirty? Seven?"

"How about six-thirty?" he asked. "That will give me time to clear off my desk and walk over."

"Okay. I'll see you there," she agreed.

For her lunch with Miranda she had dressed in a cream silk top and a straight rust-colored skirt covered with a sheer layer of chiffon the same color as the underskirt and dusted with tiny off-white lilies. Kate thought it was acceptable for dinner at the intimate little restaurant Brant had chosen, with some minor adjustments. She draped a scarf of orange-and-rust silk over her shoulders and donned a pair of amber-and-gold earrings, and then redid her makeup. She was nervous, and she hoped a little polish would hide that fact from Brant.

Brant had probably been in this same predicament plenty of times, she thought, as she left her apartment. The line between what was acceptable behavior for men and women who worked together had grown so blurry in the last decade. She had suffered a similar quandary the year before when she'd been attracted to a guy who worked for the City Planning Commission about whom she was writing a story. He asked her out a week later, and she went. It hadn't been exactly the same, of course. She had not worked with him for long. She only interviewed him once, briefly. And on their one and only date, he'd gotten completely sloshed and she politely requested that he take her home and never call her again. But the situation reflected the one in which she currently found herself.

Kate approached the restaurant with a determined stride. She could do this, she told herself, again. When she saw Brant, however, a flash of awareness traveled through her. She had made a glaring error in her calculations. The attraction she felt was different with him than it had been with the guy last year, or anyone before that or since. He was beautiful.

He stood when she started toward the table, and greeted her by leaning over and brushing her cheek with his lips. Her body took fire at that light kiss. "Hello, Brant." Kate prayed he would attribute her breathlessness to events preceding her arrival.

"Hi," he said impassively. She sat opposite him, and they each picked up one of the menus that the host had placed on the table when he seated her. "I hope you're hungry," he said.

"I am," she responded.

"Good. I really like the food here. Skipper brought me, once, and I always meant to come back. It was so fantastic."

So he *was* making some kind of statement by choosing this place, Kate thought. Well, that was what she had wanted to know. That . . . and whether he would be a help or a hindrance to her if her investigation of his friend yielded answers that he didn't like.

The waiter seemed to have been waiting for her. He appeared as soon as she had glanced over the menu. "Our specials today are tomato and basil bruschetta to start, and risotto with shrimp and asparagus in a saffron cream sauce," he began to recite.

She stopped him there. "That's what I want," she said.

"Which?" he asked.

"Both," Kate clarified.

"That was quick," Brant commented. Then, speaking to the waiter, he ordered "The same for me, please."

"Would you like to order wine?" the young man asked.

Brant held up the wine list for her approval, and Kate nodded. "The Montepulciano," he ordered.

"That comes only, I think, by the glass," their server said. He checked the wine list to confirm it and then asked, "Two glasses?"

"Yes," they said simultaneously.

The waiter chuckled and took the menus from them. "I'll be right back with your drinks."

"Good," Kate almost said, but she managed to restrain herself. She did feel the need for the calming effect of alcohol, but she didn't want to tell that to Brant.

If he felt any of the awkwardness that she did, he showed no sign of it. He seemed completely composed. "So," he said equably, "what did you want to talk to me about?"

"The story," she stated, determined not to lose sight of the chief reason for this dinner, despite the enticement he offered sitting just across the small table from her.

"I got that," he said patiently. "It was clear from your telephone call." He spread his napkin in his lap, and took a piece of bread from the basket on the table. "Can you be a little more specific?" he asked, a look of intelligent inquiry in his coffee-brown eyes.

"Well," she began, only to be interrupted by the arrival of their waiter with two glasses filled with ruby-red wine. She took a sip as soon as he put it in front of her. Then Kate launched into the speech she had decided on. She'd practiced it on her way to the restaurant. For a man who called me a race traitor, you're awfully forgiving of Skipper. This strike is about hiring minorities, or working with them, or whatever, and Skipper's decision to hire welders who are primarily Hispanic will impact on African-Americans in the union. What about Skipper's obligation to his own?"

Brant looked taken aback by her blunt question, but it didn't take him long to come up with an answer. "I think that by backing the Hispanic workers, he's living up to a principle that affects us all. All minorities. If you want to look at it that way."

"And you do?" she pressed.

"No, but you asked why I don't call him a traitor for hiring another minority. That's why."

Their appetizers arrived, and Kate waited impatiently for their waiter to depart before she inquired, "But didn't you say before that you thought he was a smart businessman to make that decision?" It was Jennifer who had said that Skipper's decision was clever from the business angle, and Kate didn't have her notes in front of her, so she wasn't sure if Brant had ever actually said the same thing. But he had implied it. Of that she was sure. Besides, tonight she was really trying to make a different point anyway. How could he accuse her of supporting racism in order to get ahead, and not hold Skipper Arnold to the same standard?

His response made it clear that he understood what she was really asking. "I'm sorry if I upset you by saying

that. But I do think they're two different things." He
picked up a piece of bruschetta as he continued. "You
work for a racist institution called the media. Leopold
Arnold blazed a path for men like me to compete with
white developers and contractors and construction workers." He bit, with gusto, into the crunchy toast covered
with diced red tomatoes that shone with the oil in their
dressing. The tantalizing aroma of garlic wafted over to
her from the bruschetta he held.

Kate's appetite warred with her righteous indignation
and won. She picked up a slice of her own bruschetta
and waved it at him as she argued, "You are not seriously
suggesting—?" She interrupted herself to take a bite of
the garlicky concoction.

"Good, isn't it?" Brant asked.

It was, indeed, delicious, but Kate had a point to make.
She washed the bite down with a little wine and recom-
menced her inquisition. "His success excuses anything he
chooses to do? Because he isn't exactly the voice of black
New York. He succeeded like the white men with whom
he competed. He got the job done, on schedule, within
the budget. He made his employers happy. And he did
that by hiring the people available, regardless of their colors—which, back when he was starting out, was white."

Their dinners arrived, and Brant waited politely until
they were both served before he responded. "I'm not excusing anything. To my knowledge, Skipper Arnold has
always stood up for our community."

"But I don't? Because I work for a newspaper?" Kate
asked, her indignation dwindling as she contemplated the
delectable dish of risotto that had been placed in front of
her.

"All I said was that the newspaper wouldn't have gone
after Skipper if he were white. And I think the reason
that that offended you so much was because, deep down,

you agree." Having made his point, her companion took a bite of the risotto. He closed his eyes in appreciation as he savored the mouthful.

"No. I don't," Kate said weakly, but the fire had gone out of her.

"Okay. I believe you," he said.

She didn't believe him for a moment, but the tempting scent of saffron wafting up toward her from her dinner was too tempting to resist. Besides, she was hungry. And, worse than that, she was suffering from the worst case of sexual frustration that she had ever experienced. She felt weary, worn-out, and in definite need of the one form of immediate gratification available to her.

She carefully cut up a large prawn into bite-size pieces, saying, "I just wanted to know if you agreed that Skipper should be held to the same standard that you and I adhere to."

"Absolutely," Brant said without hesitation.

"Great," she said, scooping shrimp, asparagus and creamy risotto onto her fork and lifting it to her mouth. "That's all I wanted to know," she lied, as she started to eat. "By the way, are you busy tomorrow night around seven?"

"No," he said. "Why?"

"I have an appointment to interview Skipper. I thought you might like to come." She might be making a mistake, but Kate trusted Brant, and she thought it might be helpful to have him at the interview. Even if he did nothing but observe, he could tell her afterward what he thought of his hero's demeanor. He was more familiar with Skipper than she was. His comments could be useful.

More importantly, he would know if Leopold Arnold was answering her questions truthfully or not. As a lie detector, he wasn't perfect, but Brant knew Skipper. He could gauge, better than she could, his friend's demeanor, and attitude. She could really use that. Besides, she had a feeling, in her gut, that she needed him there. And Kate tried to listen to her gut. It had gotten her this far.

Nine

The sky was darkening by the time they arrived at ten minutes to seven for the meeting with Skipper. The lobby was deserted except for the uniformed guard sitting behind a huge black marble reception desk where they signed in and received their visitor passes. The cavernous lobby with its twenty-foot ceilings, marble-tiled walls and floors, and beaded moldings, was impressive. Skipper had certainly chosen to make a statement by locating his offices in this building.

Brant stood leaning against the desk as Kate signed in.

"Will Jenny be joining us?" he asked.

"No, she just sets up these interviews. She doesn't monitor them," Kate said testily. She led the way to the bank of elevators that would take them up to the forty-ninth floor, where Leopold Arnold's corporate headquarters was situated. Brant followed silently—a strong, solid presence at her back. She pushed the call button, and they waited for the doors to open. Kate's nervousness had nothing to do with the man standing behind her this time. She was excited about speaking with her subject. It was a coup for her just to have gotten the interview.

In the elevator with Brant, Kate was momentarily diverted by the thought of their ascent. She'd always taken the ride for granted. If she'd ever thought about the height of any office before, it had only been to hope it would have a nice view. The worst-case scenario she'd ever imagined was having to walk back down if—God forbid—something happened to the elevator. Now, the mere act of riding the lift seemed somehow dangerous, as if she were courting disaster, rather than taking advantage of a simple technological innovation. She observed Brant as they came smoothly to a halt at the designated floor, but the man who'd inspired her morbid thoughts only stepped calmly out of the oak-paneled elevator.

Kate was annoyed with herself for losing focus just as she reached this important landmark interview. It would provide the backbone for her article—one way or the other. She followed Brant through the empty reception area, down a wide, lushly carpeted hallway, to the open door of Skipper's office. Her companion stepped aside to let her go in first. Kate took a deep breath and entered the expensively furnished room. The furniture was an eclectic and elegant mix of contemporary and antique. It was surprisingly harmonious. A modern Italian desk, a curved arc of polished blond wood, was the centerpiece of the room, and the high-backed leather chair behind it complemented the modern design. A detailed model of the completed L.A.C. Parking Garage was displayed on an intricately carved fourteenth-century mahogany sideboard, which she guessed was also Italian. She wondered if Skipper Arnold placed it there for her benefit.

"Hello, my dear," Skipper greeted her. Handsome, self-assured and distinguished in the way only the most powerful men could be, his welcoming smile was warm and certainly seemed sincere, as did his invitation for her to ask him about anything at all. He waited for her to be seated before he sat back down himself. His old-fashioned gentlemanly manners reminded her of her uncle Jake.

"I have nothing to hide," he said.

"Good, because I have plenty of questions," Kate warned him.

"Shoot," he commanded.

She turned on her small tape recorder and placed it on the desk. "Some background first, okay?"

"Okay."

"I was curious about how you got your start in the business."

"I began as a laborer's apprentice. They still have them, but it was more common in the forties and fifties."

"That is when you came over from the islands?"

"Yes."

"How old were you?"

"Seventeen," Skipper said. "There was no work at home, so I hitched a ride on a cruise ship as a bus boy in the kitchen."

"How did you end up in construction?"

"A friend of the family. We called him Uncle Dory, but he wasn't blood. You know how it is. He let me sleep on his floor until I found a job. He got it for me. The apprenticeship."

"And that was cool?" she pried.

"Not exactly. But that was how we all got work. After the war, it was easier, of course. My first job was actually building houses on Long Island for the returning soldiers. Do you know anything about how Levittown was built?"

"I went to school with a Levitt, a grandniece of the builder. The whole town was planned by the government and built as housing for all the soldiers looking for work in and around New York City after WWII. Whites only, back then."

He looked a little surprised. She supposed the anecdote was a standard, since it sounded patriotic, and established his credentials at the same time. "That's right," he said, bemused. He recovered quickly. "That development was one of the first of its kind."

"Is that where, ahem, you got in trouble with the law?"

Again, he looked a bit shocked. "You've really done your research, haven't you? No one has ever asked me about that. I'd almost forgotten about it."

"It was a long time ago." She tried to soften the blow.

"It certainly was. I was only . . . what . . . seventeen, I think." He stood up and wandered away from the desk. "Is it a matter of public record?"

"It was a juvenile record, but it wasn't sealed. I'm not sure why. Anyway, I was just curious about how it affected you. Why did you stay in construction after that first experience? Your own boss tried to cheat you. I would have thought that would have discouraged you."

"I was young, and I had already fallen in love with the business. I still love it. You have to be a builder to understand. Brant can probably explain it better than I could."

"I think I understand," Kate said. She was dying to ask about the Federal investigation, and the strike, but thought it wiser not to start accusing him outright of illegal or even unethical behavior. They seemed to have established a rapport. "So, how did you go from laborer's apprentice to owner and CEO of L.E.O. Enterprises?"

"I started small, but I knew there were going to be more Levittowns. Back then, the idea of constructing whole neighborhoods for fixed-income residents was very experimental. There were only a few projects here in the city. So I focused on becoming an expert in the area. The projects today are synonymous with poverty, crime, everything negative, but they were an amazing, hopeful innovation then. After a few years of working twenty-four hours a day at anything I could get, I convinced some contacts that I could make them money if they backed me to build one of the projects, and that was it. It worked."

Kate had known the basic story but hearing Skipper tell it put it in a new light for her. His enthusiasm was reminiscent of Brant's excitement about his work. She was tempted to pump him for more, but, fascinating as this was, it was background. She had to get to the real story. The story no one else had. "You're obviously proud of your achievements, and you have every reason to be," she started to say.

"I'm not exactly proud of what the projects turned into—but who could have predicted it? We built those places to last. And they have. Unfortunately, the residents are disempowered, voiceless, and almost hopeless today. But that can be changed. That wasn't what was supposed to happen."

"I understand," she said sympathetically. It was true. She knew the frustration he felt. She was also trying to do something that would help people, and sometimes ended up hurting them. "I know you've been very involved in trying to renovate and revive some of the worst of those areas of the city." As head of his publicity department, Jen disseminated information on her uncle's good works to the press at regular intervals, and her best friend the reporter was, of course, at the top of her mailing list. "I am curious about is the investigation last year into the construction site at 115th Street."

"Those allegations were never substantiated," he said calmly, his expression unchanging.

"I know. I wonder how they could try to indict you without evidence?" Kate was an experienced investigative reporter, and she knew how to appear completely ingenuous while asking even the most intrusive question. She'd practiced that particular questioning expression in front of the mirror countless times when she'd first started interviewing her subjects.

"Neither did I." She did not think she fooled Leopold in the least, but he answered her query without hesitating, a slight twist in his lower lip the only indication that he recognized the guile in the way she phrased the question.

"What did they have?"

He arched an eyebrow at her, mirroring the questioning expression she had so recently worn. "I wouldn't know exactly," he hedged.

"Well, what did they present to the grand jury?"

"A disgruntled former employee," he said with a smile.

"That's it?" she asked, shocked. Grand jury evidence was kept in strict confidence, and of course, jurors couldn't discuss the cases they sat on, but rumors did abound, and her sources had indicated that the Feds had obtained audio or videotape on Skipper, as well as some canceled checks and deposit slips to prove their case.

"That's what they presented," he said smugly. She knew there had to be more to the story, but she wasn't going to try to get that information from him. The man was not a fool. Besides, she couldn't print accusations that had already proven to be unfounded. She let it go. "Is that all?" he asked.

Kate was surprised to find that more than half an hour had already passed since the interview had started. She'd told him, through Jen, that this was only going to be a short meeting, so she couldn't very well drag this out any longer. It was time to take the bull by the horns. "Concerning the strike at the Ninth Avenue site," she began.

He seemed to sit up a little straighter in his chair. "What about it?"

"I wanted to know if you have anything to say," she prompted.

"Only that I had to choose between two unpleasant alternatives," he said. "I could either side with the general membership of the union and support a policy of discrimination against the Hispanic membership, or I could support that minority. In keeping with my oft-stated view of discrimination, I chose to side with the minority." He forestalled her next question by raising a hand and continuing. "My critics claim I hired nonunion welders because it was cheaper, not because they were Hispanic. I didn't. Just as this unexpected opportunity arose to bring in some of the work underbudget, some unforeseen expense will probably come along to balance it out."

"But even the Hispanic membership of the union has issued a statement condemning your choice of action. Julio Gonzalez had set a time for another press meeting right before he died, and there can be little doubt that he was going to use the venue to continue to urge the Hispanic community to close the site down, given the statements he had issued previously."

"No one knows what Julio would have said. But it's beside the point. If there had been a workable third alternative, perhaps I would have taken it. I don't know. Given the current impasse, I stand behind my decision."

"Had you met Julio?" she probed.

"Only in the normal course of business," Skipper answered, glancing at his watch. "I'm sorry, but I have to get to another meeting before nine. If you need more information, you should speak with Jennifer Collier. I believe you know her."

"Perhaps we can set up another interview?" Kate pressed.

"Perhaps. Call my secretary, and if there is time in my schedule, I'll be happy to speak with you again. It's been a pleasure." He was clearly dismissing them.

There was nothing Kate could do but accept it. But

she had gotten what she wanted. She bid Skipper Arnold good-bye and followed Brant out of the office and down the hall, her mind working busily. Even Skipper's more evasive answers provided interesting fodder for the article. It was amazing how his mannerisms brought her uncle Jake to mind. She hadn't seen the elderly Southern gentleman in years, but speaking with Skipper made her recall her father and his brother, relaxing on Jake's porch on the old family farm in North Carolina. She loved those summers.

"I take it, from that grin, that you're happy now?" Brant asked, sounding for all the world like her old aunt Sophie used to whenever Kate won an argument with her.

"Yes. It went really well, didn't it?"

The elevator arrived, and they stepped inside. Kate felt exhilarated. They both reached out at the same time to press the Lobby button on the panel, and before he could drop his hand, she seized it and gave it a squeeze. She was too happy to keep it bottled up inside. "We did good, partner."

He took his hand back and put it in his pocket. "I wouldn't know," Brant said. "Since I've never done this before."

"We did," Kate said emphatically.

"He told you everything you wanted to know?" he sounded skeptical.

"He told me enough. It will make a great article. Can you believe he confirmed the union's report that hiring nonunion welders will double the investors' projected profit?"

"He also said that that could be offset at any time by unforeseen costs. I've seen that happen time and time again. Anyone in construction can tell you that."

"But he admitted he wasn't sure he did the right thing!" she exclaimed.

"Sure. Why not? I always found Skipper to be a pretty straightforward guy."

"So you said." Kate was about to point out that Mr. Arnold hadn't been exactly forthcoming on the subject of his incarceration, and he'd glossed over the question about Julio, but just then the elevator car suddenly came to a stop.

When the doors didn't open, they both looked at the elevator panel, with the one "L" lit at the bottom of the array of numbers. Kate looked up at the display above the door, which indicated that they were at the fourteenth floor. Still, the doors didn't slide open. Just as Kate started to feel the first touch of nervousness, the elevator moved with a jolt that knocked them into each other. Then the floor dropped out from beneath their feet, throwing them so off balance that they both fell. After a few seconds, it stopped. Dazed, Kate saw that the light above the door lit up the number ten. They had dropped three floors.

She pushed herself up onto her knees, and asked Brant, "Are you all right?" Her knee ached, but otherwise she felt okay, if a little panicky. What the heck was happening?

Brant had worked his way up onto one knee, but he seemed to be having trouble breathing. "You're not claustrophobic, too, are you?" she asked.

He shook his head. "No. No."

She helped him up. He'd been so calm on the way up in the elevator, but perhaps his acrophobia could kick in in an elevator if the lift decided to malfunction on the fourteenth floor. "What's the matter?" she asked. He waved her away with one hand. "Brant? Is it your . . . little problem?"

He was breathing normally again. "You hit me in the solar plexus. That's all. How's your elbow?"

Kate flexed her arm. "Fine," she said. "How are you feeling now?"

"Okay." He reached for the emergency panel and it clicked open. He picked up the phone, listened, and finally said, "Yeah. We're stuck, apparently on the tenth floor. We're fine." He seemed completely sincere, and amazingly tranquil considering they'd just plummeted thirty feet down an elevator shaft and still hadn't left the elevator car. Kate would have thought this was an acrophobic's worst nightmare. However, she had no desire to point this out to Brant if he hadn't realized it for himself.

She was scared. And as long as he seemed to be in control of his phobia, she didn't want to jar him out of his stupor, or whatever it was that allowed him to keep his composure. She needed to be calm, and his self-control gave her the strength to keep ahold of herself, despite their precarious circumstances. "So," she asked casually, "what do you think might have caused that to happen?"

"I won't know until I know what did happen," he responded openly. "I'm guessing there was some kind of power failure, or short, at the elevator's main control panel. Of course, we can't know until it's been checked out."

"When do you think they'll be uh . . . checking it out?"

"There is nothing much else we can do until we hear from Maintenance or Security, or whomever," Brant answered sensibly. "So we might as well get comfortable."

Kate couldn't believe he was so unaffected by their situation. She was very much aware of the fact that they were dangling from a steel cable in an elevator shaft. She wanted out. Now! He seemed unconcerned. It had to be an act.

But she took her cue from him. "Sure," she said with

all the bravado she could muster. Kate sat on the marble tiled floor of their cage and looked up at him. Some of her doubt must have shown on her face, because Brant smiled wryly as he sank down beside her.

She held out her hand, and he took it in his. "Don't worry," he consoled her. "I'm sure they'll have us out of here in a minute."

"I would really like to know how this could happen," Kate said. "This building is state-of-the-art. This has got to be one of the most luxurious elevators in the world. How could they skimp on the maintenance?"

"There is no point in speculating about this," he answered. "Anything could have happened."

And still could, Kate thought, but she kept it to herself.

He continued. "It could be any number of people, besides building maintenance, that overlooked something they were supposed to do. I know the company that makes these elevators, and they are top-notch. Usually there is a service contract, and an expert crew to service the elevators in these high-rises. Or the problem could be with the computer that runs the elevators—either human error, or just a glitch in the program."

"For all we know, New York could be in the grip of a citywide blackout," Kate added, playing along.

"I'm sure it's nothing like that," Brant hastened to say. "There is probably a very simple explanation for all of this."

Kate didn't see what difference it made. They were still trapped, whatever the reason. However, she realized suddenly that Brant wasn't as unconcerned as he pretended when he remarked, "There is absolutely no need to panic." She was sure he said it to himself as much as to her.

"No. Definitely not. Probably nothing at all," she agreed, and was rewarded with a relieved smile.

Kate wanted to reach out to him again, but she wasn't sure that it would be helpful to offer sympathy. She, herself, could definitely use some simple human contact. But Brant might react better to something else. Offering him a challenge, or starting an argument, could work, maybe, given their relationship up to this point, she thought. But she found she couldn't do it. She sat frozen on the marble floor staring up at the light on the console.

Kate craved a distraction from the fear she felt welling up inside her. She needed to think about something other than their current tenuous position. All that came to mind was the man sitting next to her. She focused on Brant. His eyes, his mouth, his broad shoulders. She had read somewhere that danger caused the human animal to become aroused. Perhaps it was a survival instinct. Whatever the reason, she felt desire shimmer through her. But she didn't know Brant, or his phobia, well enough to know if he would appreciate her touch right then. Even if her body and mind were screaming for his.

"Brant?"

"Yeah?"

"Give me your hand." He reached across the small space between them and she clutched at him, concentrating all her attention on the lifeline he offered. The feel of his skin against hers calmed her fear. The panic subsided. But her need grew stronger with every passing minute. When she looked up from his strong, large hand to his face, she saw in his eyes the same stark burning desire that she felt.

"Brant?" she said again.

"Yes, Kate?"

"Please?" she said softly, pulling him to her with the hand she still held in hers. She didn't close her eyes. She didn't even blink. She watched his mouth as it floated toward her. He licked his lips, and she did the same. He kissed her, gently, on the corner of her mouth. She felt his lips against hers, as full and warm as she had imagined they'd be.

He pulled back and opened his eyes, looking up from her mouth to her eyes. She couldn't know for certain what he saw there, but she knew what she felt. She wanted him to kiss her again. She leaned into him, her eyes sliding closed, her head tilting to the side as he bought his mouth down full on hers. His lips slanted over hers, and she felt them sweeping across her round mouth, sucking her top lip softly between his. The tip of his tongue grazed her teeth, and she felt his raspy warmth against the roof of her mouth.

She braced herself with her free hand, straightening her arm as her elbow threatened to buckle. She felt the smooth cool stone beneath her fingers contrasting with the smooth warmth of Brant's hand, which she still held in hers. And overwhelming all of these sensations was the feel of his hot, silky mouth drawing her breath from her body, sparking a fire in her blood, and making her crave the feel of his flesh against hers.

It didn't register right away that the elevator had begun to move again. When she realized that it had, she slowly withdrew from him and, even more slowly, opened her eyes to look up at the console. She felt, rather than saw, his head turn to the panel to watch the lights blink on and off: seven, six, five, four. Soon they would be out of this elevator car, back on terra firma. And then she was going to have to explain herself. Kate didn't notice when Brant stood up. It was only when he waved his hand in front of her eyes that she came out of her trance. He was offering to help her up. She had just gotten to her feet when the elevator doors slid open.

It didn't take long to find out what had happened. Brant spoke briefly to the security guard, the same beefy guy who had checked them in to the building a couple of hours ago. In twenty minutes, they were in the control room talking, on the telephone, to the elevator company's maintenance guys. One of the elevator cables, it turned out, had been tampered with. It looked like the accident was indeed a veiled warning after all.

"I know what you're thinking," Brant said as they left the building. "You think Skipper had something to do with this, don't you?"

"Bingo!" Kate answered. "Don't you?"

"No, I don't," Brant said, but he didn't sound completely sure this time. "It could have been . . . lots of things." He was trying to convince himself as well as her. "Maybe someone was after Skipper, and we weren't even supposed to be there."

"You heard what the man said. You need a pretty serious knowledge of the building, plus identification, to get into that room and the elevator shaft. On top of that, how many people would know Skipper was in his office working late tonight, meeting us? This was no random attack. It was timed—meticulously timed, I'd guess—to catch us on our way out. And only Skipper knew we were going to be here tonight."

"I'm sure other people knew his schedule. A lot of people."

"You just said it could have been done by someone who didn't even know we were meeting him. I may not be Barbara Walters, but I think I probably rate a mention on his calendar," she said sarcastically.

"So, whoever did this knew we were going to be here. I still think it's more likely this was some sick joke on Skipper, not some threat to us from him. Do you realize how paranoid you sound?"

"You were in that elevator with me, big guy. You know this isn't paranoia. It's fear, plain and simple."

"It's over now, and we're fine. I just don't think you should make more of it than it is."

"And how could I do that?"

"By jumping to ridiculous conclusions. What possible reason could Skipper Arnold have to destroy his own elevator?"

"Did you forget why we're here? I'm writing a newspaper article about the man. Maybe this was a warning."

"Why would he agree to the interview if he didn't want to talk to you?" Brant asked, reasonably enough. "No one forced him to do it."

"I don't know. Maybe he wants me to do a story on him—but not *my* story."

"He doesn't even know what you're planning to write," Brant chided her. "No one does except you, right?"

"All right, I get it," Kate said, frustrated. "You don't think this . . . accident . . . was related to our visit here, or my article. I do. I guess we'll have to agree to disagree. It's not like that's a new concept for us."

Brant wasn't satisfied. "I don't want you running off, half-cocked, to investigate this alone."

"Do I detect a note of concern? That's sweet, but it's unnecessary. I don't need a protector. You've been a big help to me, and I appreciate it, but I can handle this all by myself."

"I don't think so," Brant said.

"And just what is that supposed to mean?" she asked, truculent.

"I'm not going to let you dig into this can of worms on your own," he said.

"I hate to break this to you, but I don't need your permission to do anything," she exclaimed. "You don't have a say in the matter. I'm a big girl. I've been taking care of myself for a long time now, and I don't need any assistance from you."

"If this little stunt was, as you suspect, an attempt to scare us off, I'm afraid you won't help yourself any by sticking your nose in where it doesn't belong. If you're going to go looking for the psycho who tampered with our elevator, I'm going with you," Brant said decisively.

"I don't need a bodyguard," Kate protested.

He muttered something under his breath. Kate thought she heard the words, "No, what you need is a keeper."

As she was about to launch into a full explanation as to why she truly didn't need his help, she realized that he could prove to be useful, and she stifled the rest of her objections. She hadn't asked for this, and she could easily have done without it, but . . .

After the past few hours, Kate supposed a big, tall, strong man could prove to be useful, in certain situations.

Ten

Neither the private company that provided security nor the management company that was responsible for maintaining Skipper's building would admit to any knowledge of, or any interest in determining, the cause of the incident—as they insisted on calling it. The building owners did offer a modest settlement in exchange for a promise not to sue them, supposedly at the insistence of their insurance company. Kate demurred and requested more information about the individuals who had access to the controls, including their names and phone numbers so she could question them herself about who else, authorized or unauthorized, might have been there that day. The management company declined to grant her request. She was able to intimidate the receptionist into giving her the name of the firm that installed, and repaired—when necessary—the elevators in Skipper's building.

Unfortunately, she was confronted with another brick wall when she tried to get information from the company, Thomson Brothers, Incorporated, about the accident. They were not insured against sabotage as they explained ad infinitum and in great detail. They were responsible to the building management company, who were, in turn, responsible for investigating the incident. Brant wouldn't discuss the matter on the telephone, and Kate wasn't ready yet to set a time to meet with him. He hadn't mentioned the kiss she had given him and she didn't want to push it. He sounded completely unconcerned about what had happened to them, but called her regularly and insisted she tell him where she was and what she was doing. He also told her he planned to accompany her to any interview that might have the slightest connection to the incident, which she liked to call her "brush with death."

After being given the runaround for a day and a half, Kate decided to try another approach. Taking Brant in tow on Saturday night, she tracked Jennifer down at Le Bar Bat, where her friend was attending a private party. Kate had to do some fast talking to get into the bastion of pop music, trendy cocktails, and designer clothing. She very nearly didn't make it past the trio of pompous, vicious, black-clad hulks who guarded the door to the club. They detained her with such relish that Kate was tempted to inform them that they were making a mistake if they thought their piddling jobs gave them any real power over anyone, especially her. Petty tyrants such as these young men were to be found outside every club in Manhattan, exercising their authority to admit or reject prospective patrons with an almost religious fervor. They thought they were arbiters of good taste and high fashion, hired for their ability to recognize style and grace, but they were really just heartless, arrogant, hangers-on—a nuisance Kate could have done without. Unfortunately, they were considered an absolute necessity by the club owners. After all, what was the point of having a guest list if just anyone could get in? For that matter, where was the thrill to getting in if someone wasn't kept out?

Fortunately, these particular doormen were impressed enough by her press card to finally admit her to the inner sanctum. Le Bar Bat was a night spot on West Fifty-seventh

Street, relatively well-known to New Yorkers, less so to out-of-towners. It's location, roughly halfway between the Copacabana at Fifty-fifth and Eleventh Avenue, and the strip of tourist-filled celebrity hangouts such as The Hard Rock Café, Planet Hollywood, and Jekyll and Hyde on Fifty-seventh between Broadway and Fifth Avenue, made it the perfect spot for industry parties. It was well designed for such functions. All three floors could be used for a big affair, or smaller groups could choose to reserve only one. The large open rooms had black tiled floors and crimson walls, and the lighting fixtures were well hidden and ineffective by design. The smattering of adornments on the walls were barely visible in the darkness, and black shrouding draped at intervals along the walls created an even darker, eerier ambience.

"Hey, girl. Still working?" Jen asked, as Kate bore down upon her purposefully. Jennifer wore a "clubbing" outfit that was very different from the informal attire she'd worn to Body and Soul. The scrap of silk that comprised her top was probably a designer piece. A tight black leather skirt and expensive black heels showed off her long legs. Brant let out a low whistle when he saw her. She looked at him with a mixture of surprise and speculation in her gaze. "I guess you are, since he's with you."

"Brant has appointed himself my guardian—at least until we find out who might want us dead."

"Leave me out of your fantasies," Brant said. "I'm just making sure you don't provoke someone to arrange an accident."

Jennifer watched the exchange with an amused expression. "And just how do you think you will accomplish that? Are you going to gag her?"

"Hey! You're supposed to be on my side," Kate whined.

"I calls 'em like I sees 'em," Jen retorted. "You could drive a saint to murder."

"I came here for help, but I can see you're not going to be much use to me."

Suddenly Jennifer was serious. "What do you need, Kate?"

"Do you think you could help me get a look at Skipper's books?"

"Why do you want to do that?" her friend asked, intrigued.

"Yeah, why?" Brant echoed, not intrigued, but suspicious.

"Have you ever heard the old adage, *Follow the money*, folks? That's what I want to do. There's a lot of profit in the L.A.C. Parking Garage job, and I want to know where it's going, and why."

"Do you even know what you would be looking for?" Jen asked skeptically.

"That's where he comes in." Kate nodded toward Brant. "Since he insists he has to watch me day and night, he might as well make himself useful."

Jennifer was distracted by that remark. "Day and night?" she said, looking reflectively from one of them to the other.

"She's exaggerating," Brant said. "For effect."

"I'm not the one who decided I needed a baby-sitter," Kate observed. "You volunteered for this."

"Yes, I did. And I'm beginning to wonder why I should watch your back."

"Katie is irritating, and annoying, and outspoken, I know," Jen said soothingly. "But she's worth it. Trust me."

"Trust you? You got us into this mess in the first place," Kate joked.

"One of these days, you'll have to thank me. You two make an adorable couple," Jennifer replied.

"Thank *you?*" Kate snorted. "For what?"

"For introducing you to the sweetest man in the construction business," Jen answered, unabashed. "And one who is, moreover, luscious, gorgeous, and a hard body."

"It's always nice to be appreciated," Brant said wryly. "But I'm not sure you two are aware that this is the year 2001. Men are no longer regarded as slabs of meat."

"You have some objection to being described as a beefcake?"

"How would you like it if I called you cheesecake?" he countered.

"I'm not white enough to be cheesecake," Jennifer said philosophically. "Besides I think you've got this new millennium all wrong. You men are no longer allowed to treat us as objects, whereas *we've* got a lot of time to make up for."

"An unenlightened woman, eh?" he quipped.

"I think I'm very enlightened. I am also completely determined to make the most of the new world order for as long as I can."

"How politically incorrect of you," Brant said sarcastically. "And I doubt it's necessary. I'm sure you wouldn't have any trouble getting men to do anything you want."

"Really? Then may I trouble you to fight through this crowd to the bar and get me a screwdriver?"

"At your service, mademoiselle," he responded promptly.

The minute he left them alone, Jennifer dropped her carefree facade and leaned closer to Kate to say softly, "So, what have you got?"

"I told you. I haven't made much progress. Skipper appears to be a hardworking, well-respected businessman, at the top of his form, and at the top of his field. There were some questions he didn't answer fully during our interview—like whether he had met Julio Gonzalez recently—but all in all he's been very forthcoming and doesn't act like he's got anything to hide, let alone a murder."

"Why do I sense a 'but' coming on?" Jennifer asked.

"This elevator accident wasn't an accident," Kate said, not bothering to hide the fact that she was troubled. "I'm convinced it was meant to scare me off, perhaps to stop me from digging deeper. And I can't think of anyone but Skipper who would bother. He's the only one with anything to lose."

"Well, you never know about that. . . ." Jennifer said, looking toward the bar where Brant stood waiting for their drinks. She refocused on Kate's face as she expounded, "Brant might just have a little something on the line here, too. Uncle Skip can make or break him, professionally." Her friend seemed intent not only on destroying her mentor, but she also insinuated Brant might be involved somehow. Brant! The man whose integrity she recently described as ironclad.

Kate shook her head. "I don't get it, Jen. You're the one who introduced me to Brant because you thought he was one of the good guys. And now that I've gotten to know him, I'm sure you were right. How can you imply. . . ?"

"I'm just trying to help," Jennifer said evenly. "You're very involved in all this, and I'm not sure you can see the big picture. I'm an objective observer, just trying to get at the truth." Kate wondered, all of a sudden, if Jennifer Collier had always been like this. She didn't like to be manipulated, and she had a strange feeling that that was exactly what was happening. Her old college roommate definitely had some agenda of her own.

Kate couldn't deal with that thought. She decided to

keep the discussion on track. "So? Do you think you could get me a look at the books?"

"What are you hoping to find, a canceled check to an assassin?"

"I told you, I'm just following the money trail now."

"I don't know what good it will do. Skipper isn't stupid. He probably wouldn't put anything incriminating in the books."

"Probably not, but it's as good a place as any to start, don't you think?"

"It shouldn't be too difficult. I think I can even get the bookkeeper to make me copies of all the papers connected with this job. The guy has been asking me out for months. Guess I could finally say yes." She shook her head in feigned remorse, but added, with a twinkle in her eye, "The things I do for you."

"Thanks," Kate said sardonically. "That will be a big help," she said with a little more sincerity.

"That's what I'm here for." Brant was starting back toward them, and Jennifer lowered her voice even further to ask, "Does he know about Julio?"

"I don't know if there's anything for him to know," Kate confessed.

"Good," Jen said approvingly. "What he doesn't know can't hurt him. Or us."

"I feel a little strange agreeing with that, but, for the moment, I think this is best."

"What's up?" Brant said as he rejoined them.

"I'm going to do what I can," Jennifer explained. "At least as far as this investigation is concerned. There's not a lot I can do about the rest. You're going to have to handle Katie here yourself, big guy." She looked up at Brant from under her long, lush eyelashes—a maneuver Kate had seen her use a hundred times before with great success. This was the first time she could remember resenting her friend's habit of flirting with anyone and everyone.

"I don't care to be *handled,* thank you," Kate stated.

Brant held his hands up defensively in front of him. "Hey, I didn't say it. She did." He absolved himself. "She's your friend."

"And I want it to stay that way," Jen announced. "So be good." She slipped away from them to talk to a tall, white man in a black leather outfit.

They waited for a bit, then Kate said, "I don't think she's coming back."

"Mmm-hmm," he murmured. "So . . . do you want to dance?"

"Uh, sure," Kate agreed hesitantly.

It felt absolutely exquisite, dancing with Brant again. She hadn't remembered how good he was. Or she had, but she hadn't consciously realized it. Her arms remembered, and the rest of her body. She let him hold her close, and it felt terrific. Perfect. Until she caught a glimpse of Jennifer through the crowd, watching them. Even from a distance, she thought she saw a feline smile on her college roommate's face.

So what, Kate thought. *We're just dancing. It's no big deal. No harm, no foul.*

"I really want to kiss you right now," Brant said.

All she could think of to say was, "Oh, no." She had been wrong. This was dangerous. Kate tried to pull away.

"Not exactly the response I was hoping for," he said, seemingly unperturbed.

"This is a mistake," Kate said, still trying to extricate herself from his arms.

"Why?" He bent his head, stark desire burning in his eyes. She looked away, and his lips caught her on the forehead. The brush of his mouth against her skin was disturbingly intimate, surprisingly arousing.

"Brant—" she warned.

"Hmm?" he murmured into her hair.

"We should go," she said weakly.

"I don't think so." He slid one arm behind her waist, holding her to him, then he brought his free hand up to her chin and turned her face back to his, making it impossible for her to turn away again. "Not yet," he refused.

He lowered his head slowly and Kate's breath caught in her lungs as she waited for that lingering, deliberate descent to end. Brant touched his mouth to her cheek, then brushed lightly over her eyes, forcing them closed. He left a trail of kisses behind as his lips traveled down to her chin and slipped past the curve of her jaw to her neck. She couldn't fight him. She wanted him to kiss her. She took his hand from her chin and held it in her own and raised her head, exposing her throat to his questing lips.

He took his time; tasting her, and nuzzling the shallow indentation above her collarbone. Then he worked his way back up her jawbone. He nipped her there lightly, catching a tiny fold of skin between his teeth. A wave of heat curled through her body. She gasped, and then, finally, he covered her open lips with his own. He forged deep within, his tongue twining with hers, sending her blood rushing and her senses reeling. She forgot where she was and what she was doing there. Forgot everything but the reckless hunger that surged through her and made her oblivious to anything but the fervent need to respond, to discover just how deeply she could delve into the honeyed warmth of his mouth.

They parted reluctantly, breathing raggedly. Kate licked her lips. She could never get enough of the feel of his lips or the touch of his tongue. But sanity slowly returned.

"That was . . ." he began, then faltered, searching for words.

"Definitely a mistake," she finished. But worth every minute of the sleepless night that loomed ahead, she thought to herself. She found she could not muster one iota of regret for succumbing to the temptation he offered.

"Incredible, I was going to say," he corrected her.

"An incredible lapse of judgment," she countered.

"You've got to admit, we've got some serious chemistry," he remarked.

"We are clearly attracted to each other," Kate agreed. There was no point in denying the obvious. "But it doesn't change anything."

"What doesn't it change?" he questioned. "Our relationship?"

"Yes."

He smiled. "So you admit that we have one?"

"But we shouldn't," she said hastily. "We're working together."

"I quit," he said instantly, leaning toward her.

Kate turned her head and his lips grazed her cheek. "That's the problem. I'm afraid that's exactly what would happen," Kate explained. She pulled back from him a little, so they were separated by more than a few inches. "I know this isn't as important to you as it is to me, but we have both put a lot of work into this story. I don't want to blow it now. Not when we're so close."

"Close to what?" he asked impatient.

"I don't know, exactly. But someone tried to blow up our elevator, so we definitely stepped on someone's toes. And the interview with Skipper provided some useful information."

"Forget the elevator," he commanded. At her look of annoyance, he added quickly, "Write about the interview with Skipper, with me, with whomever."

"I'm going to."

"Perfect. That takes care of that. Why can't we—"

She cut him off. "I'm not going to throw away the chance to do a story as big as this one just because of a little sexual attraction."

"A little?" he said, incredulous.

"Focus, Brant. Please?" He nodded. She went on. "We are working together. Your help has been invaluable. I'm very grateful. Really. I am relying on you to keep doing what you're doing. I could write this story without you, but I don't want to. And if we . . . get together . . . we'd be jeopardizing that."

"I don't see how. Obviously, I'm not about to walk away," he rebutted. "Not after that."

"I know, but it could happen," she tried to clarify.

"I could give up on this harebrained article tomorrow," he observed. "Whether we're together or not."

"You could, of course," Kate conceded. "But I don't think you will. You've been great so far. All I'm saying is, it's better if we don't complicate things. Maybe after I file the story, we can talk about this some more."

"I think all this talking is what's causing the problem," he protested, pulling her close again. "I never should have stopped kissing you." He lowered his head, dark eyes intent. She held her hand up in front of her face, to stop him from kissing her again, and he captured her hand, and kissed it.

"Brant, I know I started this. In the elevator. I've been meaning to talk to you about that. I'm sorry I . . . did it. I was scared. I know that isn't any excuse, but I wasn't thinking. I was just reacting. It was pure instinct."

"You didn't start anything," he said soothingly. "I felt the same way. I think what just happened here is proof of that."

"But we're not stuck in an elevator now," Kate replied

more sharply than she intended. "I mean . . . this is different. I—we—did make a mistake—"

"Twice," he interjected.

"But my brain is working now. And it's overriding my . . ." She was about to say her body, but it didn't seem like a good word to bring up at the moment. "Our—those instincts."

"That's a shame," he said lightly. "Your instincts are good."

"We barely know each other. A little attraction isn't enough to . . . to . . ."

"What?"

"I can't let myself get sidetracked. I admit I'm tempted, too, but . . ." She let her voice trail off.

"Fine" he said in response. Surprisingly, he didn't sound angry.

"Huh?" That was one response she wasn't expecting.

"Forget it. I'm sorry I brought it up. Let's just dance."

She looked up into his face. He met her searching gaze with a frank, open one of his own. Kate was still suspicious. It hadn't seemed like he agreed with her arguments. Why was he giving in now?

She opened her mouth to ask him, then shut it again. *Better to leave it alone,* she thought. She had gotten what she wanted.

Eleven

Kate Ramsey had succeeded in turning his life upside down in just over two weeks. By noon on Monday, Brant was more than a little dismayed by some of the stuff he was discovering about Skipper Arnold. He chose to pursue his own line of inquiry about the man for a day or two, without Kate's disapproving presence to distract him. He wanted to be objective about this, and Kate's palpable distrust of Skipper had, he felt, been coloring his judgment of the man lately. But what he knew of the developer didn't quite mesh with the stories he was hearing. Most disturbing of all were the rumors of bribes the developer may have paid to various city officials and union reps on the L.A.C. Parking Garage contract. Brant had worked with, and for, Skipper in the past, and had never felt compromised in the slightest.

He knew that the city's construction industry was rife with corruption, but Leopold Arnold had seemed to him to be above all that. Brant knew firsthand how difficult it was to succeed in this business without breaking and twisting and manipulating the rules. Kate's example of the contractor who was convicted of bribery and yet managed to arrange through the prison work furlough program to be employed on some of New York's biggest construction projects illustrated perfectly how easily the construction business leant itself to corruption. Brant, himself, had skirted some dangerous pitfalls when he'd first begun making his way in the industry—especially after he began his own subcontracting business.

In the beginning he had not known how to react to the various immoral builders who offered him contracts, nor what to do about the illegal transactions he'd witnessed. As time went on, Brant chose his own road and stuck to it. But even now, there were those whom he had met who made it clear they thought he did himself, and his relatively young company, a disservice by clinging tenaciously to the code of ethics he'd been taught by his father.

He wasn't naive. Brant knew he could have made more money, gotten more—or bigger—contracts, and prospered in general if he had been willing to compromise his principles. But that wasn't how he was raised. He couldn't imagine going home to his parents and having them congratulate him on success that had been achieved in a manner they would have thought less than honorable. He couldn't have bought their Christmas gifts with money he'd earned in an unscrupulous fashion.

Until he met Kate Ramsey—and even afterward—he was sure that Leopold Arnold felt exactly the same way. But now he wasn't so sure. By Tuesday afternoon, Brant knew he couldn't wait any longer to speak with her. Not about their relationship, but about Skipper. He called and asked her to come to his office to discuss the article. She paused a moment, but she agreed, as he had known she would.

He was sure that he had access to the information she wanted. He had spoken to enough people to know that there was some truth to the rumors about his mentor, and that, with a little judicious digging, and the right questions to the right people, Kate would have her story. He just couldn't decide whether to put her in touch with his friends. He was sure that Skipper had nothing to do with the elevator accident, or anything else like that. He just couldn't picture that powerful, successful, charming gentleman sinking to the level of a common criminal. Certainly it was ridiculous to suspect that the developer would feel that threatened by the reporter.

Leopold Arnold was the embodiment of the American dream. Brant couldn't bear to think of him as a sleazy profit monger who was motivated solely by greed. Skipper wasn't venal or mercenary. The builder who took him under his wing, taught him, worked with him, and generally supported his aspirations and his goals could not be what they said he was. But Kate's instinct had been to believe the rumors. That, combined with the information he'd obtained, caused Brant to wonder how well he actually knew the man.

Kate Ramsey was one of the most intelligent people he'd ever met. She had her prejudices. That was undeniable. But she seemed fair, and, more importantly, scrupulously honest. He wished he could be as forthright as she had always been with him and tell her straight out that he'd begun to wonder about the gossip surrounding New York's premier black developer. But Brant couldn't bring himself to admit to her that her suspicions might be correct. Kate was already so sure of herself, and so disparaging of the man he admired more than anyone else in the business. He didn't want to give her any more fodder for her suspicions.

Besides, she was convinced Skipper had sabotaged the elevator in his building, and, despite all his unanswered questions, Brant did not think for a moment that Skipper would dirty his hands with an attack on anyone, let alone a lone journalist writing one trivial article in the *New Amsterdam Press*. Even if the story was picked up by every news venue in the country, Leopold Arnold would not be impacted. He and his business could survive anything the media could do to him. But Kate was totally convinced that the accident had had something to do with Skipper. And Brant wouldn't mind finding out what exactly had happened in that elevator shaft, either. So perhaps they could figure it out together. He liked working with her. Despite her stubbornness, her sharp tongue, and her short temper, he felt drawn to her.

He kept telling himself that nothing serious could develop between them. He didn't chase women who weren't interested in being chased. Not since his college days anyway. The thrill of the conquest, in and of itself, no longer satisfied him. He carefully chose the women he dated, opting usually for those who were like him: independent, and ambitious, but even-tempered and sensible—polar opposites of Kate Ramsey. He liked his women sophisticated, cool if not cold, and a little smarter than him, but basically controllable. They respected him, and he respected them, because they understood each other, could please each other, and anticipate each other's needs. These relationships were satisfying, comfortable, predictable. Kate was trouble. He knew that from the moment he met her. She was not comfortable, and she certainly wasn't predictable.

But she was fun. Even when she was being impossible, argumentative, and unreasonable, there was something alluring about her. It was probably unconscious, but she roused the demon in him with her constant challenges. He was tempted to try and tame her. He certainly planned to get to know her better. He wanted her more than he had wanted a woman in a long time.

Brant knew himself well enough to know that, whatever else was going on between them, Katie aroused some powerful feelings within him. Whether it was curiosity or

plain old-fashioned lust that he felt, he wasn't about to
walk away without exploring the attraction. And soon. He
didn't know why she was so leery, but he wasn't about
to wait for her to finish the article she was writing before
trying to further their relationship. If she wanted to hold
him at arm's length until this investigation into Skipper's
business practices was concluded, she was going to have
to do it without his help. He had backed off once, but
he had no intention of letting her deny their mutual attraction for very much longer, especially since they were
forced into such close proximity by the work they were
doing together. It was ironic that the very thing she said
was keeping them apart was also thrusting them together.
She herself admitted the chemistry between them was
strong. She was as attracted to him as he was to her,
although it was clear that she wasn't happy about it.

He could not resist her. She was too enticing. It didn't
help at all that when he saw her that evening in his office, she looked utterly adorable. She was a tiny little
thing next to Brant. The top of her head barely reached
his shoulder, but she was all woman. She smelled like
lilies. Her smooth hair was pulled up and back into a
crown of shining ebony, in the same style she'd worn a
few nights before to Le Bar Bat. Her latest business suit
had an even shorter skirt than the first one he had seen
her in. This one was pleated black linen that fell at midthigh. The pleats should have made the skirt seem more
demure than the straight skirt she wore at their first meeting, but they didn't. It flared when she walked, flashing
a glimpse at her chocolate-brown thigh. In fact, it was a
more risqué outfit all around. Her suit jacket wasn't
skimpy. It fell to just below the rounded curve of her
posterior, two or three inches above the skirt's daring
hemline. As if that wasn't enough to jump-start his imagination, the deep vee of her jacket showed off her

décolleté while concealing any hint that she wore anything beneath the textured linen. Not a scrap of lace or silk peeked out from behind the low neckline.

She was anxious—that was clear from her behavior. Instead of her usual brazen attitude, she was a little diffident. When she was seated, she looked everywhere but at him, but snuck sidelong glances at him when she thought he wasn't looking. He knew perfectly well that Kate was afraid that he was going to bring up the nightclub, and their dance, and he didn't bother to put her mind at ease, because he did plan to bring it up again, in due time. But that wasn't why he'd asked her for this meeting. His invitation had nothing to do with how cute she was when she was nervous, or how much he wanted to kiss her again.

In order to distract himself from those thoughts, Brant brought up the subject he wanted to discuss. "Why are you so convinced that Skipper arranged the accident in the elevator?" he demanded.

"Besides the fact that we were leaving a meeting with him, in his office?"

"It's a long way to go from a meeting—which, at the time, you thought went very well—to an assassination attempt."

"The interview went great, from my standpoint, not only because of what Skipper did say, but also what he didn't."

"So? That still seems like a stretch to me."

"I guess so, but . . ."

"But what? What do you have against Skipper?"

Katie took a deep breath and expelled it. "I have reason to believe he was involved, somehow, in the death of Julio Gonzalez."

Brant was more than shocked. "How could you make an accusation like that?"

"Leopold didn't get to be what he is today without stepping on a few toes," she said.

"How do you know. . . ?" He suddenly realized someone had aimed Kate at Skipper like a hunter sending his hound after his quarry. She was a reporter; she didn't just pull her stories out of thin air. Someone had to be telling her something. "How do you know someone isn't just trying to set him up? Make him look bad?"

"That's why I'm investigating. But the more I look into his life, the easier it is to believe my sources."

"If you already know what you're going to write, what am I doing here?"

"I'm not sure. I'm trying to find out what is really going on. How much of this is supposition, and how much is real."

"But you're sure he's . . . a bad guy? And that's what you intend to write?"

"I have no real evidence. I need confirmation of the story."

"Then how can you be so sure? You don't even know the man, beyond his press releases."

"And you do? You couldn't possibly be wrong about him?"

"Anything is possible."

"That's exactly what I've been saying. I have no reason to wish Skipper Arnold ill. I just want to know if he had anything to do with this man's death. He might. It's possible. If he did, that would make a hell of a story."

"And if he didn't?"

"If?" She glommed onto that tiny little word. "I would have thought you'd be more definite than that."

"I believe you're looking for the truth. I just don't understand. Why this story? There's got to be more to it than an exclusive. You wouldn't sacrifice a man's reputation just to build up your own."

"Thanks for the vote of confidence," she said wryly, standing and walking away.

"So, why is this story so important to you?"

She kept her back to him, pretending to look out of the trailer's one tiny window. "Ever since I read about how Julio died, I felt I had to get to the bottom of this. Did he die because he was a drunk, or were some other factors at work in his death?"

"That's it? That's your explanation?"

"What do you want from me? You asked. I answered."

"That's not an answer."

"It's the only one I've got." She was lying. Whether to herself, or to him, he didn't know, but he didn't believe her. And that was a first. Whatever else he might have said about Kate Ramsey, the one thing he was completely certain about was her innate honesty. There was something she wasn't telling him. And it was important. It was the reason they'd been thrown together.

"Why do you hate Skipper so much?" he pressed. This was crucial. Before he could make one more statement to the woman, he needed to know why she was so hell-bent on crucifying Leopold Arnold.

She turned back to him, resting her hip against his drafting table and crossing her arms. "I told you. I don't hate him. How could I? I don't even know him." The sincerity in her voice was unmistakable. She didn't care about Skipper. So who did she care about?

"It can't be Julio," Brant said, thinking aloud. But he couldn't think of anyone else who was involved in this.

"What can't be Julio?"

"The reason you're fixated on writing this particular story."

"I'm like this on every story. It has nothing to do with who the victim was. To be honest, from what I saw of him, I didn't even like the man. Drunks kill themselves all the time—usually the slow, painful way. It's a very destructive disease. I don't know why this one got to me. But it did."

That made sense to Brant. Julio Gonzalez wasn't exactly the type to inspire a woman like Kate Ramsey to obsession. "He barely rates a mention in the article anyway. It's Skipper Arnold as a killer that will sell newspapers. No one will even remember Julio's name. He wasn't important enough," he said, thinking aloud.

"A man doesn't have to be rich and successful to be important. Everyone is important to someone."

"Did you know him?"

"Who?" she asked, distracted.

"Who?" Brant repeated, confused. They were talking about Julio Gonzalez. What was she thinking about? He asked. "Who were you talking about?"

"Julio" she said quickly. It was a good thing she wasn't a liar. She wasn't very good at it. "I never met him, but he had a wife, children."

He couldn't let it go. "Who *were* you talking about?"

"No one."

This time he could tell she was lying. Not to herself, to him. She was definitely thinking of someone. "Who was it?" Someone important to her, he was sure. A man. Probably an alcoholic. There was something about the way she said, *"Drunks kill themselves all the time,"* that made him think she was speaking of a personal experience. Someone had died. "Your father?" he guessed.

She nodded, dispassionately, as if they were discussing her shoe size, rather than the death of a parent. "My father," she confirmed.

"I'm sorry," he said, feeling it wasn't enough, but certain that her father's death had something to do with her pursuit of this story. He came out from behind his desk and approached her, very slowly.

She seemed so detached. Brant thought he understood a little of what the loss must have meant to her. Usually so fiery, Kate was suddenly like a different person; impassive and unemotional. She and her father must have been very close for her to become so apathetic at the mere mention of him. His heart went out to her.

"I don't know what I'd do without my dad. Even today. I'm thirty-four years old, and I still call home and talk to him, and my mother, almost every week." Brant felt compelled to reach out to her. He needed to touch her. He reached out his hand and felt her silky smooth cheek against the back of his fingers.

She closed her eyes and lowered her head into his palm. "My dad raised me. My mother died when I was very little. I don't remember her. He never recovered."

"I'm so sorry," he said again. He could imagine her as a little tomboy, her father's little ball of fire, a miniature version of the spirited woman he knew.

She turned away from him. "It was years ago," she muttered.

The sight of her—back straight, head up—and so utterly alone, tugged at his heart. He didn't think. He closed the distance between them, and hugged her from behind, wrapping his arms around her torso and pulling her close into his body.

She didn't resist. She leaned back, against him, and tilted her head back onto his shoulder. Her eyes were closed, her mouth sad. He leaned down, over her shoulder, and kissed her cheek, the same soft chocolatey cheek he'd touched with his hand. He rubbed his cheek against hers. She relaxed against him, and he became thoroughly aware of the lush curves of her body, which rested against him. She was so vulnerable, he was afraid to move. She touched her lips to his skin, and he couldn't help but respond. He kissed the corner of her mouth.

She tasted even better than she felt. He couldn't get enough of her. Katie didn't move an inch when he kissed her jawbone and the delicate skin beneath her ear. He didn't want to take advantage of her, but he couldn't refrain from going just a little bit further when she stood so quietly, so willingly, in his arms. His lips retraced their path back to her cheek and then he gently kissed that beguiling mouth that had tantalized him for so long—before, during, and since their previous kisses. This time it felt right.

"There's no need for you to feel sorry for me," Kate said.

"This isn't pity," he assured her, turning her around to face him. "This is that chemistry we were talking about."

He kissed her again—a quick buss full on her mouth that left her smiling. "That's better," he said. The shadows were gone from her eyes.

"I still don't think we should get involved," she declared. But she reached up and looped her arms around his neck. He watched her teeth play with her lower lip while she considered.

He wrapped his hands around her slim wrists and waited expectantly. "No?" he asked. "Don't tell me. You're afraid of commitment," he joked.

"Something like that," she replied seriously. "I've never managed to make a relationship work. And this one . . ." She shook her head doubtfully.

"I'm not asking you to marry me," Brant said. "Just . . . open up a little."

She pulled his head down to hers. "Like this?" She held his gaze as she parted her lips, only a millimeter away from his.

"That wasn't exactly what I meant," he murmured, the husky rasp of his voice evidence of how she affected him. "But it's a start." He couldn't hold back. He covered her open lips with his own, and her tongue darted into his mouth salaciously, demolishing the last of his self-control. He ravished her mouth, with lips and teeth and tongue. His hands left her wrists and slid down her arms to encircle her slim waist and pull her close, then he bracketed her hips between his palms. She moaned, and his tongue surged within to catch the sound. He savored the sweet familiar taste of her, the feel of her soft flesh beneath his splayed hands, her flowery scent.

He buried his face in her neck, breathing deeply. "This isn't why I asked you here," he told her.

"That's good, because it's not why I came," she replied, gasping as he bit her gently on the neck. "You said you had done some more research, for the article," she prompted him.

"I wanted to know why you were so determined to nail Skipper first," he tried to explain.

"Now you know," she said glibly.

He had not forgotten. "I don't know what I'd do without my father," he said apologetically, hugging her close. "My family's support means everything to me."

She squeezed him tighter. "My father supported me. He just couldn't stop drinking." Kate's grip on his waist didn't loosen. "I always knew he loved me. Unfortunately, love wasn't enough to stop him from killing himself." She looked up at him, her clear brown eyes solemn. He wanted to tell her that maybe that was why she wasn't able to commit to a relationship. To tell her it could be different for them.

He almost did it, but instead he just said, "I'm sorry, Katie."

"I stopped feeling sorry for myself a long time ago." She could pretend to be as unaffected as she wanted, but he didn't believe it for a minute.

"You're such a tough guy," he teased, smiling.

"That's me," she retorted. "Tough as nails."

"You feel nice and soft to me," he contradicted her, and lowered his head to kiss her again.

"Wait" she ordered. "What did you want to tell me about Skipper?"

"Later," Brant promised. "I'll tell you later."

Twelve

By the time they came up for air, Kate had almost forgotten about her dad. She had loved that old man. Her whole life had revolved around him. But she knew she had to move on. Thinking about him, and especially about his death, was painful. Brant was certainly doing a good job of distracting her from those thoughts, though.

"You're pretty good at this," she said, feeling surprisingly happy.

"Just wait. I can do better," he promised.

He kissed her again—with a sweet, lingering pressure that she felt down to her toes. "Mmm," she murmured against his lips. "You were right. That was nice."

"Better?" he asked playfully.

"Not bad," she answered in the same light tone.

"You *are* tough," he said. "That was one of my best." He kissed her eyes, cheeks, and the corner of her mouth. His strong arms held her close, and the warmth of his body seeped through her clothes, then her skin, and heated her blood.

"Maybe we should get out of here," she said languidly, her palm brushing lightly over his chest.

"Is there any place specific that you want to go?" he asked with a look of bland inquiry.

She froze, her hand still inside his shirt. "What?" She

pulled away from him. "I just thought . . . Oh, never mind," she answered, reverting to the slightly antagonistic tone she always used with him.

"How about my place?" he suggested with a wink, catching her hand in his and pulling her back toward him.

Kate didn't appreciate the joke one little bit. "Jerk," she said. "Just for that, I don't think I will go with you." She snatched her hand out of his grasp and stepped away from him, feeling torn between the desire to kick herself and the desire to kick him. In his arms, she felt as though she had known him for years, as though maybe they were meant to be together. She told him about her father!

A minute ago, she had wanted to thank him for being so sweet, but his teasing had ruined the mood. With one foolish remark, he reminded her that they didn't really know each other. He was just making a little joke, and she really believed him. For that split second before he explained himself, she felt hurt. That second had been long enough for her to remember she barely knew him. They had been thrown together by circumstance, and she wasn't even sure she really respected this man, or could trust him. What had happened between them was an aberration; it wasn't supposed to happen.

"I'm sorry. Really. I was just kidding," he tried to reassure her. "Please come home with me."

She felt herself softening. "Only if you tell me what it was you found out about Skipper," she bargained.

"Deal!" he agreed, and hustled her out of his office before she even had time to button her blouse back up.

"Hey!" she protested as he half helped, half dragged her out of the door of the trailer. He hustled her to the street and quickly hailed a taxi and escorted her into it. "Broadway and Eighty-sixth," he told the taxi driver, then turned to Kate. "Wanna neck?"

"No," she said with all the dignity she could muster. "We have business."

He sighed, but didn't seem surprised. "One more question," he delayed. "I still don't understand why you decided Skipper was guilty. Why not go the other way and prove his innocence?"

"That would be way too easy. Everyone wants him to be innocent."

"Even the people who suspect him of killing a man? Even you?"

"I don't know what I want. But A, the cops want to close their case. B, the union doesn't want a connection proved. C, Skipper wants to get on with business as usual. And D, lots of other people want him to remain an American success story. Like you." She didn't mention to him that Jennifer wanted to continue working as his public relations director sans guilt. "Julio was drunk. He drove off the road into the guardrail. He died. Much too easy. Anyone who knows me can tell you I never go easy."

"That I believe. But Skipper Arnold a murderer? I can't believe you're even considering it."

"I have my reasons."

"Is someone steering you in this direction?" he asked. Kate didn't move a muscle. "Whoever that person is, they've got to have a reason. He or she is using you to get to Skipper. Are you sure you want to pursue this?"

"I'm not sure of anything when it comes to this story. I'm not sure I can even trust my own instincts. That's why I'm not sure about Skipper. That, and the fact that I lack a single shred of evidence."

"What if you found some evidence? Not of murder, but of . . . malfeasance?"

"I'd write the story," she stated without hesitation. "What else?"

"How can you be so certain when the situation is so complicated?" Brant questioned.

She examined his face as she asked, "Would you still think I shouldn't publish it if I had proof positive that Skipper was . . . say . . . paying graft?"

"Maybe not," he said thoughtfully. He leaned forward in the seat to instruct the cabbie. "Pull over at the far corner." Brant took his wallet from his pocket.

"There's no question about it. People have a right to know," Kate said succinctly as the taxi came to a halt.

"I'm not saying you're wrong." Skipper paid their driver, and Kate opened her door, ready to slide out. But he wasn't finished. "I'm just saying it doesn't seem as simple to me as it does to you." Kate climbed out of the taxi and waited for Brant on the curb. He took her arm and guided her toward the door of his apartment building as he continued. "Men like Skipper Arnold broke down barriers for us, all of us, thirty years ago. They provided inspiration, and they deserve a little gratitude."

"You think he did it all for the cause of brotherhood?" she said sarcastically as they walked into his building.

The doorman waved, and Brant acknowledged it with a nod, but he continued with his argument. "You're so sure he didn't? He's still helping us today. In my case, he came to me directly and encouraged me to start my own business. It's ironic that it was a strike that started all of this, because the debate that's raging is about sponsorship, to a large extent, and Leopold Arnold has sponsored a lot of men, and women—black, Hispanic, Asian, all kinds—because that's the way he is. He's all about solidarity."

He directed her toward the elevator, which was waiting for them with the door already open. They stepped inside. "So we should let it slide," Kate said wryly. "Because Leopold Arnold saw a promising young black engineer, and he approached him with some advice and support. That didn't cost him a thing! In fact, if a white man did it, you'd call it exploitive."

"I'm not saying we should let it slide. I'm just wondering what will be achieved by your exposé. If Skipper has been doing anything illegal, the Federal investigation will smoke him out. You did say there's an investigation going on, right?"

"Right. But we can be influential in affecting that investigation. If we publish an article saying Skip committed murder right under their noses, that will certainly put the heat on the police." They had arrived on Brant's floor, and he ushered her out of the elevator as Kate said, "And if we print a news item that explains that Skipper is being vilified solely because of the color of his skin, then the law will probably back off."

He jumped in. "If Skipper has been doing something unethical, he's not the only one. According to you, every contractor in the construction business is probably corrupt." They had stopped in front of the door to his apartment. "Why pick on him?" Brant asked, digging in his pocket for his keys, rather than looking at her.

Kate had noticed something odd. "That's the second time you said 'If,' " she commented. He looked up at her, then down at the keys in his hand.

"You noticed that, huh?"

He fit the key in the lock as she pondered the change. He was no longer protesting that Skipper was innocent. He was arguing generalities and principles. As he opened the door, she asked, "What happened to all your faith in your friend?" He waved her inside, but she stood stubbornly in the doorway waiting for his answer.

"Nothing," Brant finally said. But he avoided her eyes. "I still have faith in him. I'm just . . . I'm not as sure as I was. Don't just stand there in the hallway. Come on in," he commanded, reaching inside to turn on a light switch.

"What brought this on?" Kate asked, entering the foyer. She knew he must have discovered something big because it was clear from their discussion that he hadn't been swayed by any argument she had made during the last few weeks.

He didn't answer her, just walked past her and led the way into the living room where he busied himself turning on more lights. Kate waited and waited for his explanation. The longer she thought about it, the more convinced she became that he knew something. It was the only thing that made any sense. She would have bet her first Pulitzer that Brant wouldn't believe ill of Skipper, ever! Not even if she presented him with incontrovertible evidence. So if he was wavering, it had to mean he had uncovered something quite damaging. He stood by the window, looking outside. They were on the seventeenth floor, a fact that only briefly caught her attention, so engrossed was she in the conversation they were having. He seemed equally preoccupied.

"Brant!" she finally snapped at him. He jumped a little, at her harsh tone, she supposed. She had spoken more sharply than she intended—but Kate was frustrated by his continued silence. She *knew* he knew something that he wasn't telling her.

The reporter in her finally came to life. She wasn't going to get anywhere by haranguing him. "I'm sorry. I didn't mean to bark at you." She joined him at the window and looked out at the city lights below and the distant lights of New Jersey, across the Hudson River. "Okay?" she asked, after a moment.

"Yeah," he forgave her. "I'm sorry, too. I don't mean to disappoint you, but I think it would be premature to say any more."

"Okay," she said. "But can I just ask you one question?"

"I don't promise I'll answer it, but sure," Brant said.

"Why do you have an apartment on the seventeenth floor?" she asked. She could tell by the look on his face, he was taken aback by the question. His look of surprise was replaced with one of appreciation.

"I'm trying to overcome my fear," he said.

"Speaking of which . . . You know that you can tell me anything, don't you? Off the record, if you want," she offered. It chafed at her to treat him so circumspectly after what passed between them twenty minutes earlier. He was more than a source to her. He was *the* source— the linchpin of her investigation. And he had promised.

"What does 'off the record' mean to you?" he asked, after a moment.

"It means I can't use the information you give me— except as a starting point to track down other leads." His role in her work on this article had changed, from liaison to trusted adviser, almost a partner. At least that was how it felt to her. "You do know you can trust me, don't you?"

"Of course," he said quickly, perhaps too quickly.

"I haven't given you any reason not to," she said defensively.

"No, but there have been other people whom I trusted when I shouldn't have." She wasn't sure what he meant, but she reached out and touched the back of his hand to reassure him. He looked down at her, and then back out of the window. "I had a friend when I first started in the business. Tom Miller. At least . . . I thought he was a friend, until I found out he was putting his name on my work."

"I know how that feels, believe me," she sympathized. "I would never do anything like that."

He nodded, but . . . she could tell that he wasn't completely convinced. She couldn't blame him, but she felt frustrated—as a journalist—at his reticence. More than that, Kate felt hurt—as a woman—by his mistrust. She found it hard to accept that the intimacy they had shared wasn't enough to topple the barriers between them. He still saw her as the enemy.

This was a new experience for her. She might have her reservations, but he was the one putting up roadblocks. Now she knew how it felt. Just when she was beginning to feel like she'd gotten close to him, he retreated. Kate had done the same thing to men who cared deeply about her, while she and Brant barely knew each other.

She couldn't bring herself to hold it against him. "You don't have to worry. I would never betray anyone's trust like that," she assured him.

"I know," Brant answered. But still he didn't tell her what he had found out that had made him start to doubt his hero.

Kate couldn't think of anything else to say to him. She turned away from Brant and took in the apartment. Because he had positioned himself at the window, her attention had been focused on the view outside ever since she'd entered the place. Now she took a look around. It was roomy, even by New York standards. The living room in which she stood was about twenty by thirty square feet and was dominated by the picture window in the west wall. The sturdy couch of rich reddish brown leather faced two deep comfortable armchairs across an oval cherry wood table. Glass and cherry wood shelving filled with books and knickknacks stood against one wall, facing the waist-high counter positioned between the living room and a spotless black-and-white kitchen with gleaming stainless-steel fixtures. But the furniture in the living room, including the small round glass-topped telephone table, the end tables, and the slim elegant desk against the wall, was all more traditional, carved woods with slender curved legs and brass accents. He liked red wood and black-and-white photography, and the effect was clean and beautiful.

"Nice place," she commented. Kate felt restless and unsettled, and she wandered toward the state-of-the-art stereo console on the bookshelves and leafed through his collection of compact discs.

"What do you think?" he asked.

"About?"

"My music," he clarified.

She looked again at the titles. "Interesting," she answered.

"Why don't you play something?"

"All right." Kate chose a CD featuring the Nat King Cole Trio, her father's favorite recording artists. Nat's beautiful baritone filled the room.

"Wanna dance?" He held out his hand.

"What? Here?" She remembered the last time they had danced together, at the club.

He glided a step closer. "Would you do me the honor?" he repeated.

"Oh. That is—" She faltered as he moved toward her with athletic grace, closing the distance between them. "I'm not sure." She resisted the urge to back up. "I don't know what I'm doing here."

"I thought we were finishing what we started. At my office," he said. "Isn't that why you came?"

"Yes, but . . ." Kate hadn't changed her mind exactly. She still wanted him. But the conversation they'd been having had made her feel nervous and unsure of herself. She had opened up to him, and he seemed to like that. In fact, he'd been quite clear about his feelings. He wanted her. And she certainly wanted him. But he wouldn't tell her what he knew, which made her feel bad about her abilities as a journalist. There was one thing Kate had never doubted. She was good at what she did. This man made her doubt herself, and that didn't make her feel very sexy.

"What?" He stopped a foot away from her and waited.

"Maybe we should just stick to the job at hand?" Kate vacillated. She looked away from his intent gaze.

"This isn't my job," he said softly. "I'm only here to help you." Brant took her hand and raised it to his lips. She watched helplessly as he bent his dark head and kissed her hand. "I'm having trouble concentrating on Skipper Arnold, or anything else at the moment," he confessed, his gaze locked on her face.

"I, um, know what you mean," she murmured in reply as she looked down at their linked hands.

"So how about that dance?" he asked, drawing her even closer.

"It wouldn't—" Kate cleared the lump from her throat. "It wouldn't help the situation," she protested weakly.

"Why not?" he asked, his free arm slipping around her waist to rest lightly on her back. "It'll be a nice change of pace from all the running around we've been doing."

"Yes," she breathed, raising her hand to his shoulder. "But—"

"Sticking our noses where they don't belong," he added.

"That's what I do," Kate reminded him.

Brant started to sway, slowly, to the rhythm of the music. "But not every minute of every day. No one can work all the time," he said reasonably.

Kate didn't agree with him entirely. "I'm something of a workaholic, though," she confessed. She followed his lead, swaying to the music of the jazz trio.

"You're not working now," he pointed out. He rested his chin on the top of her head.

"I love this recording. Where did you get it?" she asked, trying hard to sound as if she wasn't deeply affected by the contact between them.

He made no attempt to pretend he wasn't similarly affected. "I don't remember," he murmured into her hair.

Kate was supremely aware of the raw scent of the man, the hard muscles of his thighs against hers, the strong shoulder beneath her hand.

"No more questions tonight, okay?"

"I just wanted to know—" she began.

He cut her off. "Okay?"

She sighed. "Okay, but—"

"No buts," he ordered.

Kate rested her forehead against his chin and enjoyed the feel of his muscular body against hers. She surrendered to the sensations that suffused her and let her mind drift. Wrapped in his arms and seduced by the earthy strains of the music, she felt surrounded, immersed in a haze of sensual pleasure.

"That's better, don't you think?" Brant asked, breaking the spell.

She retreated as far as his solid hand behind her back allowed. "What are we doing?" she questioned.

"I like dancing with you," he answered simply. "I like doing everything with you. Even fighting."

"Thank you, I think," Kate responded dryly.

"Ever since we met, I've been hoping to cease the hostilities and get to know you, the woman, not the reporter."

"I am a reporter," she replied.

"There's more to you than that," he insisted. "I'd like to know the rest of you." He pulled her close again.

"I hate to break this to you, Brant, but what you see is what you get. Sleeping with me won't give you any great insight into my character. Just like it won't tell me anything new about you."

"There's not much to know about me." He kissed her temple. "I'm not a very complicated person. You, on the other hand, act so hard, so tough, and I know you're not."

She stiffened. "Why do all men think that if they can get a woman into bed, they will know everything about her?"

"We don't. I certainly don't. I want to be close to you, that's all. Without all the nonsense between us."

"At least you're honest about it," she said grudgingly.

Taking her by surprise, he kissed her gently. "I try," he said.

She shook her head, staring up at him, bemused. He bent his head again and caught her full lower lip between his and gently sucked on it for a second. He made a small appreciative sound, like a child tasting something sweet and new. "Mmm." He licked his lips as he looked up from her mouth to her eyes. His arms tightened around her. They felt like a band of steel. Strong. Inescapable.

His gaze darkened with pure, undiluted desire. It sparked an answering flame in Kate. "But—" She started to protest again.

"No buts," he said hastily, and took her mouth again in a steady, determined onslaught that prevented any further protest she might have made. He coaxed her lips apart beneath his and slipped his tongue inside to explore the warm wet recesses of her mouth, leaving her aflame, and unable to deny herself any longer.

Kate reached up to grasp his chin and push his head back. "This doesn't mean you know me, any better than you did before," she insisted. Then she pulled his mouth back down to hers and kissed him with the same urgency and thoroughness that he had shown her. She itched to feel his bare skin beneath her palms. She acted without thought. Her fingers moved, of their own volition, to the buttons of his silk shirt. The mother of pearl slipped easily through the holes, and then she was touching his chest. She felt his muscles flex beneath her fingertips.

She gloried in the corded strength of his neck against her cheek, and lost herself in his taste, his texture, his strength. He shrugged out of his jacket, and she pushed the shirt off his shoulders and gasped at the sight of coiled sinew beneath lustrous café au lait skin. He was a large man, both tall and broad, and her imagination had barely done his body justice. She was right about his musculature, and about the texture of his bone and flesh beneath the staid three-piece suits he always wore.

Now that she knew, it only made her more eager to see every inch of him. She pulled his shirttail out of his waist band. He kept his lips on hers, shifting slightly so she could reach the knot of his tie, and loosen it, without ever breaking the contact between them. She pulled his shirt cuffs over his wrists and hands without undoing the buttons and thought she heard them pop off, but that only excited her more. He let her escape him just long enough to pull the shirt off. His lips returned to hers while he helped her divest him of his slim leather belt, removing it with a snap after she released the catch. She started to unbutton his pants, but he covered her hands with his own, stopping her.

"My turn," he said. Brant's hands went to the closure of her suit jacket, an eye hook, which he released quickly. He skimmed the black linen off her, and she let it fall to the floor, revealing the tiny satin camisole she wore beneath.

"I was dying to know if you were wearing anything under that jacket," he said. He lifted her easily, and carried her to the couch, then laid her down and sat beside her, looking down at her. She reached for him, but he pushed her shoulders back down against the cool leather.

"Wait," he urged. His fingers spread across her throat, and trailed down over her collarbone and her breasts. His large hand nearly spanned her chest, the heel touching one nipple, and his fingertips grazing the other, but he just wafted past the sensitive buds, drifting down, over her rib cage to rest his open hand on her midriff.

Kate lay pliant beneath that gentle touch, her own hands roaming boldly across his chest and abdomen, but she could not wait much longer. "What am I waiting for?" she asked.

"You're so beautiful," he said softly. As he sat staring down at her, Kate started to feel self-conscious. It didn't lessen her desire for him, though. If anything, she felt more excited, as if she were going to burst out of her skin if he didn't kiss her again soon. She couldn't tear her eyes away from his mouth.

She shifted restlessly, and her hands went up and around to the nape of his neck to draw his head down to hers, but he resisted easily. "I want to look at you. I want to watch your body respond to my touch." His voice was a husky rumble. He didn't even have to touch her; her body responded to his words alone.

"Don't," she moaned. "I can't stand it."

He still held himself away from her. She tried to raise herself off the couch, but he wouldn't let her. "Just for a little while?" he appealed. She subsided, waiting.

It seemed like forever before he moved again. The hand at her waist floated back up between her breasts to her collarbone. Kate held her breath. Then he dipped his fingers beneath her satin camisole to cup one of her breasts in his large hand, stroking the tip with his thumb. She expelled the air in her lungs in a shaky rush. Though he was finally touching her, she felt the pressure within her build. The texture of his palm and calloused fingers against her breast, and the rhythmic slide of his thumb across the swollen nub caused heat to pool in her stomach and lower. She arched into him, her entire body aching for his touch. Kate wanted to feel him against her. Inside her.

He lowered his head to her other breast and closed his mouth over the tip, sending a surge of liquid heat from her heart to her toes. She half moaned, half growled in frustration, the sound escaping without her permission and against her will. She looked down at the top of his head, nestled against her chest, and the sight of his dark curls, the slope of his mahogany cheek, and his full lips pursed on her nipple made her blood sing even faster through her veins.

"I can't wait," she gasped.

Her hands went to his waist, and she pulled him onto the couch, atop her, delighting in the weight of his body as it covered hers. He looked up at her, and she saw in his eyes the same heated passion that she felt. The sienna depths, alight with desire, ignited a flame within her, and suddenly her hands were releasing the top button on his slacks and pushing the fabric aside so she could reach his hard, pulsing flesh. She encircled his male heat with her fist, and felt him buck away. She felt a sense of intense loss and profound anticipation as he slid down her body.

His mouth traveled down to her belly, and below. He clamped one steely arm around her waist and held her writhing hips still enough so that he could slide her short skirt, and the scrap of lace and satin underneath, down her legs and off her. The proceedings slowed but only slightly as he ripped open a small cellophane packet with his teeth. He dipped his hand between her thighs and cupped the moist center of her being in his huge palm. "Now, Brant," she ordered. "I can't stand it anymore." He raised himself slightly and positioned himself at the entrance to her body, and they joined together in a rush that felt like the beginning and the end of the world at once.

She sought for, and found, his firm lips. She forged within. Then he, in turn, probed the hot, wet depths of her mouth. They dueled with tongues and thighs and hips for supremacy. Their hands danced over each other's arms, backs, and buttocks, grasping for that intangible goal, the release that loomed so close and then receded with every thrust of soft flesh against hard muscle. Locked together, they struggled to surmount the blissful torment that held them in its throes. And ascended from their sweet hell at last, with one final, joyful stroke into each other.

When Kate found herself again, she was lying in Brant's arms, their bodies so intertwined, she felt his every gasping breath. "Oh, my," she breathed. "My, my, my."

"Yes," he agreed. "We do seem to work well together."

Thirteen

Kate awakened with a start. She had been dreaming about Jennifer Collier. Perhaps it was the natural result of Brant's questions about her sources, or maybe it was the story he told of his former friend, Henry Milsome, but she suddenly realized Jennifer had, indeed, been manipulating her throughout the entire investigation of Uncle Skipper. Some small part of her must have been aware of it for a while now, but, for some reason, it was starting to really bug her.

Kate remembered, back in college, when Jen told her about Uncle Skip. Even then there was something off about the way the girl talked about her mentor. And once, when Jen was ragging on her mysterious benefactor, one of their friends joked that perhaps Jennifer should tell the old man, instead of telling them, what she thought of him. Of course, the coed said, Jennifer should wait until a couple of days after the check for her substantial monthly allowance was cleared at the bank. Jennifer didn't join in with the laughter inspired by this clever idea. Instead she said something about Skipper owing her that money. When Kate had asked about it later, Jen told her she must have misunderstood. Kate thought she was just embarrassed at being called out for being disrespectful toward a man she was indebted to for her tuition.

Like most of the undergrads at their school, Kate had a warm, but increasingly distant connection with her parent, and a complete mistrust of anyone who stood *in loco parentis,* so Jen's hot-and-cold relationship with her mother seemed perfectly normal—as did her blatant disregard for her wealthy, beneficent, and slightly shadowy father figure, Leopold Arnold. In the light of everything that had gone on since that first meeting in the Fluffy Pastry Café, including the introduction to Brant, the pressure to expose Skipper, and the elevator mishap, Kate began to wonder about Jen's affiliation with this man.

What exactly was the nature of her alliance with Leopold Arnold? And why did her old college roommate feel he was obligated to her?

Kate ticked off what she knew of the history between pair: Skipper paid for Jen's higher education; Jennifer worked for him; and they even socialized with each other, insofar as the differences between their ages, their occupations, and their social circles permitted. With her eyes newly opened by Brant's interest in her unknown source's motives, Kate was determined to uncover the mysterious reason for Jennifer's recent revelations about her shady Uncle Skip.

Jen had not called her back the last few times she left messages for her, and Kate had a feeling that she was going to have to chase her friend down. But she didn't have time. Brant showed up at her door before she finished her first cup of coffee.

"Come in," Kate said, surprised and happy to see him.

He walked briskly past her and into the apartment. In the middle of the living room, he swung around and pulled her close. "Hi," he said, giving her a kiss.

"Well, good morning to you, too," Kate answered, pleased at the display of affection and curious about his strange mood.

He walked away from her. Then he turned back to face her and squared his shoulders. Clearly, he had made a decision. "If we're going to do this thing, we should just do it."

"I'm all for that," she answered.

"Come on. I've got someone I want you to meet," he urged.

The someone turned out to be another subcontractor. This one, however, was not quite as big a fan of Leopold Arnold as Brant was. His name was Dell Kaplan.

Rather than going to another building site in midtown Manhattan, as they had for her last two interviews, they took a taxi downtown. Brant was strangely silent. He seemed busy with his thoughts. Loathe to disturb him, Kate watched the scenery change as they drove down through her neighborhood, just below his on the Upper West Side, past Central Park, and then through the theater district. There was little traffic as they passed through Chelsea and into Greenwich Village. They turned east on Tenth Avenue and drove past brownstone buildings, which grew more and more elegant and aristocratic as they neared Fifth Avenue in the heart of the Village, where they stopped. He led her into one of the slim, five-story, brick buildings, which was distinguished from the others by the brass plaque on the door, which proclaimed "Dell Kaplan, Architect."

"This is the reporter I told you about," Brant announced, after introductions were made. "Tell her what you told me, Dell."

"You're the one writing the article about Arnold?" the small, thin, fair-skinned man asked. He rushed on without waiting for her response. "I can tell you two things about the big man. One is that he's got this city wired. He's got people on the city council, the zoning commission, and in city planning."

Kate extracted her tape recorder from her purse and turned it on. She didn't want to interrupt the flow of his story by asking him to repeat himself. Kate wasn't taking any chances, although there didn't seem to be any danger that he'd change his mind. He was eager to talk.

She rephrased his statement in the form of a question so she could record his answer. "When you say he's 'got people' on the city council, and in planning, and zoning departments, what exactly do you mean?"

"They're on his payroll, that's what I mean. You know how he gets all those plum sites and contracts—he's got an inside track." Dell had a thin face, mean eyes and thin lips. He sounded as if he knew what he was talking about.

"How do you know this?" she asked.

"I used to work for him," the man answered. A disgruntled former employee was not exactly the best source for her exposé of a man as powerful and well connected as Skipper. She had to be careful.

"When was this?" she asked delicately.

"I was with him for seven years. I quit two years ago," Dell supplied. Kate breathed a sigh of relief. "I couldn't take it anymore. He's not a bad guy, but my wife thought he was a hero, and I couldn't explain to her why I didn't want to have him over to the house or take her out with us. I wouldn't make excuses anymore."

"I understand," Kate said sympathetically. "You said there were two things you would tell me." She was thrilled with the information he'd given her so far, but before she started questioning him more closely about the specifics, she wanted to know how big this was. How rotten was Skipper?

"The strike is a big load of manure," he erupted. "He bribed the union guys to take a hard line on the Hispanic thing."

"He did?" That would explain why Julio had to be eliminated. "Who? Do you know?"

"All of them? Different guys from both sides. When the union thing came up, he was happier than a pig in . . . you know what. He loves to hire nonunion labor, just like anyone else in this business, but you rarely get the chance."

"So when this Hispanic faction started complaining about being underrepresented, Skipper fanned the fire?" she reiterated.

"The fire was already burning. He just had his guys add a little gasoline," Dell responded.

"Was Julio Gonzalez one of his?" Brant asked.

"I don't know the names. I'm not sure if he was one of Arnold's guys. They met, though. Leopold has all the meetings right out in the open. Trying to look like he has nothing to hide. And he doesn't hand over cash, either. Cars, apartments, stuff like that. Gifts that are easy to turn over. He 'makes arrangements.' That's what he calls it. I saw him arrange to buy one guy a Donna Karan wedding dress for his kid. Those things cost like high five figures, you know."

"So these bribes would be hard to trace?" Kate said, disappointed.

"Not really. He's Mr. Open Book. All you'd need to do is check when he met with the city council guys and see who received gifts soon after. The meetings are probably all in his appointment book. As I said, he doesn't try to hide it. He doesn't think he's doing anything wrong. That's why I know about it. He said this stuff in front of me. He winked once or twice in the beginning, so I'd appreciate his cleverness, I think. When he saw I wasn't interested, he didn't talk much about it to me—but I knew what he was doing."

"If you haven't worked for Skipper in two years, how did you know about the union payoffs?"

"I knew. As soon as I heard about the dispute, I just knew. Everyone knew."

Brant spoke up again. "I didn't catch on."

"You didn't want to see it. It was right in front of your face. You were at the groundbreaking ceremony on that parking lot job, and I heard them talking about it there."

"I can't tell you how helpful you've been, Dell," Kate told him. "Are you willing to go on record with this?"

"If you can keep my name out of it, I'd appreciate it," Dell said, embarrassed. "But if you can't, I'll understand. It's time this came out. Arnold is not the hero he pretends to be, and people should know it. I'm sick of being compared to the jerk."

If Kate hadn't already surmised that it was his bruised ego that motivated the subcontractor, Dell's last revelation would have given him away. His wife must have really given him a hard time about quitting his job with L.E.O. Enterprises.

For her purposes, a bruised ego was as good a motivator as any, and better than most. Righteous indignation had a long shelf life. Attacks of conscience in a source tended to fade once they spilled their guts and relieved their guilt, and any revelations were soon off the record. People who wanted revenge were vulnerable to manipulation. Even a simple apology could make them rethink their position. Dell wouldn't be changing his story because Skipper offered him his job back or told Dell some sob story about how he couldn't control himself. Dell wouldn't rest until his wife knew the truth. Even after that, he would probably use this as ammunition in future disagreements.

Kate didn't really care why she had gotten so lucky.

This was the break she'd been hoping for. She assured Dell that she would try to keep his name out of the article, and she and Brant left.

"Incredible!" she said to Brant as they went home. Kate let out a satisfied sigh, as she settled back into her seat in the taxi. She leaned over and gave him a kiss on his opal-smooth cheek. "Thank you," she said.

"I'm not sure I believe him," he said hesitantly.

"You don't?" she asked, honestly amazed. "Why not?"

"I don't want to," he answered candidly. "Anyway, he obviously resents Skipper."

"That doesn't make him a liar," Kate argued.

"No . . ." He let the single syllable drag out for a while, then clipped it off with a snap of his jaw. "But it gives him a reason to lie. Even if it's true, it will be hard to prove."

"Or disprove," she chortled.

"What does that mean?"

"If I can find enough 'coincidental' gifts or favors, it will serve as circumstantial evidence. Close enough to get the Feds' attention, that's for sure. Especially since they're already looking."

"So that's it?" Brant queried. "One unhappy ex-employee accuses the old man, and you're ready to start slinging mud with the rest of 'em."

"This one guy is answering questions raised by others. And I'll research his allegations first. Overall, though, I think I'm being fair enough to Skipper. He's rich. He's powerful. And he's enjoyed a lot of success. You're right that it shouldn't make him a target—but he doesn't get any special privileges, either. Not from me. That's your department," she retorted coolly. "He's not my hero."

"I don't think he's my hero anymore, either," Brant said sadly.

"I'm sorry," Kate commiserated. When he looked at her skeptically, she added, "I really am."

They had arrived at her apartment building, and she handed the cabbie a ten-dollar bill. "Keep the change," she told him.

She and Brant climbed out of the taxi. "My refrigerator is empty, but I can offer you a cup of coffee," Kate said. He nodded in agreement, and fell into step beside her as she turned to lead him inside.

They climbed the single flight of stairs to her small one-bedroom apartment, and she went into the tiny kitchen to start the coffee. There was no door between the four-foot-by-four-foot closet that served as her kitchen and the rest of the apartment, so she could watch him wandering around her place, looking it over, as she ground her coffee beans and spooned them into the filter. A wide double door, when closed, separated the living room and bedroom, but Kate kept it open to give the illusion of more space to both areas. Luckily, the apartment was relatively neat. She had cleaned up less than a month ago, and she didn't entertain much. The desk was, as usual, piled high with her papers and books, but it was not really noticeable in its little corner.

Having Brant in her apartment gave her ideas. Images of him, fulfilling her fantasies about him, filled her mind and made her cheeks warm, but she didn't think that was what was on Brant's mind at the moment. "Penny for your thoughts," she said, as she came out of the kitchen and sat on the couch while she waited for the coffee to drip.

He threw himself onto the couch beside her. "I still can't believe I could have been so wrong about Skip."

"I am sorry," she said soothingly.

He didn't look as if he believed her. "You already said that."

"I don't need this story so badly that I want anyone to suffer needlessly. At least not any innocent bystanders. I've seen enough of that." She had piqued his interest, she could see that. Kate felt compelled to go on. "When I won the American Society of Journalists and Writers Award, I thought the story was pretty straightforward but the wrong guys got fired. Those guys were only trying to do their jobs, minding their own business. They were expendable, and the day after the story hit the wire, they were gone. It didn't matter that they were minor cogs in the machinery and their bosses were the ones making the real money—the abuses could be traced back to them, and only to them, so they lost their jobs. The next time I wrote an exposé, I followed the money, and got proof of whose pockets it was going into. That time the little guys lost their jobs, too, but at least it was because the company went under. Unfortunately, they were refinanced and open for business in under a year. I'm sorry that you're unhappy about Skipper, but this time, I'm making sure that the man who's responsible is the one who gets the blame. If he doesn't go to jail—as he so richly deserves—at least he'll be too hot to get any more city contracts."

Brant nodded his understanding. "If he's guilty, then that's only right." Suddenly he was looking at her differently. "I really wanted to bring you home last night," he said.

"Thanks for letting me leave," she answered. "I needed . . . time to think."

"What did you think?" he asked.

If her skin were lighter, she'd have been bright red. "Umm . . ."

"Sorry," he said, but he was laughing.

There was nothing she could possibly say to him. She'd nearly run out of his place the night before, bewildered by her reaction to him. She had never been so intensely moved before by a man. This was something she could not have predicted, and she had no idea what it meant. He was strong, attractive, sympathetic, and intelligent, and she felt drawn to him, but Kate did not trust her feelings, or her physical response to the man. She had been wrong about every man she had ever depended upon.

And this one was the least promising one she had ever met. Sure he was a handsome devil, but they argued about everything. And she could potentially be courting an even greater danger. She might destroy his idol. Though he had said he wasn't sure about Skipper anymore, she had no way of knowing if he would ever forgive her for placing the final nail in his hero's coffin.

"What would it take to convince you that Skipper was a garden-variety lowlife." Kate was genuinely curious. Brant was such a staunch supporter of Skipper's that if she could get enough evidence to change his mind, she would almost certainly have enough to convince her editor to go ahead with the story.

"I don't know." Brant shook his head. "I do remember once I saw him arrange for a friend's apartment to be remodeled. And there were other times."

Kate looked at him, mouth agape. "He actually did this in front of you? Arranging things for people?"

"He looked satisfied, happy, gratified that he could help. That's how it always seemed to me. Maybe the reason Skipper doesn't think he's doing anything wrong is because he isn't."

"Tell me you're not going to try to justify his behavior."

"I'm just saying that there's nothing wrong with doing a friend—or even a business associate—a favor."

"Leopold Arnold is one of the most successful developers in New York City, and if he got that way by doing supposedly harmless favors for his friends and contacts,

I have to wonder what he's getting in return. If he's friendly with a city planner, does he get a head start in compiling bids? Maybe even a nod and a wink when he guesses the right number? And do those 'arrangements' Dell mentioned include committing violence of some kind? Against his friends' enemies perhaps?"

"You can never know that," Brant maintained.

"Actually, I can make a pretty good guess. If his bids are accepted when he makes his little arrangements and they're not accepted when he doesn't . . ."

"We don't even know where to look."

"Yes, we do. Dell told us, remember? We start with Skipper's appointment book."

"How do we do that?"

"You'd be surprised what people will tell you if you know how to ask," she explained. "I'll take care of it."

"Mmm-mm," he murmured. He looked at her, bemused. "You're something else, Katie."

"Thanks," she replied, embarrassed.

"I meant to say that first thing this morning. I guess I was a little nervous." He paused to clear his throat.

"You? Nervous?" She laughed.

"About what Dell would have to say," he continued. But she had already started speaking. "Why?" she began. Then, as she realized he hadn't been speaking about their encounter the night before, but about their interview this morning, she bowed her head, mortified.

"What were you going to say?" he coaxed.

"I was just going to say you had nothing to worry about," she said lamely.

"Thanks," he said, arching his brow at her. "It's always good to hear."

"Men and their egos," she complained, as if to some unseen audience.

"What can I say?" he joked. "On behalf of my sex, I apologize."

"Not good enough," Kate grumbled.

"Let me make it up to you," Brant said, taking her hand in his and lifting it to his lips. "I didn't mean to embarrass you." He kissed her palm.

"That's all right. I don't need any help from you," she said petulantly. "I can embarrass myself just fine."

He was kissing the inside of her wrist, and the sweet suction made her insides melt.

"Stop that," she ordered feebly.

"What, this?" he asked, kissing her wrist again.

"Yes."

"But you taste so good," he argued. "I can't stop." He pulled her over onto his lap, and she didn't fight him. The feel of the hard bars of his thighs beneath her own brought back the tumult of the night before in a flood of detail. The memory of the way he had looked at her, and touched her, and felt inside her, triggered a response within every cell of her body, and Kate could not deny her hunger for the sensations he evoked in her. Her arms went around his torso, and her lips explored the corded muscle in his throat. He smelled of spice and raw man, and she drank it in, reveling in the taste of his skin and the feel of his shoulder against her cheek.

"We should probably wait until I find the evidence against Skipper," she mumbled as his lips found her earlobe. "Then you can decide whether you really want to get involved."

"Or we can just fool around until then," he suggested. "Nothing serious. Just a man and a woman doing a little necking, as dad would say."

"I do like your neck," Kate commented.

"I like yours, too." He gently bit the sensitive skin, then soothed the area with tender kisses. "And your chin."

He nipped her there, just below the corner of her mouth, then touched the spot with his tongue. "And your lips."

He kissed her, deeply, thoroughly, then pulled back to ask, "Okay?"

"Huh?" Kate was busy guessing where those white teeth would descend next.

"How does that sound to you?" Brant quizzed her.

"Fine. Just fine," she answered, content. His plan could work out fine. In fact, she liked it. She liked it very much.

Fourteen

Jennifer had to know about Uncle Skip's dirty dealings. At the least, she had to have had an inkling that something wasn't kosher. So why had she sent Kate on this merry chase at all, if she didn't plan to give her all the information that she had? Kate could have been tracking down the real story of these possible bribes all along, instead of chasing her tail.

She called Jennifer the day after the very illuminating meeting with Dell Kaplan and, once again, got her friend's answering machine. This time, Kate left a message that was unmistakable. "Stop screwing with me, girl. I am at the end of my patience. If I don't hear from you today, there will be hell to pay. You know I will come and find you."

When Jennifer returned her call, she was the soul of innocence. "What's up?" she asked, as if surprised by Kate's tone.

"Don't yank my chain, Jen," Kate said, determined this time to get some answers. "You know that you've been playing with me. Why didn't you tell me about Skipper?"

"I did," she protested.

"You needed to know exactly what Skipper was doing. That's what you implied. You had to know something about what was going on. My sources tell me he's not particularly discreet about how he does business."

"That's right," Jen admitted. There was no hint of remorse in her voice. "But that doesn't include this business with Julio Gonzalez. That's different."

"You had to know whether or not he bribed the guy."

"I wasn't sure. I did know there was something going on with him. Then he turned up dead."

"I don't think there's anything to that. There's no evidence, whatsoever, of any foul play in his death. But there's plenty to incriminate your uncle Skip in some pretty serious mess."

"Oh, that," Jennifer said, as if they were discussing the weather, rather than a number of felonies that she had knowledge of, which she had concealed from both Kate and the police.

"Yes, that," Kate said, unrelenting. "Are you seriously going to pretend that *that* wasn't what you expected me to discover all along?"

"No, no. I know you're a good investigative reporter, so I figured you'd dig up all of Skipper's dirty little secrets. I just thought the possibility of two murders would pique your interest more than some run-of-the-mill graft would."

"So you admit there was no basis to your suspicions?"

"Basis?"

"In *fact.*"

"That's exactly what I hoped you would be able to discover."

"If you really did suspect Skipper of murder on top of everything you knew about him, why didn't you go to the police?"

"The police? What makes you think they'd investigate on my say-so?"

"That simple graft, as you call it," Kate said, her voice

heavy with sarcasm. "Bribery, corruption, criminal facili-
tation! Skipper was involved in some heavy stuff, and
you could prove it."

"Oh, that." Jennifer dismissed the idea. "I might stop
working for the man, but I wouldn't turn him in—not for
just greasing the wheels. No matter who I worked for,
they would probably be guilty of at least that. Murder is
something else."

"You wouldn't turn him in? You wouldn't report the
alleged illegal activity of your mentor and employer to
the police, or the Feds who were investigating? You would
protect the man you asked me to investigate so you could
work for him without any qualms? Why do you care if
he was involved in Julio's death—which, by the way,
doesn't seem likely—if the rest doesn't disturb your conscience?"

"Come off it, Katie. You know I always said Skip was
a sleazebag. I'm not an idiot. I knew he wasn't a saint
when I took the job. I told you as much."

"Not a saint!" Kate reiterated, disbelieving. "We're a
long way past 'not a saint,' Jen. And I believe your exact
words when I asked you why you went to work for a
man you didn't respect or trust were, 'It's just a job. I'm
not selling my soul to the devil or anything.' And if you
still think that's true, I've got news for you, Jennifer Collier. Leopold Arnold may not *be* the devil, but they're
pretty close to kissing cousins."

"Uncle Skip didn't have anything to do with Julio's
death though, did he?"

A thought struck Kate. "Skipper didn't make any of
his little *arrangements* for Julio?"

Jennifer's silence was her answer. Finally the other
woman admitted, "He arranged for the purchase of the
Jeep Julio was driving when he died. A very economical

purchase. I believe it cost Mr. Gonzalez five thousand dollars for that brand-new Wrangler."

"That's why you suspected him, isn't it?" Kate pursed her lips and whistled silently. "I can't believe this! Why didn't you mention this when we first discussed it?"

"I don't have any proof. The sale was handled by a third party, and Julio paid in cash. On paper it looks suspicious, but not illegal, and I don't believe there's anything that ties the Wrangler to Uncle Skip."

"Except you," Kate pointed out.

"Me?"

"Yeah. You. You are the evidence."

"Honey, if you think I'm talking to anybody but you about this, you have got one heck of a surprise coming," Jennifer stated emphatically. And no matter what Kate said to her, Jen wouldn't budge.

"If you write the article, and turn up the heat, maybe? But just to get the ball rolling, I don't want to put my job, or my relationship with Skip, on the line. I think I've done my part where that's concerned."

"But, Jen—" Kate tried to argue.

"I hope you don't think I'm being silly, but I can't take the chance."

"No, I don't think that," Kate reassured her.

Kate met with her editor to discuss the story with him and gave him the story in broad strokes, including the absence of any evidence indicating that Skipper had something to do with Julio's death. Despite that, she knew her story of graft, bribery, and corruption intrigued him. Charles was clearly interested, as she had both hoped, and dreaded, he would be.

"I can't get anyone to go on record with any of this, except one source who is willing but would rather be anonymous. He doesn't have hard evidence, but I've confirmed his allegations through independent sources."

"The legal department won't like that. They don't particularly care to use reluctant sources in stories about powerful multimillionaires. Can you get anyone to go on record? A disgruntled ex-employee? Ex-girlfriend?"

Kate thought about mentioning Jennifer, but decided against it. Her friend might have tried to manipulate her, but she couldn't let go of the loyalty she felt she owed her old college roommate. "I can get them to talk to me, but only off the record. Leopold may be a crook, but he seems to inspire a lot of loyalty in the people who know him. I'm trying to get more, but . . ."

"Try his competition," Charles suggested.

"How would they know. . . ?"

"This is one of the most important developers in the city. The people he's up against are not lightweights. They're as powerful, and as well connected, as he is. They'll have a good idea where the bodies are buried."

"Isn't that just a case of the pot calling the kettle black? Everyone will know they are more interested in getting rid of him than in bringing the truth to light. They could just be passing along rumors. That would suit their purposes."

"So?"

"Who will believe them?"

"Our readers," he said complacently.

"I'm not really comfortable with that."

"I'd prefer someone from within Arnold's organization, too," he said. Once again, Kate thought of Jennifer. "But you say they are too, ahem, loyal to talk, and we need confirmation of the facts from somewhere."

"Somewhere?" she questioned.

"That's why they call it an exposé, Kate. It's easy to confirm the facts *after* reputable sources start talking to the press and the cops, but by then there isn't anything to expose."

"So you're saying we don't care where we get confirmation?"

"Not if the source is reliable."

"By 'reliable,' I gather you mean rich and powerful?"

"I mean well-known, and high profile. Recognizable names are all we need. Skipper plays with the big boys. Let them help."

"I don't like it," Kate protested.

"That's too bad. You've spent too much time and energy on this investigation to get squeamish now."

"I'm not feeling squeamish. I don't want to print anything I can't back up."

"Neither do I. But backing up the facts doesn't mean you have to prove the allegations are true. You know that. It's not your job to question the motives of your sources, just to find people who will let us quote them. All we need is a reasonable belief that the story is true in order to print it."

"That's just it. I'm not sure that is a good enough reason to print it."

"Okay," he said, resigned. "What are we talking about here, Kate?"

"I guess I'm . . . not sure this story won't do more harm than good."

"You're not a social worker, you're a journalist. There are rules to our business, and one of those rules is that we print news items that are likely to be of interest to our readers, whether we like the people involved or not."

"It's not that I like him. I don't, particularly. I don't know him very well." Something Brant had said the night that they met came to her. Leopold Arnold had a lot of enemies, people who hated him not only because they envied his success, but because of the color of his skin. Someone else would eventually get the story, and at least then he wouldn't be pilloried by one of his own. "I don't know if he deserves to be ruined, especially by me."

"You're the one who got the story. You're a good reporter. You may even be a great reporter. We're not trying to solve the world's problems here, we're just doing our part to make sure things work the way they're supposed to. Once in a while, we get to actually make a difference."

"So we do our job, no matter who gets hurt?"

"That's how it goes, sometimes."

Brant would definitely not approve. Which did not stop Kate from going to see him that evening and relaying a slightly edited version of the conversation she had had with Charles. She knew what he would say, but she couldn't resist starting the dialogue with him. She might find what Charles had to say somewhat distasteful, but it was the realistic view and she didn't altogether disagree with her editor. Nor could she completely discount Brant's opinion. Perhaps there was even a little part of her that wanted him to talk her out of doing what she knew she had to do.

He did try. "But you know your boss is wrong. I know you agree with me or we wouldn't be talking about this," he argued, frustrated. He was standing in his kitchen, opening a bottle of red wine, while she sat at the tall kitchen counter, watching. "Why should his enemies get to publicly denounce him, without any evidence?"

"He can sue them, if they're lying."

He filled the wineglasses, and placed hers in front of her. "And your newspaper?"

"No, he can't sue us, not as long as we believed the story was true, and got collaboration from other sources." She took a sip of the rich ruby liquid, and felt it warm in her throat.

"So your newspaper can say anything they want, about anybody."

"Of course not. But we can report a story if we believe it to be true."

"So you'll print those accusations? Just to sell newspapers?"

"I believe the story is true. That's why I'm writing it. I am supposed to present the facts. It is not my job to prove or disprove them," she explained.

"So they can say anything they want about him," Brant protested. "And if it sells enough newspapers, you'll print it. I can't believe that's legal."

Kate jumped off the tall bar stool she'd been sitting on and went around the island into the kitchen. She answered him as she opened the refrigerator and inspected its contents. "All I have to do is get someone who is reasonably likely to know to tell me that the rumors are true."

"And that's it?" he asked in disbelief.

"That's it. How about if I make us an omelette?"

"Fine" he answered. "And you talk about how dirty the construction industry is," he said dryly under his breath.

"We've already had this conversation," Kate said as she took the ingredients for dinner out of the refrigerator. "I'm not going to play the 'whose business is worse?' game. I just wanted to tell you what my editor suggested. That I confirm my facts by interviewing Skipper's competitors."

"So why ask me about it?" His disgusted tone left no doubt as to his aversion for the task ahead.

Kate considered whether she was making the right decision continuing with the course of action she had chosen. She didn't have to ask him what she had come to ask him. Instead they could eat, make love. She pretended to be absorbed in dicing the tomatoes to buy time to think. Brant had been informed about what she planned to do next and why she had to do it. She didn't have to include him further. But she did. "I thought you might give me some names," she told him. "You said there are people who want to ruin him. Let them put their money where their mouth is. If they're willing to go on the record, I can give them their fifteen minutes of fame."

"You should know by now that I wouldn't help you with something like this." She looked up at him briefly, then back down at the scallions on the counter in front of her.

Kate knew it wasn't fair to test him like this, but she had to know if there was any chance for them to work out their differences. Otherwise, she was wasting her time fooling around with him, in any way. "I will find out from someone else, if you want. I just thought you might want to tell me who the men are who want to crucify Skipper because of his race. When I call them for the article, they'll have to speak up, or shut up. They'll have to go on the record, or they'll have to stop libeling him."

He considered it, but shook his head. "You'll have to ask someone else."

"That is commonly referred to as a cover-up. Do you really want to be party to that?" she asked, disappointed.

"If you wanted to expose anyone else—" he started to say.

"Anyone white for example?" she interjected, beating the eggs furiously.

"No, *not* anyone white. Anyone *else*. Just not Skipper. I'm not talking about color now. I'm talking about a friend," he replied, exasperated.

"So all this time you've been talking about racism and the media, and me, you were just trying to protect him?" she asked dubiously. She turned on the burner with a vicious twist. Luckily the knob didn't come off in her hand.

"No. I meant what I said. They—you—probably would not have gone after Skipper if he hadn't been black."

"But that's past, and now we know he is guilty. We can't just ignore that. At least, I can't."

"I don't want to, either, but what you're talking about—going to his enemies and giving them an advantage like that . . . it's not right." She knew how Brant felt, but she couldn't think of any other way.

"Can't someone else do the story?" he asked.

"No," she said. "It's my job."

He nodded. "I can understand that," he said after a moment.

"At least we agree on one point," Kate said, relieved. The pan was hot enough, the butter melting, so she started adding the ingredients. "We—you and I—don't cover up for black men who happen to be crooked, just because they are black."

"But I'm not sure we really do agree," he said. "Because you're still going to do this story, aren't you? Even if you have to get it this way."

She looked up at him. The omelette was cooking. She could give him her full attention. She hesitated. "I don't know. Probably."

"The way I see it, you may ruin him, and in the long run, it's because he's a successful black man and that kind of story sells."

Stung, Kate could only flounder. She flipped the omelette over, and still couldn't come up with a good rejoinder, so finally she answered him with a question. "Did you support Clarence Thomas, too?"

"No, but that was different," he said wearily.

"I know it was. It was easier. It wasn't just white conservatives against a black Supreme Court nominee. Anita

Hill was the accuser, and she was more believable than he was. And she was black, too." The omelette was finished. Perfect. She eased it onto one plate and then cut it in half and slid that portion onto the other dish. She brought both around the counter and placed Brant's plate in front of him, then sat beside him.

She took a sip of wine. "It wasn't a question of wanting a black judge on the court, no matter what he did, but a question of supporting a black woman who reminded us he was a conservative, and a Neanderthal. But it was tempting, because it was time for another qualified man of color to sit on that bench. Really, it was an offshoot of the same debate we're having. How far do you go to put a black face in the picture—especially one that ought to be there? For me, the answer was to wait for a qualified black man, or woman, to be nominated." She took a forkful of her omelette and tasted it. It wasn't bad.

Brant's dish was half-empty already, and he cut off another bite as he shook his head. "How long do we wait though, Katie?" he asked.

"We don't just wait. We make it happen."

"And if we don't support each other as a race, then how can it ever happen? If we are a part of the same racist institutions that can attack us so easily, then we can only hinder that progress."

"No, we don't. We fight. Just like we fought to get hired by those racist institutions. We won. Now we have a voice, and we use it to fight discrimination, and prejudice, and racism every minute of every day. But I don't believe that fight includes giving preferential treatment to men like Leopold Arnold just because of the color of his skin."

"I know what you're saying, and basically, I agree with you, but . . ." He let his voice trail off as he ate the last of his omelette.

"That's good enough for me," Kate said, feeling much more cheerful all of a sudden. She reached over to kiss his cheek. For all their differences, it seemed they did agree on the important points. She took another sip of her wine. "Would you like the rest?" She slid her plate toward him, and he took it.

"Sure," Brant said. "It's great. You didn't tell me you could cook."

"I can't, much. This is one of about three recipes I can't ruin. You put in a few too many peppers? So what? It doesn't matter. It still tastes good. Mostly, I order in, though," she admitted.

"I like to cook," he volunteered.

"Are you any good?" she asked, wriggling her eyebrows suggestively.

"My repertoire extends a little further than three dishes," he boasted. "But this is very good."

"Thank you, sir. We aim to please." Kate felt giddy, and it wasn't the half glass of wine she'd sipped while cooking dinner. She felt comfortable with this man, in his kitchen, sharing a meal and chatting about the domestic arts. On her way to his apartment, she hadn't thought this evening could possibly end this way. And the night wasn't even over yet.

"Hey, Brant?"

"Yes, Katie?"

"After dinner, do you wanna mess around?"

A big, lascivious smile was all the answer she needed. "Well, come on. Let's get these dishes washed," she exhorted, clearing the countertop.

"You want to do my dishes?" He looked more than a little bit surprised.

"It's not my life's ambition, but we had a rule in my house, growing up. When there's a chore to be done, just do it."

"This isn't your house," he pointed out.

"True," Kate said, turning her back to the sink and leaning against it as she looked over at him. "It's yours." Brant didn't move. Apparently her industriousness had not inspired him. "You wash up. I'll watch."

He stood. "I can think of better things to do." He wiggled his eyebrows suggestively.

"Watching you do household chores will be a pleasure, I assure you."

"That the kind of thing that turns you on?"

"A man up to his arms in soap suds is hot, honey," she teased.

"I could wear an apron, if you really want a thrill," he offered.

"Oooh," Kate cooed. "You'd do that for me?"

"I would," he declared. He moved around her to the sink, and she went to the stool he'd been sitting on. "Unfortunately, I don't own an apron." He rolled his sleeves up to his elbows. Kate admired his forearms, a part of the male anatomy that she felt was generally overlooked and often underrated. Nice masculine forearms were right up there with a good, tight backside, as far as Kate was concerned. Brant got a ten for both, she thought as he turned toward the sink, his back to her.

"Work it, baby," she called out.

"It's not polite to leer," he scolded, looking over his shoulder at her.

Kate grimaced when he turned away. "Just trying to do my part," she replied facetiously. "To help," she added.

"Finished," he pronounced, turning off the water.

"That was quick," she said, pouting in mock disappointment.

"It doesn't take all night to wash a few dishes. But

there are things we could do that would take all night . . .
if we wanted to do them right," he said.

"I was enjoying the view," she complained.

"And now it's my turn. Up!" he commanded. Obediently, Kate stood. "About-face . . . and . . . march." She
sashayed toward the living room, hips swaying like the
back of a taxi taking a turn too fast.

Fifteen

It was surprisingly easy to get Leopold Arnold's calendar of appointments for the last year. She used Jennifer's computer to access her calendar, including dates with Leopold, and through that link, a friend of hers talked her through the process of downloading Skipper's appointment book. Kate went into the offices and just asked outright for some of the information she needed. She spoke to his secretary—who was very friendly and cooperative, and was able to take her through Skipper's schedule very thoroughly.

Once she knew about his meetings, it wasn't at all hard to find out which people among those with whom he lunched were involved in contracts he went after, including the L.A.C. Parking Garage contract. She was able source out which city government officials he saw, and how often, and Kate found it almost as simple to discover through public records about some of the favors Skipper had done for those people. She even got the name of the title holders on the vehicle that Julio Gonzalez was driving when he died. The pattern was very clear, now that she knew what to look for, but it would still be very hard to prove. Skipper's "favors" for his friends were not easy to trace. Cash gifts were like that. But the evidence she came up with didn't leave any questions in her mind.

She tried, but she couldn't write the article. Even after having gathered all the facts, she couldn't seem to get the words onto paper.

Kate couldn't stop thinking about Brant, either. She knew that was what was holding her back. She tried to call him, but she found herself unable to do it. She stared at the telephone, despondent. She was mortified at her weakness, but she couldn't help how she felt. She wanted to speak with him, needed to hear his voice, even picked up the phone once and started to dial, but she dropped the receiver before she could finish dialing his number.

This wasn't her. Kate felt like one of those helpless, vulnerable women whom she despised as a rule. She was ashamed of herself for behaving this way. Still, she didn't write the story. Brant wouldn't approve. She was sure of that. She was just as sure that her own opinion differed from his. It was her responsibility to expose Skipper's illegal activities. It didn't matter that Leopold Arnold had worked incredibly hard to overcome almost insurmountable odds to achieve his success. Nor was it important that he was a black man who inspired and supported men like Brant. Of even less import was the fact that Skipper had lived by his own particular code of honor, breaking only those rules that he felt were unimportant. He couldn't be excused because he chose to live by his own set of rules. No more than she could live her life by Brant's rules.

It wasn't because she feared his disapproval that she didn't go forward with the story. Their beliefs were different. Very different. He didn't even respect her work.

No, Kate corrected herself. *That isn't, strictly speaking, the truth.* Brant might feel the media was inherently racist, and the *New Amsterdam Press* was a voracious, profit-driven, unprincipled institution, but he respected her writing, and he seemed to have come to understand her motivation for doing what she did. His views on the entire subject of the media had changed since they'd known each other. She'd have bet her first cover story for the *Washington Post* on it.

She knew that, because her views had changed, too. She felt conflicted about exposing Skipper. After years of being influenced by Jennifer Collier, of having her ideas shaped subtly yet purposefully, she would not have thought she could ever admire the developer. But she did. She admired his business acumen. She appreciated his intelligence and acknowledged his perseverance. There were even aspects of his character that deserved admiration; he had courage, and foresight, and was intelligent and loyal. She understood why he did what he did, and why he didn't think it wrong.

Kate finally decided she needed Brant's input before she could decide what to do with the information she had gathered.

She went to his apartment a couple of days after she finished compiling her research. She thrust the accordion file full of Skipper's complete history at Brant as soon as he let her into the apartment. "Here," she said churlishly. "Have a look." She perched on one of the stools at the kitchen counter, turning her back on him.

"Kate, calm down," Brant urged. He put the folder on the cherry wood table and came over to put his hands on her shoulders. "What's the matter?" He started to massage her neck.

"I wish I could tell you," she muttered softly.

"So tell me," he pressed.

"I can't," Kate whined. "I—I'm . . . all mixed-up. Between you and Jennifer—"

"Jennifer?"

"Collier. My source. Also my best friend."

"Jennifer Collier put you on to Skipper Arnold. That

doesn't make sense." He looked suddenly as perplexed as she had felt since this whole thing began.

"Tell me about it," she retorted petulantly.

"But she's like a daughter to him. Skipper worships the ground she walks on. And Jennifer seems equally devoted to him. I mean . . . she makes the odd crack, and she teases him a lot, but . . ."

"I thought you would guess . . . when you were trying to figure out who my source was. She did introduce us, after all."

"Yes, but you guys are old friends. I figured you approached her."

Kate shook her head. "Nope."

"She came to you?"

"Yup."

He walked away from her. "With a story on Skipper?" He turned back to her. "She actually accused him of murder."

"Yup."

He was silent for a moment. "I don't get it," he finally said. He started to pace and repeated, "I don't get it. Why didn't she tell you about the whole operation? She had to know about it."

"I asked her that myself. I gather she felt that *that* would be a betrayal of his trust."

"Whereas accusing him of murder isn't?" he asked, incredulous.

"Don't ask me to explain." Kate shrugged. "I've been on that particular roller coaster since the beginning." It felt good to have someone to share it with, finally. But it was only the start of her problems. "Then there's you," she added.

He stopped pacing abruptly and faced her. "Oh," he said simply. There was a wealth of understanding in the single syllable.

"Yeah." Kate was too flustered to try to play games with him.

"Me," he reiterated. The beginnings of a smile tugged at the corner of his mouth. "Am I on that roller coaster ride, too?"

"You are the loop the loop. You've got me all turned around, upside down, inside out."

"You do it to me, too," he confessed.

"I do? I'm happy to hear that. But it doesn't really solve my problem," she said glumly.

"You're doing it right now."

"Sorry," she said, but the apology lacked sincerity even to her own ears. She was too busy feeling sorry for herself to pity him.

"You make me feel like no one else has," Brant continued, easing the constriction in her throat.

She suppressed a smile. "Breathless?" Kate queried hopefully.

"Dizzy," he said.

But it didn't work. She was too pleased at his admission for his wording to faze her. " 'Bewitched, bothered, and bewildered,' as they say in the song," she prompted.

"Fine" he acceded. "You're the one with the vocabulary. I'm a structural engineer. I'm not so great with words."

"But you're good with your hands," she countered.

Brant smiled. "We have to be. In my line of work."

"That's right, you need good eye-to-hand coordination to draw your little designs, don't you?"

"We call them plans."

"Speaking of plans . . ." Kate drawled.

"Later. I want to talk some more about this roller-coaster ride," Brant said firmly.

"Professionally, I don't know what to do about this article," she said, frustrated.

"I don't understand. I thought you said you were going to write it, no matter what."

"I am. I will. That hasn't changed. The thing is, I can write this, like any other story, about a hundred different ways. It's pretty simple to slant a story one way or another. It's all in the words I choose."

"I thought you said the facts were the facts," he said, tapping the accordion file in which she'd put the results of her research.

"They are. And they should be known. But . . ."

"But what?"

"But there's more than one way to present this . . . information. Is Leopold Arnold a hardened criminal, with earlier arrests, a murky past, and a proclivity for shady business dealings, or is he an aggressive genius getting buildings built despite the hundreds of obstacles of dealing with a bureaucracy that may be more corrupt than he is?"

"Well, if those are my only two choices, I'd have to say the second is nearer to the truth."

"Face it, darling, there is no 'truth' to be found here. There are lies, however, and I want to get to the bottom of all of it. Mostly, I want to know who sabotaged that elevator."

"Isn't the bottom of it in here?" Brant asked, picking up the accordion file.

He sat on the couch and started to take out the manila folders in which she'd organized the information she'd amassed on Skipper Arnold. "Jennifer Collier? You made a file on your friend?"

"Well, she was a source," she excused herself guiltily.

"You've never had a friend give you a lead before?"

"My friends help me out. Sure. But this is different. I don't like being used. Do you?"

"Jen does owe me an explanation," he conceded.

"Something better than she's given me," she agreed. "But I don't think she's going to give us one. I've asked."

"I haven't," he said grimly. He flipped open the folder and started to read.

"What makes you think that will make any difference?" Kate asked.

"She knew I loved Skipper. She had to have some reason for making me a part of this betrayal."

"Jennifer likes to get her own way, but I can't believe she'd manipulate us so blatantly."

"This is strange."

"What?"

"Did Jenny ever tell *you* about her brother? Because she never mentioned him to me."

"No," Kate said. "I found out when I looked into her past. But he died before I ever knew her, and she doesn't like to talk about her childhood. Her mother is an alcoholic, and her father left when she was a baby. I can understand why she doesn't want to discuss it."

"She told you about her mother, and her father, right? She made up this whole story about Skipper? She seems to have confided her life story to you. Why leave out her big brother?"

He pointed at a line on the page of the report in front of him. "Do you know this company is one Skipper owned?"

Kate sat beside him and read the name. "That was fifteen years ago."

"Her brother worked there."

"She works for Skipper, too. It makes sense. He's a friend of the family."

"Still . . ."

"It doesn't matter. It's not up to Jen, it's up to me. I have to decide what I'm going to write."

"Maybe I can help," Brant offered, leafing through more of the papers in front of him.

"I don't know if that's such a good idea," Kate said hesitantly. She had come to him for help. But she already knew his opinion. She had hoped for . . . for something else. Permission to do something she was perfectly aware that he wouldn't want her to do, maybe. But she wasn't ready to ask for it.

"Then what are you doing here?" he asked.

"It's not what you think," she told him.

"I don't think anything. I asked because I wanted to know," he said.

"I don't want to do the wrong thing." She wanted to make a difference, but her articles weren't enough. She couldn't control the outcome. And this time, because of him, she was afraid to try. In the past when she published her investigative reports, they had not always had the intended effect. The wrong people sometimes got hurt.

When she didn't continue, he prompted her. "I thought you said there was only one right thing to do."

"I know. But it doesn't always work out the way you think it will. It's not that I'm naive. I've worked hard to get to where I am today. I know we can't always do everything we want. I'm a big girl. I can live with that. What scares me is, I'm afraid it will happen again."

"What will happen again?"

"Someone getting punished for someone else's crime. Someone who doesn't deserve it."

"Skipper?"

"No."

"Who then?"

"You, maybe. Or . . . I don't know. Jennifer? Those strikers? His other employees?"

"Why Jenny?"

"Why didn't she tell me about his criminal behavior?

The only reason I can come up with is that she was implicated somehow."

"And you don't want to expose her?"

"I don't know if she'll be a scapegoat because she's more vulnerable than he is. I've seen it happen before."

"What makes you think she needs a protector?"

"I don't know if she did anything or not. I just know I don't want *her* to take the fall for *him.*"

"That's right . . . You don't have a very high opinion of people in the construction business, do you?" Brant said, tongue-in-cheek.

"Hardhats are okay. It's the contractors and the developers who are the real problem in the construction industry," she joked, attempting to lighten the mood.

"I'm a subcontractor," he pointed out.

"That counts. You're one of *them,*" Kate said, feigning disapproval.

"I'll change," he said. "I'll demote myself. I'll be a hardhat again."

"I like them," she teased.

"Why is that, Ms. Ramsey?"

"Nice pecs," Kate said playfully.

"I never would have thought you'd go for brawn over brains," he shook his head. "*Tsk, tsk, tsk.*" He clicked his tongue.

"Everyone's got their little weaknesses." She was unapologetic.

"And yours is . . . muscles?" he said, suddenly sounding pleased. "So it's not strength of mind you're interested in, it's strength of body."

"Shapes and proportions are important, too," she commented. "I could never marry . . . say . . . a sumo wrestler."

"I'll remember that," Brant said, "when I start bulking up."

"You're going to start working out?" she asked. "For me?" She put her hand over her heart.

"I'm already working harder and making less money as a hardhat, for you. I'm not going to have the time or energy to work out, too."

"How?" she asked. "A construction worker in this city has to work on skyscrapers. You've got a little problem in that area, remember?"

He shrugged. "I've done it before. When I started in the business, I had to get up on the buildings. There was no way to stay on the ground back then. I managed."

"Well, I'm not taking responsibility for this. I don't want anything to do with you getting yourself killed." A hint of seriousness crept into her voice against her will.

"Darling, I'm so glad you care," he said wryly. "I didn't think I stood a chance with you, after you found out *my* weakness, but now that I know what you want in a man . . ." He let his voice trail off, and reached for her, wrapping his hand around the back of her neck and pulling her close. She ducked out of his grasp and put her hands against his shoulders to keep a little distance between them.

"Enough," she said, laughing. "Get serious."

"In a minute," he promised. "First come here."

Kate gave up—for the moment. She wrapped her arms around his neck and kissed him, hard.

Sixteen

She watched Brant sleep. He looked delicious, and she was tempted to awaken him, but she didn't know if he would appreciate it. She could wait. Somehow he had set her free. Kate had come to him, she now knew, for absolution, and, in a way, he had given it to her. Or, perhaps the debate with Brant had just cleared her mind, finally. Whatever the catalyst, she felt at peace. She knew she had a ways to go with her article, but the tension she had felt was gone. Kate had always trusted her instincts before, and as she lay, looking at his face, she realized she was ready to do it again.

She realized he was awake when he pulled the sheet up over them, his eyes still closed.

"Thanks, sweetie," she told him as she covered her shoulders.

"You're awake," he announced. He still hadn't opened his eyes.

She nipped his shoulder playfully. "Somebody stole the covers."

"Were you cold?"

"No, I was just teasing." He seemed to doze off, and Kate lay contentedly staring up at the ceiling.

A thought occurred to her. "I've invited a few friends over to dinner at my place tomorrow night. Would you like to come?" she asked softly, unwilling to wake him if he were trying to sleep.

"Sure," he answered. After a few seconds he suddenly said, "Sorry."

She thought he was going to say he couldn't come, but he didn't. "You can't come?" she inquired.

"Yes, I can."

"Then what are you sorry for?"

"My stomach's growling. Can't you hear it?"

"No."

"I'm hungry," Brant said.

"I take it that you're a man of rather large appetites," she couldn't resist joking as she turned her face into his shoulder to hide her smile.

"Are you laughing?" he asked.

She chuckled against his skin, allowing a snort to emerge as her answer.

Brant groaned. "What can I say, babe? You bring out the, umm, beast in me."

Just then his stomach rumbled loudly. They both lost it. Kate laughed so hard she couldn't breathe. Brant covered his face with a pillow, but his massive chest convulsed again and again so that even if she hadn't been able to hear his muffled guffaw from beneath the goosedown, she would have felt every spasm of laughter. It was contagious. Each time she saw his chest move, it set her off again.

Brant finally stuffed a corner of the pillow in his mouth in order to stop. "Cease and desist," he commanded firmly when he had himself under control. As laughter threatened to overwhelm her again, he clapped a hand over Kate's mouth. "It's clear to me from this that I'm actually giddy with hunger. I must eat."

She nodded and he removed his hand. "Okay, let's eat," Kate said.

He threw her his robe. "It's my turn to cook for you," he said as he strode out of the bedroom. Kate scrambled out of bed and into a terry-cloth robe. She had seen what he had in his refrigerator a few days before. She wanted to see what he was going to make without any ingredients. By the time she reached the kitchen, he was already at work. Miraculously, he'd produced spinach when she thought she had used all his supply in her omelette. He also had Canadian bacon, cheese, flour, butter, and other ingredients, but the most interesting thing he'd laid out on the counter was a rolling pin.

"I'm impressed," Kate said.

"Are you vegetarian?" he asked perfunctorily as he portioned out a small pile of flour from the bag, made a slight depression in the top, and poured a little water into it. He started to mix the dough very confidently.

Kate was so impressed with his skill, she almost forgot to answer him. "Usually. Why?"

He smiled. "Usually? I thought the traditional answer was yes or no."

"Yeah, well. I'm not a traditional girl. Usually I don't eat the flesh of other warm-blooded creatures, but for Canadian bacon fixed by your dexterous hands, I might make an exception." She watched, fascinated, as he turned powder and water into a ball, and then rolled it out into a thin mantle of dough.

"Dexterous. I like that." He started to add other ingredients; cubed bacon, tomato, broccoli, spinach, and a block of cheese.

"I can embellish," she bragged.

Brant turned on a burner on the stove under a small pot. He put butter and water and powdered milk into the saucepan, quickly chopped the cheese into squares, and then dropped them, a couple at a time, into the sizzling pan. After he'd added all the cheese, he stirred it, and turned back to the pastry.

"Skillful, adroit, clever." She listed the synonyms quickly. "Talented, gifted, accomplished." He folded the dough, with its savory filling, into two large triangles, and squeezed two of the edges together on each, then placed them on a cookie sheet. "Adept, proficient . . . handy," she added, ending the recitation.

He dribbled some of the cheese sauce into each of the turnovers, and placed them in the oven. "Twenty minutes," he announced. "In the meantime . . ." Brant took the small pot off of the stove, dropped it on the counter, and produced some Italian bread she hadn't noticed before.

She was sure it hadn't been there when she'd cooked the omelettes. "Where did this all come from?" she asked.

"I have groceries delivered once or twice a week," he explained. "These arrived before you did yesterday." He tore off a bite-size chunk of bread from the loaf and handed it to her, then took one for himself. He dipped his in the cheese sauce, then popped it in his mouth.

"You cheat!" She soaked the crusty bread in the creamy golden mixture. The warm morsel melted in her mouth. He went to the stainless-steel refrigerator and opened it. It was very well stocked. He removed a container of orange juice and poured them each a glass. "You know I was thinking that I had missed all of this when I explored the kitchen."

"I thought so. But I enjoyed being a magician, for a minute."

"You are a magician." She couldn't get enough of the impromptu cheese fondue. "This is scrumptious." She didn't know if it was truly as remarkable as it seemed, or if she was just particularly hungry after the workout they had had. But she was willing to give him the benefit of the doubt. "Mmm," she cooed as she ate more of the concoction. "I could get used to this."

"Is that all I get?"

"Well, what do you want?" Kate asked. "I said thank you."

"Actually, you didn't."

"Oh, sorry." She sopped up the last of the cheese sauce with a bit of bread and held it up. "For you."

He lowered his head and opened his mouth, and she placed the tidbit daintily on his tongue. He caught her hand and drew her to him as he swallowed that bite of food. Then he kissed her hand.

"Thank you," Kate said.

"It's about time." He wrapped an arm around her waist and pulled her body to his. "There's a penalty for the delay."

"What is this, a basketball game?" she said laughingly as he nuzzled her neck, tickling her.

"I don't think the NBA would approve of the penalty I have in mind."

"Would I?" she asked.

"I think so," he answered, bending her back over his arm as his lips roamed lower and lower. His hand found the tie at her waist and undid it. The robe fell open, and Kate enjoyed the admiring look in his eyes before she pulled him close and kissed his chin. His hands went around her and drifted over the contours of her back to her buttocks. Just then, a bell rang.

Brant expelled his breath in a gust of regret. "The food is ready," he declared.

Kate knew just how he felt. "We should eat, then," she said practically.

He kissed her neck once, then let her go. While she

retied her robe, he placed the pastries on plates, and arranged them on a tray. "Breakfast in bed?" he inquired.

"I've grown somewhat attached to your kitchen," she teased.

"We can always come back later," he pointed out.

She followed him into the bedroom, and they climbed onto the bed. She admired the tray he'd arranged. The two plates were cornflower-blue china with an elegant pattern of hand-painted, delicate white lilies around the rims. Crystal glasses, silver flatware, and gleaming white cloth napkins bordered in the same cornflower blue, complemented the dishes.

"Pretty," Kate pronounced. Brant grunted. "You're really very artistic. That must be helpful when you draw your little designs."

"Why do you keep calling them my 'little' designs. You make me sound like some poofy fashion designer."

"Poofy is not a word I think of when I look at you," Kate said.

"What do you think of, then?"

She looked up at his beautiful brown eyes, strong mouth, square jaw, and brawny shoulders, then down at his rippling stomach, solid thighs, and muscular calves, and answered. "Nirvana."

They ate. The pastries Brant made were fantastic. The buttery crust and creamy vegetable filling with the tangy accent of Canadian bacon melted in her mouth. Despite the snack she'd devoured while they waited for their breakfast to bake, Kate was ravenous. She savored every bite, while she watched Brant do the same. It was a pleasure to observe him wield his fork, gracefully lifting the silver to his lips and placing it on his tongue. The flash of strong white teeth, the motion of his jaw, and the bob of his Adam's apple as he swallowed made her anticipate finishing the meal and getting on to dessert.

"Good?" he asked, as she placed her napkin back on the tray after dabbing her mouth with it.

"Delicious," she answered. "I could get used to this."

"We are here to serve," he said humbly.

"I love that." She reached out and ran a fingernail down his arm. "It is so hard to find a man who is nurturing, and it is one of the great joys in life," she needled him.

"Ahh," he sighed. "I have been told that I am in touch with my feminine side."

"You are," she confirmed. "Definitely."

"I'll take that as a compliment."

"It was certainly meant as one." She leaned toward him and kissed his shoulder. "It is important that we, women, reward men who demonstrate those rare qualities." She worked her way up to his throat, and pressed her tongue to his Adam's apple. She felt it jump. "Positive reinforcement is such an effective training tool."

"Hold on there," he objected, taking her by the shoulders and pushing her back a couple of inches so he could look into her eyes. "I'm starting to feel like a German shepherd. Could you possibly make it sound less like I'm in some kind of perverse obedience school?" Kate surged forward, into his chest, propelling him back onto the bed.

She leaned on her elbows on his chest. "Perverse?" she whispered in his ear.

"I know you women like to think of us as raw material," he replied, caressing the shoulder that was closest to him. "But I'm not a puppy," he continued, as he brushed the robe away from her skin, and bent to explore the exposed skin.

She moaned as he slipped his hand beneath the other side of the robe and his fingertips flirted with her breast. Still, she couldn't resist prodding him just a little bit more. "Good boy," she murmured against the top of his head.

His mouth was traveling down her arm, and he nipped her right above her elbow. "Behave," he ordered.

She giggled. "Okay," she agreed, pulling his head back up to hers. He kissed her, his tongue delving deep, entwining with hers, and the urge to goad him faded. Then she felt the evidence of his arousal against her hip, which reminded her of earlier. She smiled to herself, and he saw.

"What's funny?" Brant asked breathlessly.

"You have to admit, you guys can be a little puppyish when you're . . . excited."

He flipped Kate on to her back and held her hands down beside her head. "It is very hard to concentrate on pleasing you when you are so determined to get a rise out of me," he said.

Kate couldn't help it; she laughed at the double entendre. "I would like that," she said shamelessly, wrapping her legs around his hips.

Positioned between her thighs as he was, she thought he would be unable to resist the temptation to slip inside her, but he held himself back. "You think you're so clever," he taunted. "I know you like this banter and all, but I can only do one thing at a time, so if you want to play games, I—"

She cut him off. "I'll stop," she swore. "Please don't."

"Don't what?" he asked, tormenting her in his turn.

"Don't stop."

He waited for an interminable moment, looking down at her, then he let her hands go. Kate clasped his chin between her palms and pulled his head down to fasten her lips to his.

He slid one arm around her torso, and lifted her body into his, while his other hand trailed down over her breast and belly, straight to the core of her. She opened to him immediately, but he took his time, sliding two long, hard fingers around the nubbin of flesh that guarded the inner recesses of her body and circling it with his thumb until she bucked and strained against him. Then he finally relented and pressed firmly into the tender spot, releasing the ache that tormented her. A warm rush of sensation pulsed through her body and left her quivering. She watched as he got a condom from the bedside table, then helped him slide it on. When he came back to her, she rose up to meet him, and his iron hardness forged through smooth velvet, and retreated, only to plunge back into the silky depths again and again. Kate felt the tide within growing higher and higher, and groaned as time came to a halt while she waited for it to carry her away. She watched his eyes slide shut as he trembled, and buried himself to the hilt inside her as the wave crashed over them both. It took a moment for the sweet spasm to subside.

She lay with her cheek against his shoulder, trying to catch her breath. "Good cook, great body, and the brains to know what to do with it. Good Lord," she exclaimed. "What did I ever do to deserve this?"

Seventeen

David arrived at the apartment early on Sunday night. Kate had made her guests swear to be on time. He, as usual, was careful to keep his promise. It hadn't been David she was worried about. Tanikwa was notorious for being late, and since she lived with Marie, Kate put the chances at fifty/fifty that they'd be sitting down to eat at seven as she'd planned.

David offered his help, so she put him to work setting the table while she checked on her dinner. "Are you cooking, Kate?" he asked dubiously, sniffing loudly.

"I could," she said, pretending to be insulted.

"It smells wonderful," he backpedaled quickly.

"Thank you," she relented, smiling at him. "That's the bread. I brought some of that ready-made dough. And I brought home a vegetarian lasagna from the gourmet place up the street, which is heating."

"I'll keep your secret, dear," he promised.

"It's not a secret. I was just pulling your leg."

"Good, because I don't think Tanikwa would believe us."

"She knows I'm not domesticated. Marie is the one who wouldn't let me get away with it. She never cuts anyone any slack. I hope she doesn't give Brant too hard a time."

"I don't know, Katie. I wouldn't hold out too much hope," he cautioned. "With a name like that, he's got to be used to being tormented."

She stuck her tongue out at him. "There's nothing wrong with his name."

He shook his head. "I hate to be the one to tell you . . ."

"Oh, shut up," she whined. "You're just trying to make me nervous."

"Ah, yes, you are too placid. I enjoy you so much more when you're on edge," he said dryly. It was a running joke among her friends that Kate's temper was dangerous. She could only hope that they would not regale Brant with any tall tales.

David answered the door when Brant arrived, and they introduced themselves as she took dinner out of the oven and placed it on the cooling rack. She had told her friends to arrive at half past six, and counted on giving Marie and Tanikwa the time needed to cool the dish as a grace period. Unfortunately, they were over fifteen minutes late, and despite telling them she'd start without them, she really didn't want to serve dinner twice.

Kate blamed herself. "I should have told them dinner would be served at six o'clock," she told Brant and David, as she gave them each some Chianti and poured a glass for herself. "Or gotten it ready later." If they weren't at the table at seven o'clock, she would have to reheat the entrée.

Her friends arrived together, just as Kate was starting to get antsy. She was too relieved to be annoyed. "Let's sit down at the table," she suggested peremptorily.

"All right, all right," Tanikwa said as Kate hurried them into their seats. "Good thing I washed my hands before I came."

Marie was unrepentant. "It's not my fault. I tried to

get us out of the house on time, but this one"—she inclined her head toward her roommate—"I couldn't get
her to move her skinny little butt."

"I had to dress, didn't I?" Tonight Tanikwa had donned
her cowgirl outfit: a white T-shirt under a plaid top over
black jeans, and pointy black boots with turquoise leather
inlays. But the most startling accessory was a shiny silver
belt buckle that had to be six inches wide by three inches
tall. Large silver earrings, rings, necklace, and bracelets
with ornate patterns etched into the bright metal also
winked in the low light that Kate had thought would set
the mood for a nice, intimate meal. "Besides, I didn't
think we'd be having a feast like this," she excused herself. "What happened to our usual Chinese take-out?"
Tanikwa asked with a look of bland inquiry. "As if I
didn't know," she added, looking over at Brant.

"Eat," Kate exhorted.

"Appearances aside, this girl is not at all domesticated,"
she persevered.

"She makes a great omelette," Brant disputed.

"She does?" Marie asked, skeptical. Somehow her British accent made any answer he might give seem implau-
sible.

"Could we change the subject? I'm starting to feel insulted," Kate remonstrated.   ——

"I didn't think you were interested in the housewifely
arts," Tanikwa said snidely. "What brought about this sudden change in priorities?"

"You all make it sound as if I'm completely incompe-
tent in the kitchen. I'm not an idiot. I *can* boil water."

"I believe you. This is delicious," David said with his
customary good manners. He was a true gentleman, and
Kate had never appreciated him more.

"Thank you." She accepted his compliment gracefully,
and nodded as the others added their praises to his.

Dinner was a relaxed affair after that. At least it was for Kate. Brant was subjected to a bit of an inquisition by her friends, but he took it in the spirit in which it was intended, and really didn't seem to mind their prying. There were one or two comments made about his profession. Her gang was less than complimentary at first, but when Kate tried to rein them in, Brant jumped in.

"I see you share Kate's opinion of the construction industry," he said, noncommital in response to one of Tanikwa's barbs.

"Nothing personal, I'm sure," Marie replied. "It's just that you Yanks have such a convoluted way of doing things. The low-income housing projects end up as cesspools, while privately financed buildings that are not endowed by the government with guaranteed, if limited, funds for their maintenance end up as luxury apartments and office buildings, which the residents of this city end up paying for with their taxes."

"We don't set them up that way. We just build them," Brant pointed out.

"The developers do set them up that way," Kate interjected. "It's part of the plan from the beginning. Although I know you, personally, don't work on projects like that," she said, trying to temper her answer.

"I've worked on all kinds of buildings all over this city," Brant corrected her. "I may not be a builder like Skipper, but as a subcontractor, I'm involved with the building plans. I know that it seems like the low- and middle-income projects start out with handicaps that make it impossible for the tenants to maintain them properly, but believe me, we always hope that this particular building will be the one that breaks with tradition and becomes the model for subsidized housing."

"I don't understand," David commented. "How could

anyone but the tenants affect their own housing situation?"

"For example," Tanikwa explained to him. "The project will be built in an area that is deemed less expensive for the city to *give* away. So the people who are qualified to live there, by definition, people with few, if any, resources, are dumped into a neighborhood with higher crime rates, bad schools, and unsuccessful businesses. And that's just the tip of the iceberg."

"But the men building the apartments don't have anything to do with that, do they?" he asked innocently.

"They do," Marie answered. "We have the same thing in London—council housing. The city pays for it, and often pays the rental through the dole, but since the tenants are poor, they don't have much of a voice. The police treat them abysmally, the politicians are uninterested in their complaints, and their poverty creates an atmosphere of hopelessness. I'm oversimplifying, of course, but the builders are certainly aware of what the outcome of their efforts will be and they act accordingly, I'm sure."

"Are you suggesting that we are responsible for the predicament the people find themselves in? Because that isn't the case," Brant said.

"No, I'm not saying that," Marie said.

"Neither am I," Tanikwa replied. "But they don't help, either. They compound the problem by exploiting the system."

David couldn't stand to see their guest of honor insulted. "What do you know about it?" he challenged Tanikwa. "Brant may be completely uninvolved."

"Well, that would make Brant a rather unusual contractor," Marie pointed out.

"He's unusual, all right," Kate muttered as she cleared the table.

"I knew it," David crowed. "I'm right, aren't I?"

"What does that mean?" Tanikwa asked curiously.

Katie looked up to find all eyes trained on her. *Oh, no,* she thought. She'd been about to tell them about Brant's phobia.

"Uh, nothing," she faltered.

"Oh, no, girl, you can't just make a statement like that and expect us to believe you. You have to defend your man." Tanikwa baited her. "Let's hear the evidence. What's so different about him?"

"I just meant that David is right. We can't assume the worst about him. He may be in the construction business, but that doesn't necessarily mean he builds low-income housing."

"But he said he's involved with them," Marie pointed out. She turned to Brant. "Didn't you?"

"He said he sees the plans," Kate corrected her.

"He's right here, why don't we ask him?" Tanikwa suggested. She focused on him. "Have you ever worked on low-income housing?"

"As it happens, I haven't. But that doesn't mean I wouldn't ever work on a project like that. It hasn't come up. So far."

"Right," Marie said. "You see."

"See what?" Tanikwa was like a dog with a bone. She couldn't let it go. "That doesn't prove anything one way or the other. He's not against doing it, he just hasn't had the opportunity. That doesn't make him any different from anyone else in the business. Come on, Kate, spill it! What were you going to say?"

"I wasn't going to say anything," Kate insisted.

"Anyway, it's a moot point," David interjected. "Brant doesn't know what he'd do. As he said, it hasn't come up."

"Yet," Marie added mischievously.

Tanikwa nodded. "That's right. And he defended his buddies. He said he doesn't think it's their fault."

"I don't," Brant averred. "It's a complicated issue. I'm sure you all agree, someone *has* to build low-income housing. Who do you think should do it? Nuns?"

Kate glared at him, but he only smiled at her, clearly unaware of the danger he was in. Tanikwa sensed that there was something she wasn't telling them, and the copywriter was worse than any newshound when she went after information she wanted. There was no stopping her once she got the bit between her teeth. "I'm guessing Kate had something besides the issues in mind when she made that cryptic statement about you. Am I right?" she appealed to Brant directly.

"I have no idea," he answered, sitting back in his chair and crossing his arms over his chest. His body language clearly indicated that he wasn't about to reveal anything to his inquisitors. It was, in fact, as if he were daring her to pry further.

Kate didn't think he knew that she had almost blurted out his secret, but she was certain he was aware that, with his attitude, he was waving a red flag in front of Tanikwa, and she couldn't fathom his reasons for behaving this way. "Brant, may I speak with you in the kitchen?" she asked through a clenched jaw.

"Of course," he replied.

"What in the world are you doing?" she demanded quietly but forcefully as soon as they had reached the relative safety of the other room.

He gave her a wry look and answered blandly, "What do you mean, Katie, honey?"

"Cut the bull," she answered roughly. "Do you know I almost told them about your . . . your problem?" She almost fumbled toward the end of her query, but regained her aplomb just in time to gaze at him meaningfully as she finished posing the question.

"My little phobia," he interpreted complacently.

"Yes," she hissed. "So you want to help me out here? Change the subject or something?" she requested in a stage whisper.

"What do you suggest I do?" he asked, deadpan.

"Stop egging them on," she ordered.

"Is that what I was doing?" he asked, feigning surprise.

"You know perfectly well that you were," she retorted, exasperated. "And I think you'd better get a grip, funny man, or you're going to be sorry."

"Are you threatening me?"

"No, I'm just clarifying the situation. If you want Tanikwa tormenting you—and me!—for the rest of the evening, go right on doing what you've been doing. But I am not going to feel sorry for you if she ends up finding out the truth."

"I'm not going to tell her anything," he assured her. "If you're not sure you can resist your nosey friend, then . . ."

"Why are you doing this?" she asked, baffled.

Brant shrugged. "Just wondering if you can keep your mouth shut," he answered pompously.

Kate fumed. "I can," she vowed. She followed him back into the dining room where the others were waiting.

"So, what were you guys talking about in there?" Tanikwa asked archly.

"Nothing that would interest you."

"You never know what might interest me," she retorted.

Kate tried to allay her friend's suspicions, but it was impossible to divert her once she was convinced she was on the scent of a juicy secret. For the rest of the evening she fended off Tanikwa's inquiries with as good a grace as she could muster. But she had every intention of mak-

ing Brant suffer at some point in the near future for testing her this way, and she told him so that night. She had
a feeling he didn't believe her, which was just fine with
Kate. When it came to this kind of thing, she agreed
with the Bard—revenge *was* a dish that was best served
cold.

Eighteen

There was a piece to the puzzle that Kate had not found yet, and she had the feeling her college roommate was the key. Jen had been the one to get this whole thing started, and Kate couldn't help feeling that she had a reason. Kate took Brant with her to interview her old friend because she suspected that between the two of them they could see through any story she might concoct. Jennifer opened the door, but she didn't look pleased to see them. Her expression resigned, she ushered them into the living room and indicated that they should sit on the couch. Brant sat. At first, Kate remained standing. She felt restless, discomfitted. She stood facing one of her oldest friends, and didn't know whether she was facing a friend at all.

"You have some information for me?" Jen said.

"First, we have a couple of questions for you," Kate said.

"I've already told you everything I know," Jen answered, her voice hard.

Kate played a hunch. "What about the elevator accident?" she asked. She sat next to Brant on the couch, facing Jennifer. He looked from one to the other, but he didn't say a word.

"You weren't supposed to be hurt or anything, and you weren't," Jen said defensively.

"So you did know about it?" Kate probed.

"Do you have something to tell me, or not? I don't have time for this," Jennifer said.

"I'd like to know more about the incident with the elevator," Brant announced.

"Later," Kate said. From the closed look on Jen's face, she knew that she'd gotten as much as she was going to on that subject. For the moment. She switched tacks. "Right now, we need to talk about Julio."

Jennifer's defensive posture changed to one of tense expectation. "You found out something about his death?" she questioned eagerly.

Kate knew the time was right to drop an even bigger bomb. "Why didn't you tell us about your brother?" she asked, feeling not one iota of regret at blindsiding her.

"What was there to tell?" Jennifer asked, lowering her eyelids. But before she'd hidden her eyes, Kate had glimpsed the hope and longing she felt. "He's dead. Too."

"He died working for Skipper."

"Big Apple Construction, Skipper's first company," Brant interjected. "He lost a contract, and it went under."

"Yes?" Jennifer waited breathlessly.

"How did he die?" Kate asked.

"He was killed when he fell through some wooden lattices."

"An accident. Like Julio," Kate said, nodding as if that confirmed some suspicion she herself had entertained.

"Was it?" Jennifer asked anxiously. The pretense of tranquil composure she had maintained had vanished.

Brant's head whipped around toward her. "It was ruled an accident," he said slowly. He held out the accordion file to Kate. "Wasn't it?"

"Yes."

Jen regarded them with bated breath. Finally, she cried, "I need to know, was it an accident, or not."

Kate relented. "It seems to be."

Jennifer deflated, visibly. "That's all you were able to find out?"

"Jen, if you thought the man killed your brother, how could you—?" Kate started to ask.

"I don't know. I don't know," Jennifer groaned. "He was working for Uncle Skip, and I didn't think it could have been anything other than an accident, at first. But Skipper acted so guilty, so upset. And then he closed the company, and reopened later under a different name, and . . . I've tried to find out everything I could about it, but no one was going to tell me anything. They wouldn't talk to me at the time—"

"You were thirteen years old," Kate said.

"But I needed to know. And I couldn't get any information out of anyone. Mom was a zombie, even more than before, and Skipper was . . . He said we had to be strong. You know how men are." She appealed to Kate. "I needed a professional to check this out for me, and I knew you'd stumble across it, if you were researching Skipper. You started out just the way I hoped you would—looking into his past. But then you got sidetracked." She nodded toward Brant. "By him."

"But you were the one who got us together."

"I knew Skipper would talk to you if Brant was with you. He trusts Brant. And I knew you two would click. It's just something about you. You're both the same kind of person. Honest, upright, principled." She said the words as if they were insults. "I had a feeling you would work well together. And I was right."

"I've got to admit it, you had me pegged," Brant said.

Kate remained silent.

Jennifer went on. "But you got sidetracked by the corruption angle. And then it seemed like Brant was changing your mind," she said to Kate. "You were questioning everything, except the accident."

"But there wasn't anything there. He didn't kill Julio."

"You don't know that," Jen insisted.

"I do," Brant said somberly.

"It didn't look good." She turned to Kate again. "And you're such a bulldog. Usually, anyway. I didn't think you'd give up so easily."

"I didn't," Kate said, offended at the implication, despite the fact that Jennifer had engineered the entire situation.

"I thought it was a setup, but she didn't," Brant clarified.

"You sounded like you wanted to believe him," Jennifer accused her. "I had to do something. Especially after the interview with Skipper."

"How did you know—?"

"I listened in, from the outer office. The intercom can work as a speaker. And I heard how nice you were to him, how you just let him skate over the questions about his past. You never even mentioned Big Apple Construction."

"So you sabotaged our elevator car?" she felt betrayed.

"I just took out one of the cables. They've got a million fail-safes. I knew you wouldn't get hurt."

"You could have killed us," Brant said angrily.

"I wouldn't have done that. But I had to keep Kate on track. I figured she'd blame Skipper."

"It was all for nothing, Jen," Kate retorted.

"It was not for nothing. There will be an investigation when your article comes out. And maybe this time, they'll listen to me."

"You still think Julio's death was more than an accident?" Brant asked, shaking his head.

"I have to know," Jen said desperately. "I can't live like this. Wondering about Skipper. Hating him. It gets worse every year."

As angry as she was to find out that Jennifer had put them in danger, Kate couldn't help feeling pity for her. "Have you tried talking to a professional about this?"

"A shrink? No. I don't need a therapist, I need to know what happened to my brother," Jennifer exclaimed.

"I'm sorry, Jen, but it doesn't seem as though there's any way to find out about that. It happened so long ago, and the police report didn't indicate anything at all out of the ordinary. Your brother was only nineteen. They certainly looked into his death, with Skipper's full cooperation, by the way. But he fell through the slats on that floor in full view of a crew who all gave statements to the effect that he lost his balance. He didn't have any enemies, and he was well liked."

"His funeral was big. I couldn't believe how many people came. He was so young, but he'd touched a lot of people—guys from high school, different jobs he'd had, people from the neighborhood, and church. The guest register had three hundred names in it at the end. Mom was a basket case, but my aunt Fielding came from down South to stay with us, and we had people in and out of the house for days, bringing food and flowers. Everyone loved Bobby."

"You most of all," Brant said sympathetically. "He was your big brother. I have a younger sister. I think I can understand why you did this. But you've got to let it go. You're only hurting yourself."

"I've been living with this for too long to just give it up. I survived my mother's house just dreaming of the day I'd discover the truth about why Bobby died," Jennifer ranted. "I have spent every waking moment planning some kind of revenge for so many years that I don't know what else I have to get up for in the morning," she said, tormented.

Kate felt tears sting the back of her eyes. She had been blind. "You have to make peace with the past," she urged. Jennifer turned away. Kate knew how hard it was. When her father died, she thought she would never recover, never feel whole again. And she was a young woman when it happened, not a thirteen-year-old girl. Compared to Jen's childhood, her own hadn't been that bad. Ben Ramsey might have been an alcoholic but he was devoted to her, and he tried to make her feel as if she could do anything. She knew from the little her college roommate had told her that her mother was a mean drunk. The loss of her big brother must have seemed like the end of the world. Bobby was the one person in Jen's life whose love she could count on.

Kate knew she couldn't force Jen to get help. She had taken her to an Al-Anon meeting once, and ever since, any invitations had been politely but firmly refused. This was something Jennifer was going to have to handle on her own. Or not. There was nothing anyone could do for her until and unless she requested their help. Brant looked as helpless and dismayed as she felt as he cast about for something more to say.

Kate hated feeling this powerless. "We should probably go," she said finally. "Unless you want us to stay?"

"There's no point," Jennifer said dully.

"You could talk. We could listen. Sometimes"—she faltered—"Sometimes it helps."

The offer clearly wasn't welcome. "I don't think so. I'd rather be alone."

Kate stood and Brant followed her lead. "If I can help . . . in any way, please call me," she requested.

"I will," Jen responded, but she wasn't very convincing.

When the front door of Jennifer's little house closed behind them, Kate reached out to Brant, and he took her hand in his, then put his arm around her. The sedan they'd hired to bring them out to Long Island was parked right in front of Jennifer's walkway, and the driver jumped out as soon as he saw them and hurried to open the car door.

"Your place or mine?" Brant asked as he helped her into the car.

"Yours is closer," Kate said, nestling into his side for comfort.

"Fine." He gave the driver his address and pulled her closer under his arm.

They sat in silence all the way back to the city. The chauffeur chose to take them home over the Triboro Bridge, and they watched through the window as they descended toward the island of Manhattan and a panorama of millions of lights shining from the skyscrapers that made up the New York City skyline.

When they reached his apartment, they didn't speak much, except the little murmurs that accompanied his opening the door for her, and her excusing herself to go to the rest room. Kate looked at herself in the mirror. She looked the same as always, but she felt agitated and alarmed. She didn't know what Jennifer would do now. She didn't know what she herself would do. When she went back out into the living room, Brant was quiet, and she couldn't tell from his expression how deeply he'd been affected by her friend's confession. He seemed distracted, but he made them coffee without comment. He remembered to add milk and sugar to hers. She encircled the warm mug with both hands and inhaled the savory aroma thankfully. The deep rich flavor was comforting.

"Well, now we know," Kate said sadly.

"Maybe it would have been better if we didn't," he told her.

"How can you say that? It had to come out. Better this way than some other way."

"Why?" he asked, sounding genuinely curious. "What can we possibly do about it? We can't help her."

"You never know," Kate argued. "Maybe when the article comes out and she sees that Skipper hasn't gotten away with anything, she'll be able to come to terms with the loss. This could help her. Force her to get help, or at least confront him."

"You think she'll feel better when he is investigated for taking bribes, maybe goes to jail for it. I think she'll feel guiltier than ever, and it won't even answer her questions."

"Maybe it will. The police might investigate her brother's death, too."

"They're not going to reopen a fifteen-year-old accidental death case. You know it as well as I do."

"You don't know," Kate asserted. "You don't," she repeated. "No one does."

"Why are we arguing about this? There isn't any right answer, or wrong one. It's a terrible situation, and I don't think there's anything we can do to make it better. It just is."

She opened her mouth to contradict him and realized Brant was right. She was only quarreling with him because she felt terrible, and frustrated, and she didn't know how else to express it. "I'm sorry," she apologized.

"Me, too. I don't even know what I'm saying," he said placatingly.

"Come here, Brant," she said softly.

He came to her and wrapped his arms around her. "I'm glad we're together." He buried his face in her hair, and breathed deeply.

Kate felt a twinge of fear at the idea that he might be making assumptions that she wasn't sure were true. But she didn't protest. There would be time enough to talk about that tomorrow. For tonight, she needed him close to her.

Nineteen

She was awakened the next morning by the telephone. By the time the answering machine cut off the ringing, she had determined that she was alone in Brant's bed, while the sound of the shower running in the bathroom clued Kate in to his whereabouts. She lay in bed looking up at the ceiling. Brant came out of the bathroom clad only in a towel. The clean white swathe of plush terry cloth stood out in striking contrast to his rich brown skin.

"Morning," he greeted her, leaning over the bed to kiss her, his black hair shining wet.

"Morning," she responded. The scent of his soap and his skin was heady. "You smell good."

"Thank you," he said. "I've got to be at work by eight. Sorry."

She excused him. "Morning sex was never my thing, but I was hoping you'd make me breakfast again."

"It's your turn anyway," he reminded her.

"Nuh-uh, I cooked dinner," Kate disagreed. "It's definitely your turn. Besides, you're so much better at it than me," she wheedled.

He shook his head, ruefully. "I love you, Katie." He was smiling, but she looked into his eyes and knew that he thought he meant it. That brought her up short.

"What?" She wasn't expecting this.

"I've got to go." He was half-dressed already.

"What happened to our agreement just to fool around a little?" Kate sensed that they might be at a crossroads in their fledgling relationship.

"I guess I want to renegotiate," he said, buttoning his shirt and sitting on the side of the bed to put his socks and shoes on.

"Well, I don't," she stated decisively. "This is ridiculous. You can't just change the rules for no reason."

"I have a very good reason," he argued. "I love you, and I think you might be falling in love with me, too."

"The ego of the man," she tried to joke.

"I just want you to know how I feel." He uttered the words as if it were no big deal. Perhaps, to him, it wasn't. He brought it up on his way out the door, didn't he?

"I'm not going to talk about this, Brant. I'm just going to say what I should have said in the first place. You're nuts, boy. Now go to work!"

"I don't think so." He swept onto the bed, taking her with him, pinning her under him, and kissing her until Kate had forgotten his foolishness, forgotten Jennifer and Skipper and the article, and everything else that had brought them to this point, in this bed. All she could think of was Brant, his hard muscle against her soft flesh, his spicy male scent, his lips against her skin.

Then he did it. He ruined it. "I do plan to convince you," he said with certainty.

Kate stilled. "I thought you had to be at work early, loverboy."

"You can make fun, try to discount what I say, but I'm not giving up that easily."

"Easily? Ha!" she exclaimed. "What I want is easy. What you want is complicated. And we can't discuss this now. You're in a time crunch, remember?"

"You aren't going to scare me away, either," he said, unperturbed. "I have enough time to talk about this."

"Actually, we don't need any time at all. I'm perfectly happy with the way things are. How about we just leave it at that?" She tried to kiss him, but he raised his head, out of her reach.

"No. That's not good enough. I want you to tell me why I can't be in love with you."

"Oh, come on, Brant. Give me a kiss good-bye and go to work," she pleaded. "Forget all this nonsense."

"Give me a reason. One good reason."

"Only one. That's easy. How about this? We've only known each other a few weeks. You're not some kid. Think about it."

"I've thought."

"Think some more," she suggested. "At work maybe."

"How long do you think it takes? Seriously, Katie, my parents knew it from the moment they met." She groaned. "Maybe I did, too. I don't know. But as far as I *do* know, there's no hard and fast rule, no particular time limit."

It was a lost cause. He was definitely going to be late. Kate realized that he was determined to have this conversation, so she responded to him with complete honesty. "We don't know each other."

"We do," he argued. "I know you always bite your lip while you wait for someone to pick up the phone when you call them, and I know that right before you're about to blast into someone, your eyes light up, and I know you salivate over men who do household chores. You know I like to cook, and where to touch the back of my neck to make me crazy, and, of course, the deep dark secret that I haven't ever told a soul. How much more do we need to know?"

"That's not what I meant."

"Then what did you mean? Be specific. Why is this so impossible?"

"Okay. You asked for it," she warned him. "First of all, we haven't known each other long enough. You say you know me . . . but I've known Jennifer for ten years, and I didn't know about her brother."

"She hid that from everyone."

"I'm not saying I should have known. I'm just saying that thinking you know a person isn't the same as really knowing them. They can surprise you. You say we've gotten to know each other so well, but we haven't exactly been living together here. This has been easy. I sleep in your bed, you sleep in mine. It seems great. You cook me breakfast, you come to dinner at my place. Once. That's nothing. We've been enjoying each other's bodies. Nothing could be better than that. You don't know what I'm like when I'm really angry. I don't know your parents, who are important to you. We've barely scratched the surface of each other's lives."

"All I'm saying is that I think we're compatible. Very compatible."

"We're compatible in bed, but outside of it we want different things. Haven't you noticed that?"

"Like what?"

"Well, I may be wrong, but I've gotten the strong impression that you don't really approve of the business I'm in."

"You don't approve of what I do, either," he pointed out.

"It's not that I don't approve, it's . . ." Kate wanted him to understand her. "The construction industry has its problems, but so does everything. Journalism certainly does. So what do you think will happen if we have to justify everything we do at work to each other? We'd end up resenting the hell out of it."

"We can work that out. It's just logistics."

"It's not logistics," she exclaimed. "It's my life."

"Your life is trying to help people you've never even met, and caring about Jenny and laughing with your friends, and making love with me. Journalism is only one part of it. And I'm not asking you to give it up or anything."

"That's good," she said sarcastically.

"Don't do that," he commanded. "This isn't a joke. I meant that we would work it out. Whether you believe me or not, I do plan to work this out. We make a good team. I think we've already proven that. And I don't want to end it."

"Who said anything about ending it? I just don't want to rush into something that could lead to pain and heartache."

"So if we're just fooling around, we can't get hurt? Is that what you're saying?"

"Maybe. Yes," she insisted. "We don't need to make any confessions, or any promises. We can just be together, without any love nonsense to contend with. Why complicate things?"

"I don't consider it complicated. I love you. It's three little words. Yes, they mean a lot, but they're simple. The idea behind them is simple. I care about you. I want to be with you. I feel close to you. And if you didn't feel something for me, you would not have made a big deal of this."

"You're right. That was my mistake. I overreacted."

"But you're still upset."

"Because you haven't heard me," she claimed. "I'm just trying to be honest with you."

"That's bull," Brant charged. "You're trying not to be honest with yourself. You're afraid to care for me, afraid to admit I'm the one telling the truth. And I have to ask why? What is it about my loving you that makes you so miserable?"

"I already told you—"

"No," he cut her off. "You told me why I can't be in love. You haven't said why you can't love me, if you can't?"

"I don't trust you, yet," she answered.

"You're afraid I'll leave you. Is that it? When I—what was that example you gave—when I see what you're really like when you're angry, I'll walk away. Is that it?"

"I guess so. I don't know." Kate wanted this conversation to be over. History.

"You do know," he insisted. "Why won't you tell me?"

"Even if I did say I love you, that wouldn't be enough for you, would it? I'd have to prove it. We would have to prove it. Over and over. I don't think I'm up to it. I've never been very good at relationships, especially when they grew tense."

"It's perfectly normal for you to feel that way. Children of alcoholics—"

"Don't go there, Brant. I don't need any paperback psychology to tell me I have problems because of my father's addiction."

He ignored her protest. "You watched your dad drink himself to death and felt powerless to do anything about it. I know how you felt. I got a glimpse of it tonight at Jenny's place. But I'm not your father. You've got to give me a chance."

Maybe he was right. Maybe there was something abnormal about her, and that was why she had been so unsuccessful with men before. If she could see in Jennifer what Jennifer herself couldn't see, then maybe Brant could see something in her that she wasn't aware of. "A chance?" she asked tentatively.

"I need to be able to see you, to be with you and tell you that I love you. Can you just give it a try?"

Scary as the idea was, she nodded. "Okay." But she needed time to get used to the idea. "But let's take it slow, all right?"

He looked disappointed, but he agreed.

"You are going to be very late," she told him. She hustled him out of the apartment and took her time showering and dressing to go home. Then Kate walked all the way to her apartment. Her thoughts were all jumbled, and her emotions were worse. She didn't know what Brant wanted from her. As much as that scared her, she was even more afraid that, when she discovered what he wanted, she wouldn't be able to give it to him.

The strange side effect of all the walking, and thinking, and worrying she did during her trip home, was that when she arrived at her apartment, she knew one thing for certain. She no longer wanted to crucify Leopold Arnold. If Julio had brought his accident on himself, and it seemed more than likely that he had, then it would be irresponsible of her to point a finger at a man who couldn't very well prove he didn't commit the crime. It was so hard to prove a negative.

And once she'd decided that the one accusation was wrong, everything else fell into place. Kate couldn't live with herself if she made the same mistake again. If she published the exposé on Skipper, she was positive that it would do more harm than good. She made herself a cup of tea, and sat at the computer to start piecing together the story she wanted to write.

She considered making it an editorial, but after reviewing her research, she found she had enough for a news item about the current union membership and its representatives. For all that Skipper had taken advantage of the situation, it was the union leadership that had ensnared Julio, and the Hispanic members, and everyone else, into this mess. And they should be recalled.

Kate didn't finish work until late that night, but when she finally closed her laptop, she had written the opening portion of the story, and she was more sure than ever that this was the way to salvage some good out of the predicament Jennifer had gotten them into. Leopold Arnold would not escape unscathed, but the thrust of the piece was the advisability of voting unethical city politicians out of office, and watchdogging appointed officials to make sure they didn't profit at the expense of New Yorkers both in the construction business and elsewhere.

She was bone tired, so she got ready for bed, but she couldn't sleep. The image of Jen's dejected face would probably have been enough to make it impossible, and worry about her friend was not her only concern. She was going to have to contend with a lot more. Skipper's reaction to the article could be anything from apathy to outright anger. He could make life somewhat unpleasant for her if he used his influence to damage her reputation in his social circle. Her editor, Charles, was bound to be displeased with the results of the last three weeks of work, and probably wouldn't print the item. And he'd be peeved when she had it printed elsewhere, especially since she'd put off writing the article she'd promised him in order to research this one.

Overshadowing all of these turbulent thoughts was the memory of her discussion with Brant that morning. Three simple words, he said. But they were not simple. They were the most confusing, profane, seductive words in the English language. In theory, at least. Kate wasn't sure she would know if they were, because she didn't think she'd ever experienced the emotion that they supposedly expressed. She had never been in love. If she were in love at the moment, it was not what she had been led to expect. First off, she did not feel particularly ecstatic, a sensation she'd assumed would accompany her first fall. Added to that, she was terrified. She could not imagine what she had done to deserve his trust, let alone his loyalty. And, above all, that was what she always thought she would want in the man she loved. Devotion to her alone. Unswerving faithfulness.

Could she really believe he would give her all that? Kate had been willing to settle for much less. Why should he offer her more? She didn't think she had ever indicated to him that she wanted anything other than what they had agreed upon—mutual satisfaction. She was only now realizing that he had given her much more support than she'd had any right to expect. He stuck by her, even after she broke his heart by revealing the truth about Skipper. Perhaps Brant had been in love with her from the beginning, she mused. It had happened before. Like his parents, hers had fallen in love at first glance. They had found each other across a crowded room, just like in the schmaltzy old movies she loved to watch.

She climbed out of bed and lay on the couch, where she could watch television. She searched the classic movie channels for something in black and white. She only enjoyed watching these old movies by herself. If things worked out with Brant, would she have to give up her privacy? Kate remembered reading somewhere that love was a compromise, and good relationships were based on sharing and sacrifice. She didn't know if she could share the remote, let alone her life, and she was almost positive that she'd have trouble accepting any sacrifice he was willing to make on her behalf. So where did that leave her?

She had promised to give Brant a chance. Was that a compromise? He had agreed to go slowly because she asked. That was definitely a compromise. Maybe it would work out after all. *Pat and Mike* starring Katharine Hepburn and Spencer Tracy was playing on channel fifty-four. As she settled back to watch and, hopefully, fall asleep, Kate thought, *Katharine Hepburn didn't ever get married because she thought it was selfish for a woman with a career to have a family.* She had always thought the woman had a point. Between her screen idol and her father, she had a lot of good reasons to forget about a relationship with Brant, and go on as she had been. Alone. It would certainly be the easiest solution to the problem. But, for the first time, alone didn't seem so easy to her.

Twenty

The idea might first have presented itself to her in a dream. Whether she'd been inspired in her sleep, or not, as she went through her morning, Kate became more and more convinced that it could work.

She called Brant before she stopped to think about it. "Good morning," she said, before he even identified himself.

"This is a good sign," he said. Even over the telephone he sounded smug.

"Don't flatter yourself. I'm calling about Skipper and Jennifer."

"Oh?" he inquired, his tone doubtful.

"I think I've thought of a way to get your friend and my friend together. To talk. Maybe they can iron some of this stuff out."

"I'm all ears," he proclaimed.

She outlined her plan for him, and Brant promised to do his part. Then she called Jen. "Are you going to work today?" she asked.

"Of course," Jennifer said, as if the previous night's events had never occurred.

"In Skipper's offices?"

"As usual. Yes," she said impatiently.

"I'll meet you there at lunchtime," Kate said in her sternest voice.

"I don't feel much like socializing," Jen objected.

"This is work related," Kate coaxed.

"My work?"

"No, mine. And after all you put me through, you can make the time," she insisted.

"Fine." Jennifer sounded annoyed, but Kate was satisfied. Now, if only Brant could get Skipper to show up, she might just be able to create something good out of all of this.

Kate rode up to Jennifer's office in Skipper's building somewhat nervously, but the elevator went straight up to the forty-ninth floor without a hitch. Kate took it as a good sign. Her old college roommate could have tried to kill her again. She walked into Jennifer's office feeling quite hopeful.

Jennifer looked up from her desktop, which was bare, and said, "Hey, girl." But she didn't stand.

"Hi" Kate said. "How are you feeling?"

"Fine" Jen answered emotionlessly.

"I've written the article, but the primary focus isn't Skipper or the strike. It outlines the entire process that went into building the L.A.C. Parking Garage."

"Skipper is the builder. How can he not be the focus?"

"He's *a* builder. This is one job. I've written about how these big projects work. Including the involvement of city government and, of course, the unions."

Jennifer mulled it over for a minute. "Is this supposed to be some kind of apology?"

"For what? I did what I thought was right. I don't think I have anything to apologize for."

"Okay," she said grumpily. "Why bother telling me about it? Are you here looking for my approval? Do what you want," she ordered.

"I will, thank you. I don't need your permission and I didn't set up this meeting to get your opinion," Kate said, her pride stung.

"So why did you?" Jennifer asked.

"I can't leave it like this. I need a resolution." She held up her hand to halt Jennifer's protest. "Even if you don't. We need to clear the air, Jen."

"I'm used to things being murky," she argued.

"You are one of my oldest friends, and I can't stand to see you in pain. You hide it well, but now that I know, I can see that you are suffering. And I can't take it."

"There's nothing you can do about it," Jen said. She wasn't angry anymore. She appeared to be more disheartened than anything else. "You did your best."

"I'm not done yet," Kate vowed.

"I'm grateful for what you've done. I'm sorry I wasn't honest with you, but I think you can understand. You know what it's like to lose someone, how powerless you feel, how angry it can make you."

"Yes I do. Which is why I want you to talk to Skipper about those feelings," she suggested. Internally, she cringed in anticipation of Jennifer's response. She hid it with a casual smile.

"What?" Jen exclaimed. "Are you nuts?"

Kate rushed on. "He's right down the hall. Where he's always been. Brant is talking to him, just like I am talking to you."

Jennifer was steaming. "Who do you think you are?" she shouted. "I might have been able to find out the truth, somehow. Someday. But not if Skipper has been warned."

"We didn't tell him about Bobby," Kate pacified her. "Brant is explaining that I need to speak with him. We decided to let him read the article, since he was kind enough to allow me to interview him. He is featured prominently, if not in the best light. All Brant was to tell him about you was that you were coming with me to talk to him."

"Oh," Jennifer said, bewildered.

"I'm sure Skipper has questions, though. He will definitely wonder why you're attending this meeting, and I plan to tell him that you're unhappy working for him—if you won't. You can tell him it's his criminal behavior that upsets you, if you want to."

"You are going to drive me out of my mind, girl," Jen growled.

"This has got to come out. I think if you will talk with him honestly, he'll probably be able to answer a lot of your questions." Kate couldn't *force* her friend to confront the man but she had every intention of making it as difficult as possible not to do so.

"What makes you think he'll be honest with me?" she demanded.

"You can't be certain. But I think you know the man well enough to make a pretty good guess. Most importantly, when you confront him, this can stop festering inside you. You can think of your brother without hurting so much."

"You don't know that that will happen."

"I only know what happened to me. I bottled up all my sorrow and grief and anger at my father's death because I didn't think I had a choice. There was no one to share it with—or, at least no one whom I felt comfortable unloading all that bile on. My sponsor at Al-Anon finally got me talking, and I went to a therapist. People helped me to work through it."

"Your relationship with your dead daddy doesn't exactly inspire me to follow in your footsteps," Jen said nastily.

"I'm still dealing with my memories of Dad, but I have been able to accept his death and move on."

"You are not my sponsor, Kate. I'm not in the program, remember?"

"Tough. You are coming with me anyway. Like I said, you can keep it inside, or you can let it out, but you are going to face Skipper today if I have to drag you down that hallway by your hair. Up!" She ordered Jennifer out of her chair.

Resigned, Jennifer followed her out of the office. Skipper and Brant were waiting for them. Skipper didn't look too thrilled to see her. Kate looked at Brant, who directed a speaking glance at her. "He read it."

"Damn straight," Skipper burst out. He pulled on his tie, then tightened it, clearly trying to get a grip on his anger. The familiar gesture reminded her of her uncle Jake again. This time, she didn't ignore it. This man was part of Jennifer's family. Kate hadn't looked for the family man in Skipper before. She tried, but the impeccably dressed old gentleman behind the imported Italian desk didn't fit the image of any of the kindly old uncles she'd known. "Jennifer, have you seen this?" he said heatedly. She didn't answer.

"You are the only person who has read it . . . so far," Kate told him. "I thought you deserved the courtesy, but I don't plan to change a word of it."

"This is a smear job," he grumbled. Drawing himself up, he said with dignity, "I am not a crook."

"What do you call it?" Kate queried.

"I do what I have to do to get the job done." He looked at Brant, who remained impassive, then at Jennifer, who kept her gaze on the floor. "I don't make the rules."

"You just play the game," Kate interjected.

"Not even that. I don't seek out these people. They

come to me. Because they know I can get the job done. Because I've proven myself. They show up at my door, with a contract they are dying to give me, and expect something in return. If I don't play the game they'll just go on to the next guy."

"You cannot expect me to feel sorry for you," Kate said wryly.

"No, of course not. But I built my business from nothing. No one gave me anything."

"I know that. I know exactly where you came from. I'm the expert on Leopold Arnold, remember? With the exception of a few details, I've learned everything that ever was printed about you. It still doesn't explain *why*. You don't have to go along with them. No one is forcing you to do anything."

"Young lady," he said, his reproachful tone bringing her up short. "You have no idea what I deal with every day. If I have to bend a few rules, I'll do it, because that's the kind of man I am. I'm not going to make excuses for it."

"I'm going to show this city the kind of man you are," she retorted. "That's my job. And I don't plan to make excuses for that, either."

"Why go after me?" he asked, puzzled. "What did I ever do to you?"

Kate looked at Jennifer, who was watching Skipper. "The strike," she answered. "A couple of my favorite restaurants are on Ninth Avenue, and when I walk down there and see the men picketing the construction site, I can't help feeling sorry for them. I turn on the television and see another story about rioting, and I wonder what is going on," she responded. "You really got my attention when you hired the nonunion welders."

"Oh, that," he said, subdued.

"Yes, that. Why did you do it?"

"Because I could. The opportunity presented itself to me, and I'm not ashamed to say I took advantage of it."

"It doesn't bother you at all that men are standing outside the walls that you built around that construction site, cursing you . . . and their own brothers?"

"You don't get where I am without making a few enemies. The union isn't my problem. They have to look out for themselves."

"Was that what Julio Gonzalez was doing, looking out for the union?"

"Julio? What does he have to do with this?"

"You arranged for him to buy a Jeep Wrangler, didn't you? At a very nice price."

"He needed a car. I helped him out."

"In exchange for . . . ?"

"Nothing concrete. Good will. For the future. There will be other jobs. I will have to work with these people again."

Kate's hackles rose. "These people?" she echoed disdainfully.

He looked surprised. "Not much gets built in this city without the Professional Steel Workers Union," he commented.

"And that's all. You didn't buy his services?"

"There was nothing Julio could do for me. He had his own agenda. I just made sure there would be no hard feelings after it was all over. As you know, it didn't matter in the end."

"His death was unfortunate, wasn't it?" she said, disgusted by his prosaic tone. Kate might not have known the union representative, but she had come to feel for him and the people he left behind, while researching the article.

Apparently, it was enough to galvanize Jennifer into motion. "And my brother, Bobby," she added.

"Bobby?" Skipper repeated, obviously confused. "What does that have to do with this?"

"He died, too. Working for you."

The old man suddenly looked his age, and then some. "I remember," he said sorrowfully. "I'm not likely to forget, Jennifer dear." His voice broke, and he had to clear his throat before he continued. "When he died, a little bit of me died with him. I hoped to share my work with him. I was just starting to get my bearings, to think I might be . . . what I am today. He was supposed to live, to make his own mark on the world. He reminded me of myself at his age. Passing along what I've learned to men like Bobby, and Brant here, is what makes it all worthwhile."

Jen stood staring at him, mouth agape. Kate and Brant shared a look of triumph. They were talking. The plan was working.

Skipper started at Jennifer, his eyes filling with tears. "Jenny?"

"I thought . . . I thought . . . I don't know. All this time I blamed you."

Understanding dawned in his eyes. "For Bobby? But . . ." Kate could almost see the pieces clicking together in his mind. "Jennifer, you couldn't believe that I had something to do with Bobby's death?"

"Covering it—it up," she stammered. "You always acted so . . ."

"Guilty," he finished for her. "I *felt* guilty, because he was working for me. I was the one who had to bring him to the hospital and tell you and your mother what happened." Jennifer started to cry silently. Kate took her hand, but she didn't think her friend even noticed. "I took away the only person you trusted," Skipper continued. A sob shook Jennifer's body. Skipper approached her diffidently and, when he was close enough, he took her other hand. They led her to the sofa. He sat beside her, his eyes glued to her face as he pulled his handkerchief out of his breast pocket and gave it to her. Feeling like an intruder, Kate backed away. Brant came to stand beside her, but the other two were too absorbed in each other to notice.

Words tumbled from Skipper's mouth like water pouring through an open floodgate. "When your mom and I were growing up together, she was like a little sister to me. I couldn't stop loving her just because she grew up a little differently than I hoped. When she fell in love with your . . ." He caught himself before he finished whatever it was he was going to say, hesitated, then went on. "I couldn't protect her from your father or herself. After your dad left, when she gave up on everything, I tried to be there for you and your brother, to make her life easier. You, too. I loved you kids. You had to know that."

Jennifer turned her face into his shoulder, and he put his arms around her. "I was so proud of how you and Bobby took care of each other, and her. When he was gone, I didn't know what to do for you—how I could make it up to you."

Finished, Skipper looked at them helplessly over her head. "I can't believe you thought—" Words failed him. The distinguished old man didn't look so urbane at that moment. Kate felt sorry for him in his distress, but she was glad he and Jennifer were talking about the pain they had hidden from each other for so many years. They grieved together, and consoled each other.

"I believe you," Jennifer said, her voice muffled against his jacket. She lifted her head and tried to smile. "I believe you."

Kate sniffed. The revealing sound was louder than she

had expected, and she glanced up at Brant, to find him smiling down at her.

"You old softy," he teased gently. His eyes were suspiciously bright, though.

"Like they didn't get to you," she retaliated.

They turned to the door in tacit agreement, and Brant ushered Kate out. When he closed the door behind them, Kate leaned back against the wall. She felt fantastic. The plan had actually worked.

"I guess our work is done." She felt another sniffle coming on. "Have you got a hankie?" she asked, figuring that since Leopold was Brant's role model and he'd had one, Brant might, also.

"I should make you use your sleeve," he admonished. But he did pull a handkerchief out of his pocket.

Kate examined it. "Is this clean?"

"Give it back," he ordered, reaching for her.

She jumped back. "Just joking." Kate wiped her nose. "Want it back now?"

"Keep it," he said, grinning.

"A gift? For me? What a guy!"

"Go ahead, make fun. I'm feeling pretty good right now."

"Me, too," she acknowledged. "I guess we do make a pretty good team."

Twenty-one

Kate hung up the phone the next morning and crowed. Skipper Arnold had agreed to offer the P.S.W.U.A. an incentive to end the hostilities, in the form of jobs on his next site, if they would just agree to allow their members to sponsor experienced Hispanic steelworkers to the union in a fast-track program designed to admit qualified welders and other steelworkers without the long apprenticeship usually required.

"He's going to do it!" she announced to Brant over lunch.

"Amazing," he responded. "But you know what's going to happen now. All the other union members are going to want an equitable policy for their sponsors."

"Minority union members," she corrected him. "The program is designed to redress existing inequities." She speared a forkful of salad and ate it while he answered her. "Katie, darlin', *everyone* is a minority. The Irish will complain that they're underrepresented, and the Italians, Armenians, and Lithuanians, et cetera."

"Not to mention African-Americans," she chimed in, munching happily. "We'll get to everyone, eventually," she said confidently.

"You are such an optimist," he said accusingly.

"You've got something against optimists?"

"I don't think tough guys can be optimists," he theorized. "It just doesn't go together."

"Are you saying I'm a paradox," she asked playfully.

"Oh, you are definitely a paradox," he asserted.

"Ahhh." She nodded. "I confuse you then?" she quipped. "That must be why you dislike me so much."

"No. I find it delightful," he retorted.

"Delightful? I don't think I've ever been called that before."

"Yes, you have," he told her. "Skipper called you a delightful young woman after he met you at the charity ball."

"He did?"

"Sure. When I set up the interview with him, he said it again. 'I'd be happy to meet with that delightful creature.' His words."

"That was before I wrote the article and forced him to negotiate with the union," she concluded.

"Yes," Brant remarked dryly. "Before that."

"That means I didn't need you after all?"

"Need me?" he questioned.

"To get an interview with him," she explained. "That's the main reason Jennifer introduced you to me."

"You like to fight?"

"Skipper Arnold doesn't give many interviews. That's one of the reasons I was so eager to do the story. Why else do you think I spent all that time trying to make you see reason? I could have saved the energy I wasted trying to work with a big lummox like you and gone right to the Big Kahuna."

"Lummox?" he repeated inquiringly.

"I thought you knew. I only slept with you to get closer to him."

"You slept with me *after* you interviewed Skipper," he reminded her.

"I did?" She feigned ignorance. "Oh, well." She shrugged. "Can't be helped now."

"Can't be helped? You little . . ."

"You've got a piece of spinach stuck on your tooth," she lied, trying to distract him.

He didn't bite. "You fought with me because you enjoy fighting. Admit it, you shrew."

"I admit nothing and demand proof," she countered.

"You want proof? You can't go ten minutes without getting in an argument about something."

"I can, too."

"See?" he declared, triumphant.

"That doesn't count," she whined. "You attacked me. I had to defend myself."

"It wouldn't matter if I did nothing but bow and scrape to you. You are the most opinionated, argumentative woman I have ever met."

"That's because I have an inquiring mind," she contended.

"That's because you love it," he countered.

She decided to try something different. "So why did you sleep with me?" she challenged.

"I happen to find those characteristics sexy," he shot back at her.

"Aha!" she exclaimed, laughing. "So you admit you started it . . . as some sick form of foreplay."

"Me? You're the one! I've never seen anyone over the age of three who gets such a charge out of playing 'am-not-am-too.' "

They left the restaurant together, holding hands, and that night, after work, they met at his place and picked up right where they had left off.

"So you only slept with me to get the story, huh?" he prodded, advancing on her menacingly.

"N-no," she stuttered, backing away. "Of course not. I really like you."

"So why did you say all that to at the restaurant?"

"Just trying to get your goat. It's like you said, I enjoy quarreling with you. It's great foreplay!" Kate came up against a wall and had to stop. She held up her hands in front of her to ward him off.

He scooped her up in his arms and carried her toward the bedroom. "I don't know whether to believe you or not. I'm going to need a demonstration."

"A demonstration? Of what?"

He dropped her on the bed. "Some kind of display of affection would do the trick," he informed her. She scooted off the other side and faced him, across the expanse of the navy blue spread. "Which is it, Kate? You slept with me because you like me? Or you wanted to get the story?"

"Mmm." She pretended to consider. He started around the bed. "Both!" she answered desperately.

"How much?" he asked.

"What?"

"Both."

"I wanted the story really bad," she said, laughing.

"And me?"

"You?"

He lunged across the bed and grabbed her, pulling her down onto the king-size mattress with him. "What was it you said? You wasted all that time and energy on me?" He pinned her down, his hands around her wrists, the weight of his body on hers.

"I don't think I used the word *wasted*."

"You did, too," he insisted.

"What I meant to say was that I *spent* a lot time and energy on you," she corrected herself.

"Yes, you did. And would you say that was because you like me?" he probed.

"Yes, okay," she grudgingly admitted.

"How much?" he asked again.

"On a scale of one to ten?" she said sarcastically.

"I want an answer, you little witch. An honest one."

"Well, umm . . ." She pretended to think about it. "What was the question again?"

"There's only one way to get a straight answer out of you," he said threateningly, and he kissed her.

His lips were firm and demanding. His entire body, which covered her like a blanket, was firm and demanding. The solid, warm weight of him was strangely comforting. The burly fingers that had moored her arms to the bed so effortlessly skimmed lightly down to her splayed hands, fingertips flitting over the contours of her palms, and then he laced his fingers through hers. Kate held on tight, and kissed him greedily, groaning when he withdrew his mouth from hers. His lips trailed over her cheek, and then fastened to the sensitive skin directly below her ear in the hollow where her jaw and her throat met. She purred as he lavished attention on her neck and chin, and then he slid his hot mouth down to trace her collarbone.

"How much do you like me, Katie?" he asked. He continued to administer the sweet torture.

"No fair," she whined. "I can't concentrate on two things at once." At the moment, her attention was centered on the hard press of his arousal against her hip. "I want you," she said imploringly.

"I want you, too," he said. He raised their linked hands above her head and held them there. Her chest rose with the movement, and she watched as his avid gaze moved down to her breasts. He transferred both of her wrists into one of his large hands, and brought his free hand down to flick open the buttons of her blouse, one by one. She held her breath as he lowered his head. "First things first," he said, kissing the swell of her breast.

"Oh, come on," she goaded him. "We can talk afterward."

"Tell me now," he ordered.

It was time for her to take control. "Or else?" she called his bluff.

"Or else?" He looked up at her consideringly. "Nothing." He released her hands, eased himself off her body, and swung his legs over the side of the bed to sit with his back to her.

"Brant, I was kidding." Kate scrambled over behind him and put her arms around his massive shoulders as far as she could reach. She kissed the nape of his neck. "Of course I like you. More than I like my new laptop."

"Too little, too late," Brant said. She couldn't see his face. She didn't know whether he was serious or not.

"Brant?"

"I'm still in love with you, Katie," he announced. He still didn't look at her.

"That's good," she said with an assurance she didn't feel.

"At least you're not running for the hills. That's progress I suppose," he said tonelessly.

She grasped at the straw he offered her. "I'm not even nervous," she informed him. "Not shaking in my boots. Not sweaty. Heart rate normal. Well, almost back to normal," she amended. "You had it racing there, so it may take a few more minutes." Kate was growing alarmed at the lack of response. "Are you listening to me?"

"You're not saying anything," he answered.

"I'm trying," she said in rebuttal. "You're not helping."

"What do you want me to do?" he asked brusquely.

"I'm sorry," she replied.

"Hold me, Kate. Just hold me." He pulled her onto his lap and tucked her head under his chin. A glimmer of suspicion formed in her mind. "Are you laughing at me?"

"I had you going there, for a minute," he chortled.

She punched him in the arm. "You rat!"

"With everything you put me through, I have a right to get a good laugh out of this," he defended himself.

"Just wait. I'll get you for that," she promised.

"I had you worried, didn't I?" He smiled smugly.

"Not at all. I was just starting to think I had misjudged you, that you're not a bully, but a nice, sensitive guy," she told him.

"Right," he said sarcastically.

"I did!" she insisted.

"You thought I turned into some big wimp who was going to walk away because you hurt my feelings," he contended. "You're not helping," he mimicked her, raising his voice to a ridiculous falsetto.

"I don't sound like that," she protested, annoyed.

"You do when you're scared. Your voice rises and gets sort of squeaky and quivery."

"I can suggest a solution for that," she said dryly. "Don't scare me."

"I can't help it. You're so easy. I thought girls were the ones who were supposed to be so good at this love talk. But you suck at it," he maligned her.

"Some *girls*"—she emphasized the offensive word— "probably are. Why don't you go find yourself one of them?"

"I can't," he stated baldly. "I'm hooked on you."

"That's not my fault," she said reprovingly.

"You could be a little nicer, though," he proposed. "It wouldn't kill you."

"It might. You don't know everything," she retorted childishly.

"You want to go a couple of more rounds, or just admit you've got a crush on me, too?"

"Okay," she said.

"Okay what?" he questioned.

"Okay, I love you," she grudgingly admitted.

"I don't think I believe you," he reflected.

"I do" she insisted. "Jeez!"

"You could sound a little happier about it," he commented.

"Don't press your luck. You got what you wanted," she said peevishly.

"Thank you very much," he said graciously. He kissed her.

"You're welcome." She kissed him. "I think we should celebrate this breakthrough." She snapped her fingers. "I know! We can start by taking off all of our clothes and getting in this big comfortable bed."

"Then what?" he asked. "As if I couldn't guess."

"No more stalling," she ordered. "Let's celebrate." She let her blouse fall off her shoulders.

"Is this what it's going to be like?" he asked. "Are you going to order me around all the time?"

"Probably," she said honestly. "I thought you liked it." She removed her bra while he watched, shaking his head. "So? What are you waiting for?"

"Shrew," he accused with a big smile, but he took off his suit jacket. She enjoyed the sight of his powerful shoulders emerging from beneath pristine white cotton.

"Lummox," she shot back at him, kicking off her shoes as she unzipped her skirt. She removed a condom from his shirt pocket before dropping it to the floor, then flashed it at him. She stood looking at him, in her undies, tapping her foot impatiently. "What's taking you so long?" she nagged him.

"Nothing, my dove. I'm there," he replied, stepping out of his pants, and grabbing her up in his arms to swing her onto the bed. "How did you know this was my favorite kind of celebration?"

"I guess we do have a few things in common," she said. "So shut up and kiss me already."

"Nag, nag, nag," Brant groused. But he obeyed her, which was all she could ask.

Dear readers:

I haven't written to you before, because I didn't know you, but when I first saw my books in the library, I realized I've been writing to you all along. You are readers, just like me. As much as I hope you actually bought this book, I get an even bigger thrill from the idea that you borrowed this novel from a lending library.

Libraries are like churches to me. The silence, the smell, and the feel of them inspire awe and wonder, while the books themselves are treasure troves full of fascinating places to visit and wonderful people to meet. I hope you enjoyed meeting two more of these people—Kate and Brant. I'm pretty sure they both love libraries, too.

If you'd like to write back to me, c/o BET Books, I would love to hear from you.

Roberta Gayle

BOOK YOUR PLACE ON OUR WEBSITE AND MAKE THE ARABESQUE ROMANCE CONNECTION!

We've created a customized website just for our very special Arabesque readers, where you can get the inside scoop on everything that's going on with Arabesque romance novels.

When you come online, you'll have the exciting opportunity to:

- View covers of upcoming books

- Learn about our future publishing schedule (listed by publication month and author)

- Find out when your favorite authors will be visiting a city near you

- Search for and order backlist books

- Check out author bios and background information

- Send e-mail to your favorite authors

- Join us in weekly chats with authors, readers and other guests

- Get writing guidelines

- AND MUCH MORE!

Visit our website at
http://www.arabesquebooks.com

More Sizzling Romance From
Brenda Jackson